THE INCREDIBLE ADVENTURES OF DENNIS DORGAN

The room was an inside one; no winder, but a kind of skylight. Just the one door, as far as Dennis could make out. It was lighted with European made lamps, and they was five men in it. One was Tao Tang hisself, setting in a corner like a idol, nothing alive about him but his snaky eyes. Two was giants, like the hatchet man downstairs; one was a tall lean man dressed in decorated silk garments that must have cost plenty. The other'n was Jack Randal. He was hanging from a hook in the ceiling by cords which cut into his flesh so his wrist was trickling blood.

A voice from the dark side of the room spoke: "You have eluded us long, my friend . . ."

Ace Fantasy Books by Robert E. Howard

THE GODS OF BAL-SAGOTH
HEROES OF BEAR CREEK (coming in November)
THE IRON MAN WITH THE ADVENTURES OF DENNIS DORGAN
THE SHE DEVIL (coming in December)
THE TREASURE OF TRANICOS

Chronological order of the CONAN series:

CONAN
CONAN OF CIMMERIA
CONAN THE FREEBOOTER
CONAN THE WANDERER
CONAN THE ADVENTURER
CONAN THE BUCCANEER
CONAN THE WARRIOR
CONAN THE USURPER
CONAN THE CONQUEROR
CONAN THE AVENGER
CONAN OF AQUILONIA
CONAN OF THE ISLES

Illustrated CONAN novels:

CONAN AND THE SORCERER
CONAN: THE FLAME KNIFE
CONAN THE MERCENARY
THE TREASURE OF TRANICOS

Other CONAN novels:

THE BLADE OF CONAN
THE SPELL OF CONAN

The IRON MAN

WITH THE ADVENTURES OF DENNIS DORGAN

ROBERT E. HOWARD

ACE FANTASY BOOKS
NEW YORK

THE IRON MAN WITH THE ADVENTURES OF
DENNIS DORGAN

An Ace Fantasy Book/published by arrangement with
the Estate of Robert E. Howard

PRINTING HISTORY
Ace edition/October 1983

ISBN: 0-441-37365-8

Ace Fantasy Books are published by The Berkley Publishing Group,
200 Madison Avenue, New York, New York 10016.
PRINTED IN THE UNITED STATES OF AMERICA

CONTENTS

THE IRON MAN

INTRODUCTION

The iron man has fought since time immemorial—with but one thought in mind—to get to his foe and to crush him. The centuries, the costumes, the weapons are different. The object is the same. The gore and savagery of Howard's tales of the ring are little removed from those exploits of Conan and Kull and Bran Mak Morn.

It is common knowledge that the late Robert E. Howard was a boxing enthusiast. Indeed, he is pictured in boxing pose in more than one photograph that has survived to this day. His fellow author, H. P. Lovecraft, tied Howard's interest in sports directly to "his love of primitive conflict and strength . . ." But Howard's enthusiasm for boxing seems to go beyond the ordinary pugilist and centers itself on the "iron man"—that individual who could take any amount of punishment and stand up to it. And the iron man of fact and fiction seems not unlike Howard's super-heroes of ancient and barbaric eras.

Howard's article, "Men of Iron," which has come down to us in apparently unfinished form, details the fistic careers of a handful of fighters out of real life—fighters who caught the writer's interest. Foremost among them was the Philadelphian, Joe Grim. Grim and the men like him—Battling Nelson, Tom Sharkey, Mike Boden and Joe Goddard—became the models for Howard's fighters: Brennon . . . Van Heeren . . . Lopez . . . Costigan . . . Karnes. Unlike Howard's fictional heroes who are usually heavyweights, Grim weighed, at most, 165 pounds. Yet the giants of his day failed to knock him out, and the 210-pound Jack Johnson, one of the most devastating champions in the history of the ring, was arm-weary at the finish of his match with Grim.

Thirteen stories by Howard appeared in *Fight Stories* magazine before its four-year suspension in early 1932. After publication of the title was resumed, fourteen of Howard's fight stories were reprinted—two from *Action Stories*—all under different titles and all but one under the publisher's house name, Mark Adam.

The title story of this volume, "The Iron Man," was the fifth Howard tale to appear in *Fight Stories* and was featured on the cover of the June 1930 issue. Its hero, Mike Brennon, is a typical Howard lead—dark, with narrow grey eyes and black hair, broad cheekbones, and a firm jaw. Howard lets him move "with the ease of a huge tiger," and comparisons between him and the real-life iron men are frequent. "You're just a heavyweight Joe Grim." "Joe Goddard had nothing on you." "They'll come packing in to see me—for the same reason they want to see Joe Grim—to see if I can be knocked out." He is also "a dark, brooding figure, charged with the abysmal fighting fury of the killer."

Another heavyweight, Jack Maloney, although he has battered Brennon relentlessly in their match, falls before the iron man's savage persistence. Three years later, Howard brings Maloney back in the story "They Always Come Back." Maloney is discovered, down and out, in a Mexican bordertown by an Australian fight manager, who brings him back to prominence by skillful direction and subterfuge. Maloney is less of the iron man. His ability lies with his speed and punch, and when he does face a second iron man—"Iron Mike" Costigan, the conqueror of Brennon—he decisions him handily.

In "Fists of the Desert," the hero is Kirby Karnes, "a bronze barbarian from the desert." Karnes is another iron man who falls in with a shady manager, and in the end takes on another of his own breed . . . "a caveman, this giant from Honduras." Karnes is so rugged that his manager has occasion to say: "Joe Grim is a sissy beside him."

Karnes and his cohorts are a barbaric crew, and their exploits provide some exciting reading in the tradition of Howard's better known heroes.

Donald M. Grant
February 10, 1976

Men of Iron

What freak of nature makes an iron man? We know that the human skull is well built to withstand violence, and that the body muscles may be developed into a steel-like toughness. But this alone will not explain that strange and incredible mortal known to the ring and its followers as an Iron Man.

We know that often an ordinary man is killed by a comparatively slight blow on the head and even a skilled boxer is often knocked senseless by a blow which, landing on the right place, need not be overhard. Compare these facts, then, with the deeds of the iron men! I will mention five here explicitly: Joe Grim, Battling Nelson, Tom Sharkey, Mike Boden and Joe Goddard.

In passing, let me speak of Jim Jeffries, one of the two iron men who achieved a title. Undoubtedly he was the greatest of them all, but unlike the rest, he combined real skill and cleverness with his toughness. Just now I am speaking of men whose main, or only, asset was durability.

Joe Grim was an Italian, a native of Philadelphia. If he ever won a fight, it is not on record. He was neither a boxer or a fighter in the true sense of the word. He was wide open—a blind man could hit him—yet Bob Fitzsimmons, Joe Gans, Sam McVey and Jack Johnson failed to knock him out. Grim never weighed over 165 pounds. Consider then the fact of stacking him up against men who weighed over 200 pounds! Stanley Ketchel was accounted as tough a man as ever lived, yet Jack Johnson, rising from a knockdown, knocked Ketchel out with one blow, breaking off all his front teeth, which remained stuck in the glove. This same Johnson at his very best, weighing 210 pounds, battered Joe Grim, 165, until he was arm-weary, and failed to score a knockout. Sam McVey was a harder hitter than Johnson and much more aggressive. He had two tries at Grim and failed to stop the India-rubber Man.

Bob Fitzsimmons, without a doubt the most effective hitter in the history of the game, was matched with Grim for six rounds. Consider Fitzsimmons' record if you feel he was at fault. He was the man who knocked out the great Corbett; who knocked out Tom Sharkey, the giant Ruhlin, Ed Donkhorst the Human Freight Car, 320 pounds, whom Bob finished with one punch. Fitzsimmons gave Jeffries the Boilermaker's most vicious battle. One boxer died from the effects of his trip-hammer smashes.

Now then, look! For six rounds Fitzsimmons hammered the wide open Italian with every blow and series of blows known to the game. His deadly body blows, which had proved so effective against Corbett and Sharkey and Ruhlin, did not even jar Grim. Fitzsimmons switched to the Italian's head and knocked him down sixteen times—an average of three times to the round. At the final gong Fitzsimmons was arm-weary; Grim landed the last blow of that fight and, reeling over to the ropes, spit out a mouthful of teeth and, grinning, made his usual speech: "I am Joe Grim! I fear no man! I challenge that bigga Jeem Jeff' fora da title!"

Scientists examined Grim and found his skull to be of extraordinary thickness, his brain cell so small that the nerves were dulled. When Joe said he did not feel the blows, he spoke the truth. A blow which would have agonized or crippled the average man only produced a dull jar and slight discomfort to him.

But that scarcely explains his body which was of such chilled steel hardness that he once allowed a man to shatter a baseball bat across his stomach. He was knocked down but unhurt.

Joe Gans came nearer knocking out this marvel in his prime than anyone else. Though a much smaller man than Grim, weighing only 138 pounds, the Old Master gave Grim a hideous battering. He worked in close, found Grim had only one style, a continuous roundhouse swinging of his arms. Gans kept in close, ducking these swings, and each time he came up again and hooked right or left to Grim's jaw. For round after round this kept up until Grim's jaws swelled. In the thirteenth round they burst and the chief of police, in horror, stopped the fight. Gans himself was willing for he was sickened at the havoc he had made, but Grim was furious, insisted he was not hurt and wished to go on!

The many batterings took their toll at last, however, and Grim was knocked out by Sailor Burke, a hard-hitting second-rater who stepped off a ship to turn the trick. Grim's heart was broken.

One would think that falling four feet headfirst onto a concrete floor would at least render a man senseless. In his first fight with Joe Choynsky, Tom Sharkey had that experience. He not only was not hurt; he got up and won the fight. Choynsky was a venomous hitter. Though weighing only 170 pounds, Corbett said he was one of the hardest hitters that ever lived. The giant Jeffries always said Choynsky hit him his hardest blows. In their drawn battle of twenty or twenty-five rounds, Choynsky smashed a straight right into Jeffries' mouth which crushed the lip back and wedged it between the two front teeth in such a way that one of Jeffries' seconds was forced to cut it loose with a knife.

Sharkey was a raw novice; Choynsky a trained veteran. Choynsky smashed Sharkey over the ropes and out of the ring. The sailor landed on his head on the concrete with all the heft of his 190 pounds. That would have caved in most skulls like an eggshell. Sharkey climbed back into the ring and knocked Choynsky out.

Choynsky, hitter par excellence, met another tough nut in Chicago in the person of Mike Boden. This man was as wild and wide open as Grim—and about as tough. In the six rounds they fought, he landed not one solid blow while Choynsky almost broke his heart trying to put him to sleep—and failed.

In Australia Choynsky was twice outfought by one Joe Goddard, a man who claimed that no human being could be struck hard enough to be rendered senseless.

The Iron Man

CHAPTER 1

A cannon-ball for a left and a thunderbolt for a right! A granite jaw, and chilled steel body! The ferocity of a tiger, and the greatest fighting heart that ever beat in an iron-ribbed breast! That was Mike Brennon, heavyweight contender.

Long before the sports writers ever heard the name of Brennon, I sat in the "athletic tent" of a carnival performing in a small Nevada town, grinning at the antics of the barker, who was volubly offering fifty dollars to anyone who could stay four rounds with "Young Firpo, the California Assassin, champeen of Los Angeles and the East Indies!" Young Firpo, a huge hairy fellow with the bulging muscles of a weight-lifter and whose real name was doubtless Leary, stood by with a bored and contemptuous expression on his heavy features. This was an old game to him.

"Now, friends," shouted the spieler, "is they any young man here what wants to risk his life in this here ring? Remember, the management ain't responsible for life or limb! But if anybody'll git in here at his own risk—"

I saw a rough-looking fellow start up—one of the usual "plants" secretly connected with the show, of course—but at that moment the crowd set up a yell, "Brennon! Brennon! Go on, Mike!"

At last a young fellow rose from his seat, and with an embarrassed grin, vaulted over the ropes. The "plant" hesitated—Young Firpo evinced some interest, and from the hawk-like manner in which the barker eyed the newcomer, and from the roar of the crowd, I knew that he was on the "up-and-up"—a local boy, in other words.

"You a professional boxer!" asked the barker.

"I've fought some here, and in other places," answered Brennon. "But you said you barred no one."

"We don't," grunted the showman, noting the difference in the size of the fighters.

While the usual rigmarole of argument was gone through, I wondered how the carnival men intended saving their money if the boy happened to be too good for their man. The ring was set in the middle of the tent; the dressing-rooms were in another part. There was no curtain across the back of the ring where the local fighter could be pressed to receive a blackjack blow from the confederate behind the curtain.

Brennon, after a short trip to the dressing-room, climbed into the ring and was given a wild ovation. He was a finely built lad, six feet one in height, slim-waisted and tapering of limb, with remarkably broad shoulders and heavy arms. Dark, with narrow gray eyes, and a shock of black hair falling over a low, broad forehead, his was the true fighting face—broad across the cheekbones—with thin lips and a firm jaw. His long, smooth muscles rippled as he moved with the ease of a huge tiger. Opposed to him Young Firpo looked sluggish and ape-like.

Their weights were announced, Brennon 189, Young Firpo 191. The crowd hissed; anyone could see that the carnival boxer weighed at least 210.

The battle was short, fierce and sensational, and with a bedlam-like ending. At the gong Brennon sprang from his corner, coming in wide open, like a bar-room brawler. Young Firpo met him with a hard left hook to the chin, stopping him in his tracks. Brennon staggered, and the carnival boxer swung his right flush to the jaw—a terrific blow which, strangely enough, did not seem to worry Brennon as had the other. He shook his head and plunged in again, but as he did so, his foe drew back the deadly left and crashed it once more to his jaw. Brennon dropped like a log, face first. The crowd was frenzied. The barker, who was also referee, began counting swiftly, Young Firpo standing directly over the fallen warrior.

At "five!" Brennon had not twitched. At "seven!" he stirred and began making aimless motions. At "eight!" he reeled to his knees, and his reddened, dazed eyes fixed themselves on his conqueror. Instantly they blazed with the fury of the killer.

As the spieler opened his mouth to say "ten!" Brennon reeled up in a blast of breath-taking ferocity that stunned the crowd.

Young Firpo, too, seemed stunned. Face whitening, he began a hurried retreat. But Brennon was after him like a blood-crazed tiger, and before the carnival fighter could lift his hands, Brennon's wide-looping left smashed under his heart and a sweeping right found his chin, crashing him face down on the canvas with a force that shook the ring.

The astounded barker mechanically began counting, but Brennon, moving like a man in a trance, pushed him away and stooping, tore the glove from Young Firpo's limp left hand. Removing something therefrom, held it up to the crowd. It was a heavy iron affair, resembling brass knuckles, and known in the parlance of the ring as a knuckle-duster. I gasped. No wonder Young Firpo had been unnerved when his victim rose! That iron-laden glove crashing twice against Brennon's jaw should have shattered the bone, yet he had been able to rise within ten seconds and finish his man with two blows!

Now all was bedlam. The barker tried to snatch the knuckle-duster from Brennon, and one of Young Firpo's seconds rushed across the ring and struck at the winner. The crowd, sensing injustice to their favorite, surged into the ring with the avowed intention of wrecking the show! As I made my way to the nearest exit I saw an infuriated townsman swing up a chair to strike the still prostrate Young Firpo. Brennon sprang forward and caught the blow on his own shoulder, going to his knees under it; then I was outside and as I walked away, laughing, I still heard the turmoil and the shouts of the policemen.

Some time later I saw Brennon fight again, in a small club on the West Coast. His opponent was a second-rater named Mulcahy. During the fight my old interest in Brennon was renewed. With incredible stamina, with as terrific a punch as I ever saw, it was evident his one failing was an absolute lack of science. Mulcahy, though strong and tough, was a mere dub, yet he clearly outboxed Brennon for nearly two rounds, and hit him with everything he had, though his best blows did not even make the dark-browed lad wince. With the second round a half minute to go, one of Brennon's sweeping swings landed and the fight was over.

I thought to myself: that lad looks like a champion, but he fights like a longshoreman, but I won't attach too much importance to that. Many a fighter stumbles through life and never learns anything, simply because of an ignorant or negligent manager.

I went to Brennon's dressing-room and spoke to him.

"My name is Steve Amber. I've seen you fight a couple of times."

"I've heard of you," he answered. "What do you want?"

Overlooking his abrupt manner, I asked: "Who's your manager?"

"I haven't any."

"How would you like me to manage you?"

"I'd as soon have you as anybody," he answered shortly. "But this was my last fight. I'm through. I'm sick of flattening dubs in fourth-rate joints."

"Tie up with me. Maybe I'll get you better matches."

"No use. I had my chance twice. Once against Sailor Slade; once against Johnny Varella. I flopped. No, don't start to argue. I don't want to talk to you—or to anybody. I'm through, and I want to go to bed."

"Suit yourself," I answered. "I never coax—but here's my card. If you change your mind, look me up."

CHAPTER II

Scenting the Kill

Weeks stretched into months. But Mike Brennon was not a man one could forget easily. When I dreamed, as all fight fans and fighters' managers dream, of a super-fighter, the form of Mike Brennon rose unbidden—a dark, brooding figure, charged with the abysmal fighting fury of the primitive.

Then one day Brennon came to me—not in a day-dream, but in the flesh. He stood in the office of my training camp, his crumpled hat in his hand, an eager grin on his dark face—a very different man from the morose and moody youth to whom I had talked before.

"Mr. Amber," he said directly, "if you still want me, I'd like to have you manage me."

"That's fine," I answered.

Brennon appeared nervous.

"Can you get me a fight right away?" he asked. "I need money."

"Not so fast," I said. "I can advance you some money if you're in debt—"

He made an impatient gesture. "It's not that—can you get me a fight this week?"

"Are you in trim? How long since you've been in the ring?"

"Not since you saw me last; but I always stay in shape."

I took Brennon to my open-air ring where Spike Ganlon, a clever middle-weight, was working out, and instructed them to step for a few fast rounds. Brennon was eager enough, and I was astonished to see him put up a very fair sort of boxing against the shifty Ganlon. True, he was far out-stepped and out-classed, but that was to be expected, as Ganlon was rather a prominent figure in the fistic world. But I did not like the way Mike sent in his punches. They lacked the old trip-hammer force, and he was slower than I had remembered him to be. However, when I had him slug the heavy bag he flashed his old form, nearly tearing the bag loose from its moorings, and I decided that he had been pulling his punches against Ganlon.

The days that followed were full of hard work and careful coaching. Brennon listened carefully to what Ganlon and I told him, but the result was far from satisfying. He was intelligent, but he could not seem to apply practically the things he learned easily in theory.

Still, I did not expect too much of him at first. I worked with him patiently for several weeks, importing a fairly clever heavyweight for his sparring partner. The first time they really let go, I was amazed and disappointed. Mike shuffled and floundered awkwardly with futile, flabby blows. When a sharp jab on the nose stung him, he quit trying to box and went back to his old style of wild and aimless swinging. However, these swings were the old sledge-hammer type, and his erratic speed had returned to him. I quickly called a halt.

"I'm wrong," I said. "I've been trying to make a boxing wizard out of you. But you're a natural slugger, though you seem to have little of the natural slugger's aptitude. Looks like you'd have learned something from your actual experience in the ring.

"Well, anyway, I'm going to make a real slugger like Dempsey, Sullivan and McGovern out of you. I know how you are; you've got the slugger's instinct. You can box fairly well with a friend when you're just doing it for fun, but when you're in the ring, or somebody stings you, you forget everything but your natural style. It's no discredit to a man's mentality. Dempsey was a clever boxer when he was sparring, but he never boxed in the ring. And he swung like you do, till De Forest taught him to hit straight.

"Still, Mike, I'll tell you frankly that at his crudest, Dempsey showed more aptitude for the game than you do. Now, this is for your own good. Dempsey, Ketchell and McGovern, even when they were just starting, used instinctive footwork and kept stepping around their men. They ducked and weaved and hit accurately. You go in straight up and wide open, and a blind man could duck your swings. You've unusual speed, but you don't know how to use it. But now that I know where I've been making my mistake, I'll change my tactics."

For a time it seemed as though my dreams were coming true—that Mike was a second Dempsey. In spite of his urging that I get him a fight, I kept him idle for three months—that is, he was not fighting. For hours each day I had him practice hooking the heavy bag with short smashes to straighten his punches and eliminate so much aimless swinging. He would never learn to put force behind a straight punch, but I intended making him a vicious hooker like Dempsey. And I tried to teach him the weave of that old master and the trick of boring in, protected by a barricade of gloves and elbows until in close; and the fundamentals of footwork and feinting. It was not easy.

"Mike," said Ganlon to me, "is a queer nut. He's got a fighter's heart and body, but he ain't got a fighter's brain. He understands, but he can't do what you teach him. He has to work for hours on the simplest trick—and then he's liable to forget it. If he was a bonehead, I'd understand it. But he's brainy in other ways."

"Maybe he fought so long in second-rate clubs he formed habits he can't break."

"Partly. But it goes deeper. They's a kink in his brain."

"What do you mean, a kink?" I asked uneasily.

"I dunno. But it's somethin' that breaks down his co-ordination and keeps his mind from workin' with his muscles. When he tries to box he has to stop and think, and in the ring you ain't got time. You see a punch comin' and in that split-second you got to know what you can't do and what you can do to get outa the way and counter. 'Course, you don't exactly study it all out, but you *know,* see? That is, if you're a fast boxer. If you're a wide-open slugger like Mike, you don't think nothin'. You just take the punch as a matter of course, spit out your teeth and keep borin' in."

"But any slugger is that way," I objected. "And we're not trying to teach Mike to be clever, in the technical sense of the word."

Ganlon shook his head. "I know. But Mike's different. He ain't cut out for this game. Even these simple tricks are too complicated for him. Well, he's got to learn some defense, or he'll be punched cuckoo in a few years. All the great sluggers had some. Some weaved and crouched, like Dempsey; some wrapped their arms around their skull and barged in, like Nelson and Paolino. Them that fought wide open didn't last no time, 'specially among the heavies. The padded cell and paper-doll cut-outs for most of 'em. It don't stand to reason a human skull can stand up under the beatin's it gets like that."

"You're a born croaker. Mike's rugged but intelligent. He'll learn."

"At anything else, yes—at this game—maybe."

Not long after my talk with Spike, Brennon came to me.

"Steve," he said, "I've got to have a fight. I need money—bad."

"Mike," said I, "it's none of my business, but I don't see why you should be so desperately insistent. You've been at no expense at all, here in the camp. You said you weren't in debt, and you've refused my offers to loan you—"

"What business is it of yours?" he broke in, white at the lips.

"None at all," I hastened to assure him. "Only as your manager, I've got your financial interests at heart, naturally. I apologize."

"I apologize, too, Steve," he answered abruptly, his manner changing. "I should have known you weren't trying to pry into my private affairs. But I've got to have at least—" And he named a sum of money which rather surprised me.

"There's only one way to get that much," I answered. "Understand, I don't believe you're ready to go in with a first-string man. But since money is the object—Monk Barota is on the coast now, padding his kayo record. He'll be looking for set-ups. The promoter at the Hopi A.C. is a friend of mine. I can get you a match with him at close to the figure you named. You understand that a bad defeat now might ruin you. Don't say I didn't warn you. But you're in fine shape, and if you fight as we've taught you, I believe you can whip him."

"I'll whip him," Mike nodded grimly. I hoped he was more sincere in his belief than I was. I really felt in my heart that he was not ready for a first-rater and I had intended building him up more gradually. But there was fierce, driving intensity about him when he spoke of the money he needed that broke down my resolution. Brennon was, in many ways, a character of terrific magnetic force. Like Sullivan, he dominated all about him, trainers, handlers and matchmakers. But only in the matter of money was he unreasonable, and this quirk in his nature amounted to an obsession.

Mainly through my influence, Brennon, an entirely unknown quantity, was matched with Barota for a ten-rounder;

at ringside the odds were three to one on the Italian, with no takers. My last instructions to Mike were: "Remember! Use the crouch and guard Ganlon taught you. If you don't have some defense, he'll ruin you!"

The lights went out except those over the ring. The gong sounded. The crowd fell silent—that breathless, momentary silence that marks the beginning of the fight. The men slid out of their corners and—

"Oh, my gosh!" wailed Ganlon at my side. "He's doin' everything backward!"

Mike wore his old uncertain manner. Under the lights, with his foe before him and the roar of the crowd deafening him, he was like a trapped jungle beast, bewildered and confused. Barota led—Mike ducked clumsily the wrong way, and took the punch in the eye. That flicking left was hard for any man to avoid, but Mike incessantly ducked into it.

Ganlon was raving at my side. "After all these months of work, he forgets! You better throw in the sponge now. Look there!" as Mike tried a left of his own. "He can't even hook right. The whole house knows what's comin'. Same as writin' a letter about it."

Barota was taking his time. In spite of the fact that his foe seemed to have nothing but a scowl, no man could look into Mike Brennon's face and take him lightly. But a round of clumsy floundering and ineffectual pawing lulled his suspicions. Meanwhile, he flitted around the bewildered slugger, showering him with stinging left jabs. Ganlon was nearly weeping with rage as if his pupil's ineptness somehow reflected on him.

"All I know, I taught him, and there's that wop makin' a monkey outa him!"

With the round thirty seconds to go, Barota suddenly tore in with one of his famous attacks. Mike abandoned all attempts at science and began swinging wildly and futilely. Barota worked untouched between his flailing arms, beating a rattling barrage against Brennon's head and body. The gong stopped the punishment.

Mike's face was somewhat cut, but he was as fresh as if he had not just gone through a severe beating. He broke in on Ganlon's impassioned soliloquy to remark: "This fellow can't hit."

"Can't hit!" Ganlon nearly dropped the sponge. "Why, he's

got a kayo record as long as a subway! Ain't he just pounded you all over the ring?"

"I didn't feel his punches, anyway," answered Mike, and then the gong sounded.

Barota came out fast, in a mood to bring this fight to a sudden close. He launched a swift attack, cut Mike's lips with a right; then began hammering at his body with the left-handed assault which had softened so many of his opponents for the kayo. The crowd went wild as he battered Mike around the ring, but suddenly I felt Ganlon's fingers sink into my arm.

"Bat Nelson true to life!" he whispered, his voice vibrating with excitement. "The crowd thinks, and Barota thinks, them left hooks is hurtin' Mike—but he ain't even feelin' 'em. He's got one chance—when Barota shoots the right—"

At this moment Barota stepped back, feinted swiftly and shot the right. He was proud of the bone-crushing quality of that right hand. He had a clear opening and every ounce of his weight went behind it. The leather-guarded knuckles backed by spar-like arm and heavy shoulder, crashed flush against Mike's jaw. The impact was plainly heard in every part of the house. A gasp went up, nails sank deep into clenching palms. Mike swayed drunkenly, but he did not fall.

Barota stopped short for a flashing instant—frozen by the realization that he had failed to even floor his man. And in that second Mike swung a wild left and landed for the first time—high on the cheek bone, but Barota went down. The crowd rose screaming. Dazed, the Italian rose without a count and Mike tore into him with the ferocity of a tiger that scents the kill. Barota, blinded and dizzy, was in no condition to defend himself, yet Mike missed with both hands until a mine-sweeping right-hander caught his man flush on the temple, and he dropped—not merely out, but senseless.

The crowd was in a frenzy, but Ganlon said to me: "He's an iron man, don't you see? A natural-born freak like Grim and Goddard. He'll never learn anything, not if he trains a hundred years."

CHAPTER III

White-Hot Fighting Fury

The day after Mike Brennon had shocked the sporting world by his victory, he, Ganlon and I sat at breakfast, and we were a far from merry gang. Ganlon read the morning papers and growled.

"The whole country's on fire," he muttered. "Sports writers goin' cuckoo over the new find. Tellin' that Barota cried and took on in his dressin'-room when he come to; and talkin' about how Mike 'fooled' his man in the first round by lookin' like a dub—callin' him a second Fitzsimmons! Applesauce. But here's a old-timer that knows his stuff.

"'If I am not much mistaken,'" he read, "'This Brennon is the same who looked like a deckhand against Sailor Slade in Los Angeles last year. His kayo of Barota had all the earmarks of a fluke. He is, however, incredibly tough.'"

"Uhmhuh," said Ganlon, laying down the paper. "Quite true. Mike, I hate to say it, but as a fighter you're a false alarm. It ain't your fault. You got the heart and the body, but you got no more natural talent than a ribbon clerk, and you can't learn. You got the fightin' instinct, but not the fighter's instinct—and they's a flock of difference.

"You're just a heavyweight Joe Grim. A iron man; never was one but Jeffries who could learn anything. I'm advisin' you to quit the ring—now. Your kind don't come to no good end. Too many punches on the head. They get permanently punch drunk. You don't have to go around countin' your fingers; you got brains enough to succeed somewhere else.

"You got three courses to follow: first, you can go around fightin' set-ups at the small clubs. You can make a livin' that way, and last a long time. Second, you can sign up with some of the offers you're bound to get now. Fightin' clever first-raters you won't win much, if any, but you'll be an attraction like Grim was. But you won't last. You'll crack under the incessant fire of smashes, and wind up in the booby hatch. Third and best, you can take what money you got and step out. Me and Steve will gladly lend you enough to start in business in a modest way."

I nodded. Mike shook his head and spread his iron fingers on the table in front of him. As usual he dominated the scene—a great sombre figure of unknown potentialities.

"You're right, Spike, in everything you've said. I've always known there was a deficiency somewhere. No man could be as impervious to punishment as I am and have a perfectly normal brain. Not alone at boxing; I've failed at everything else I've tried. As for boxing, the crowd dazes me, for one thing. But that isn't all. I just can't remember what to do next, and have to struggle through the best way I can.

"But—I *can take it!* That's my one hope. That's why I'm not quitting the game. At the cost of my reflexes, maybe. Nature gave me an unusual constitution. You admit I'd be a drawing card. Well, I'm like Battling Nelson—not human when it comes to taking punishment. The only man that ever hurt me was Sailor Slade, and he couldn't stop me. Nobody can now. Eventually, after years of battering, someone will knock me out. But before that time, I'm going to cash in on my ruggedness. Capitalize on the fact that no man can keep me down for the count. I'll accumulate a fortune if I'm handled right."

"Great heavens, man!" I exclaimed. "Do you realize what that means—the frightful punishment, the mutilations? You'll be fighting first-raters now—men with skill and terrific punches. You have no defense. You sap, they'd hammer you to a red pulp."

"My defense is a granite jaw and iron ribs," he answered. "I'll take them all on and wear them down."

"Maybe," I answered. "A man can wear himself down punching a granite boulder, as I've seen men do with Tom Sharkey and Joe Goddard, but what about the boulder! You were lucky with Barota. The next man will watch his step."

"They can't hurt me. And I can beat any man I can hit. Win or lose, I'll be a drawing card, and that means big purses. That's what I'm after. Do you think I'd go through this purgatory if the need wasn't great?"

"If it's poverty—" I began.

"What do you know about poverty?" he cried in a strange passion. "Were you left in a basket on the steps of an orphanage almost as soon as you were born? Did you spend your childhood mixed in with five hundred others, where the needs of all were so great that no one of you got more than the barest necessities? Did you pass your boyhood as a tramp and hobo worker, riding the rods and starving? I did!

"But that's neither here nor there; nor it isn't my own personal poverty so much that drove me back in the ring—but let it pass. As my manager, I want you to get busy. If I can win another fight it will increase my prestige. I don't expect to win many. Later on, they'll come packing in to see me, for the same reason they went to see Joe Grim—to see if I can be knocked out. Until the fans find out I'm a freak, I'll have to go on my merits. Barota wants a return match. I don't want him now, or any other clever man who'll outpoint me and make me look even worse than I am. I want the fans to see me bloody and staggering—and still carrying on! That's what draws the crowd. Get me a man-killer—a puncher who'll come in and try to murder me. Get me Jack Maloney!"

"It's suicide!" I cried. "Maloney'll kill you! I won't have anything to do with it!"

"Then, by heaven," Brennon roared, heaving erect and crashing his fist on the table, "our ways part here! You could help me better than anyone else—you know the ballyhoo. But if you fail me—"

"If you're determined," I said huskily, my mind almost numbed by the driving force of his willpower, "I'll do all I can. But I warn you, you'll leave this game with a clouded brain."

His nervous grip nearly crushed my fingers as he said shortly: "I knew you'd stand by. Never mind my brain; it's cased in sold iron."

As he stroke out Ganlon, slightly pale, said to me in a low voice: "A twist in his head sure. Money—all the time—money. I'm no dude, but he dresses like a wharfhand. What's he do with his money? He ain't supportin' no aged mother, it's a cinch. You heard him say he was left on a doorstep."

I shook my head. Brennon was an enigma beyond my comprehension.

The rise of Iron Mike Brennon is now ring history, and of all the vivid pages in the annals of this heart-stirring game, I hold that the story of this greatest of all iron men makes the most lurid, fantastic and pulse-quickening chapter.

Iron Mike Brennon! Look at him as he was when his exploits swept the country. Six feet one from his narrow feet to the black tousled shock of his hair; one hundred and ninety pounds of steel springs and whalebone. With his terrible eyes glaring from under heavy black brows, thin, blood-smeared lips writhed in snarl of battle fury—still when I dream of the super-fighter there rises the picture of Mike Brennon—a dream charged with bitterness. Take a man with incredible stamina and hitting power; take from him the ability to remember one iota of science in actual combat and leave out of his make-up the instinct of the natural fighter, and you have Iron Mike Brennon. A man who would have been the greatest champion of all time, but for that flaw in his make-up.

His first fight, after that memorable breakfast-table conversation, was with Jack Maloney—one hundred and ninety-five pounds of white-hot fighting fury, with a right hand like a caulking mallet. They met at San Francisco.

With the aid of Ganlon and friendly scribes, I set the old ballyhoo working. The papers were full of Mike Brennon. They pointed out that he had over twenty knockouts to his credit, ignoring the fact that all of these victims, except one, were unknown dubs. They glossed over the fact that he had been outpointed by second-raters and beaten to a pulp by Sailor Slade. They angrily refuted charges that his kayo of Barota was a fluke.

The stadium was packed that night. The crowd paid their money, and they got its worth. Before the bell I was whispering a few instructions which I knew would be useless, when Mike cut in with fierce eagerness: "What a sellout! Look at that crowd! If I win it'll mean more sell-outs and bigger purses! I've *got* to win!" His eyes gleamed with ferocious avidity.

Two giants crashed from their corners as the gong sounded. Maloney came in like the great slugger he was, body crouched, chin tucked behind his shoulder, hands high. Brennon, forgetting everything before the blast of the crowd and his own fighting fury, rushed like a longshoreman, head lifted, hands clenched at his hips, wide open—as iron men have fought since time immemorial—with but one thought—to get to his foe and crush him.

Maloney landed first, a terrific left hook which spattered Brennon with blood and brought the crowd to its feet, roaring. I heard a note of relief in the shouts of Maloney's manager. This bird was going to be easy, after all! Like most sluggers, when they find a man they can hit easily, Maloney had gone fighting crazy. He lashed Brennon about the ring, hitting so hard and fast that Mike had no time to get set. The few swings he did try swished harmlessly over Maloney's bobbing head.

"He's slowin' down," muttered Ganlon as the first round drew to a close. "The old iron man game! Maloney's punchin' hisself out."

True, Jack's blows were coming not weaker, but slower. No man could keep up the pace he was setting. Brennon was as strong as ever, and just before the gong he staggered Maloney with a sweeping left to the body—his first blow.

Back in his corner Ganlon wiped the blood from Mike's battered face and grinned savagely: "Joe Goddard had nothin' on you. I'm beginnin' to believe you'll beat him. You've took plenty and you'll take more; he'll come out strong but each round he'll get weaker; he'll be fought out."

The fans thundered acclaim as Maloney rushed out for the second. But he had sensed something they had not. He had hit this man with everything he possessed and had failed to even floor him. So he tore in like a wild man, and again drove Brennon about the ring before a torrent of left and right hooks that sounded like the kicks of a mule. Brennon, eyes nearly closed, lips pulped, nose broken, showed no sign of distress until the latter part of the round, when Maloney landed repeatedly to the jaw with his maul-like right. Then Mike's knees trembled momentarily, but he straightened and cut his foe's cheek with a glancing right.

At the gong the crowd began to realize what was going on. The timbre of their yells changed. They began to inquire at the top of their voices if Maloney was losing his famed punch, or if Brennon was made of solid iron.

Ganlon, wiping Brennon's gory features and offering the smelling salts, which he pushed away, said swiftly: "Maloney's legs trembled as he went back to his corner; he looked back over his shoulder like he couldn't believe it when he saw you walk to your corner without a quiver. He knows he ain't lost his punch! He knows you're the first man ever stood up to him wide open; he knows you been through a tough grind and ain't even saggin'. You got his goat. Now go get him!"

The gong sounded. Maloney came in, the light of desperation in his eyes, to redeem his slipping fame as a knocker-out. His blows were like a rain of sledge-hammers and before that rain Mike Brennon went down. The referee began counting. Maloney reeled back against the ropes, breath coming in great gasps—completely fought out.

"He'll get up," said Ganlon calmly.

Brennon was half crouching on his knees, dazed, not hurt. I saw his lips move and I read their motion: "More fights—more money—"

He bounded erect. Maloney's whole body sagged. Brennon's rising took more morale out of Jack than any sort of a blow would have done. Mike, sensing the mental condition and physical weariness of Maloney, tore in like a tiger. Left, right, he missed, shaking off Maloney's weakening blows as if they had been slaps from a girl. At last he landed—a wide left hook to the head. Maloney tottered, and a wild over-hand right crashed under his cheek bone, dashing him to to his knees. At "nine!" he staggered up, but another right that a blind man in good condition could have ducked, dropped him again. The referee hesitated, then raised Mike's hand, beckoning to Maloney's seconds.

As Maloney, aided by his handlers, reeled to his corner on buckling legs, I noted the ironical fact: the winner was a gory, battered wreck, while the loser had only a single cut on his cheek. I thought of the old fights in which iron men of another day had figured: of Joe Goddard, the old Barrier Champion, outlasting the great Choynski, finishing each of their terrible battles a bloody travesty of a man, but winner. I thought of Sharkey dropping Kid McCoy; of Nelson outlasting Gans; Young Corbett—Herrerra. And I sighed. Of all the men who relied on their ruggedness to carry them through, Brennon was the most wide open, the most erratic.

As I sponged his cuts in the dressing-room, I could not help saying: "You see what fighting a first-string hitter means; you won't be able to answer the gong for months."

"Months!" he mumbled through smashed lips. "You'll sign me up with Johnny Varella for a bout next week!"

CHAPTER IV

Iron Mike's Dread

After the Maloney fight, fans and scribes realized what he was—an iron man—and as such his fame grew. He became a drawing card just as he had predicted—one of the greatest of his day. And his inordinate lust for money grew with his power as an attraction. He haggled over prices, held out for every cent he could get, and rather than pass up a fight, would always lower his price. For the first and only time in my life, I was merely a figure-head. Brennon was the real power behind the curtain. And he insisted on fighting at least once a month.

"You'll crack three times as quickly fighting so often," I protested. "Otherwise you might last for years."

"But why stretch it out if I can make the same amount of money in a few months that I could make in that many years?"

"But consider the strain on you!" I cried.

"I'm not considering anything about myself," he answered roughly. "Get me a match."

The matches came readily. He had caught the crowd's fancy and no matter whom he fought, the fans flocked to see him. He met them all—ferocious sluggers, clever dancers, and dangerous fighters who combined the qualities of slugger and boxer. When first-rate opponents were not forthcoming quickly enough, he went into the sticks and pushed over second-raters. As long as he was making money, no matter how much or how little, he was satisfied. What he did with that money, I did not know.

He was honest, always shot square with his obligations; but beyond that he was a miser. He lived at the training camps or at the cheapest hotels, in spite of my protests; he bought cheap clothes and allowed himself no luxuries whatever.

At first he won consistently. He was dangerous to any man. Coupled with his abnormal endurance was a mental state—a driving, savage determination—which dragged him off the canvas time and again. This was above and behind his natural fighting fury, and he had acquired it between the time he had first retired and the next time I saw him.

At the time he was in his prime, there was a wealth of material in the heavyweight ranks, and Brennon loomed among them as the one man none of them could stop. That fact alone put him on equal footing with men in every other way his superiors.

Following the Maloney fight, the public clamored for a match between my iron man and Yon Van Heeren, the Durable Dutchman, who was considered, up to that time, the roughest and toughest man in the world, one who had never been knocked out, and whose only claim to fame, like Brennon's, was his ruggedness. A certain famous scribe, referring to this fight as "a brawl between two bar-room thugs," said: "This unfortunate affair has set the game back twenty years. No sensitive person seeing this slaughter for his or her first fight, could ever be tempted to see another. People who do not know the game are likely to judge it by the two gorillas, who, utterly devoid of science, turned the ring into a shambles."

Before the men went into the ring they made the referee promise not to stop the fight under any circumstances—an unusual proceeding, but easily understood in their case.

The fight was a strange experience to Mike; most of the punishment was on the other side. Van Heeren, six feet two and weighing 210 pounds, was a terrific hitter, but lacked Mike's dynamic speed and fury. Those sweeping haymakers which had missed so many others, crashed blindingly against the Dutchman's head or sank agonizingly into his body. At the end of the first round his face was a gory wreck. At the end of the fourth his features had lost all human semblance; his body was a mass of reddened flesh.

Toe to toe they stood, round after round, neither taking a back step. The fifth, sixth and seventh rounds were nightmares, in which Mike was dropped three times, and Van Heeren went down twice that many times. All over the stadium women were fainting or being helped out; fans were shrieking for the fight to be stopped.

In the ninth, Van Heeren, a hideous and inhuman sight, dropped for the last time. Four ribs broken, features permanently ruined, he lay writhing, still trying to rise as the referee tolled off the "Ten!" that marked his finish as a fighting man.

Mike Brennon, clinging to the ropes, dizzy and nearly punched out for the only time in his life, stood above his victim, acknowledged king of all iron men. This fight finished Van Heeren, and nearly finished boxing in the state, but it added to Brennon's fame, and his real pity for the broken Dutchman was mingled with a fierce exultation of realized power. More money—more packed houses! The world's greatest iron man! In the three years he fought under my management he met them all, except the champion of his division. He lost about as many as he won, but the only thing that could impair his drawing power was a knockout—and this seemed postponed indefinitely. He won more of his fights against the hard punchers than against the light tappers, as the latter took no chances. Many a slugger, after battering him to a red ruin, blew up and fell before his aimless but merciless attack. He broke the hands and he broke the hearts of the men who tried to stop him.

The light hitters outboxed him, but did not hurt him, and his wild swings were dangerous even to them. Barota outpointed him, and Jackie Finnegan, Frankie Grogan and Flash Sullivan, the lightheavy champion.

The hard hitters made the mistake of trading punches with him. Soldier Handler dropped him five times in four rounds, and then stopped a righthander that knocked him clear out of the ring and into fistic oblivion. Jose Gonzales, the great South American, punched himself out on the iron tiger and went down to defeat. Gunboat Sloan battered out a red decision over him, but still believing he could achieve the impossible, went in to trade punches in a return bout, and lasted less than a round. Brennon finished Ricardo Diaz, the Spanish Giant, beat down Snake Calberson after his toughness had broken the Brown Phantom's heart. Johnny Varella and several lesser lights broke their hands on him and quit. He met Whitey Broad and Kid Allison in no decision bouts; knocked out Young Hansen, and fought a fierce fifteen-round draw with Sailor Steve Costigan, who never rated better than a second-class man, but who gave some first-raters terrific battles.

To those who doubt that flesh and blood can endure the punishment which Brennon endured, I beg you to look at the records of the ring's iron men. I point to your attention, Tom Sharkey plunging headlong into the terrible blows of Jeffries; that same Sharkey shooting headlong over the ropes onto the concrete floor from the blows of Choynski, yet finishing the fight a winner.

I call to your attention Mike Boden, who had no more defense than had Brennon, staying the limit with Choynski; and Joe Grim taking all Fitzsimmons could hand him—was it fifteen or sixteen times he was floored? Yet he finished that fight standing. No man can understand the iron men of the ring. Theirs is a long, hard, bloody trail, with oftentimes only poverty and a clouded mind at the end, but the red chapter their clan has written across the chronicles of the game will never be effaced.

And so Brennon fought on, taking all his cruel punishment, hoarding his money, saving little—as much a mystery to me as ever. Sports writers discovered his passion for money, and raked him. They accused him of being miserly and refusing aid to his less fortunate fellows—the battered tramps who will occasionally touch a successful fighter for a handout. This was only partly true. He did sometimes give money to men who needed it desperately, but the occasions were infrequent.

Then he began to crack. Ganlon, his continual champion, first sensed it. Crouching beside me the night Mike fought Kid Allison, Spike whispered to me out of the corner of his mouth: "He's slowin' down. It's the beginnin' of the end."

That night Spike spoke plainly to his friend.

"Mike, you're about through. You're slippin'. Punches jar you worse than they used to. You've lasted three years of terrible hard goin'. You got to quit."

"When I'm knocked out," said Mike stubbornly. "I haven't taken the count yet."

"When a bird like you takes the count, it means he's a punch-drunk wreck," said Ganlon. "When the blows begin to hurt you, it means the shock of them is reachin' the brain and hurtin' it. Remember Van Heeren, that you finished? He's wanderin' around, sayin' he's trainin' to fight Fitzsimmons, that's been dead for years."

A shadow crossed Mike's dark face at the mention of the Dutchman's name. The beatings he had taken had disfigured him and given him a peculiarly sinister look, which however, did not rob his face of its strange dominating quality.

"I'm good for a few more fights," he answered. "I need money—"

"Always money!" I exclaimed. "You must have half a million dollars at least. I'm beginning to believe you are a miser—"

"Steve," said Ganlon suddenly, "Van Heeren was around here yesterday."

"What of it?"

Ganlon continued almost accusingly, "Mike gave him a thousand dollars."

"What if I did?" cried Brennon in one of his rare inexplicable passions. "The fellow was broke—in no condition to earn any money—I finished him—why shouldn't I help him a little? Whose business is it?"

"Nobody's," I answered. "But it shows you're not a miser. And it deepens the mystery about you. Won't you tell me why you need more money?"

He made a quick impatient gesture. "There's no need. You get the matches—I do the fighting. We split the money, and that's all there is to it."

"But, Mike," I said as kindly as I could, "There is more to it. You've made me more money than either of the champions I've managed, and if I didn't sincerely wish for your own good, I'd say for you to stay in the ring.

"But you *ought* to quit. You can even get your features fixed up—plastic face building is a wonderful art. Fight even one more time, and you may spend your days in a padded cell."

"I'm tougher than you think," he answered. "I'm as good as I ever was and I'll prove it. Get me Sailor Slade."

"He beat you once before, when you were better than you are now. How do you expect—"

"I didn't have the incentive to win then, that I have now."

I nodded. What this incentive was I did not know, but I had seen him rise again and again from what looked like certain defeat—had seen him, writhing on the canvas, turn white, his eyes blaze with sudden terror as he dragged himself upright. Terror? Of losing! A terror that kept him going when even his iron body was tottering on the verge of collapse and when the old fighting frenzy had ceased to function in the numbed brain. What prompted this dread? It was a mystery I could not fathom, but that in some way it was connected with his strange money-lust, I knew.

"You'll sign me for four fights," Brennon was saying. "With Sailor Slade, Young Hansen, Jack Slattery and Mike Costigan."

"You're out of your head!" I exclaimed sharply. "You've picked the four most dangerous battlers in the world!"

"Hansen will be easy. I beat him once, and I can do it again. I don't know about Slattery. I want to take him on last. First, I've got to hurdle Slade. After him, I'll fight Costigan. He's the least scientific of the four, but the hardest hitter. If I'm slipping I want to get him before I've gone too far."

"It's suicide!" I cried. "If you've got to fight, pass up these man-killers and take on some set-ups. If Slade don't knock you out, he'll soften you up so Costigan will punch you right into the bug-house. He's a murderer. They call him Iron Mike, too."

"I'll pack them in," he answered heedlessly. "Slade's nearly the drawing card I am, and as for Costigan, the fans always turn out to see two iron men meet."

As usual, there was no answer to be made.

CHAPTER V

The Roll of the Iron Men

It was a few nights before the Brennon-Slade fight. I had wandered into Mike's room and my eye fell on a partially completed letter on his writing table. Without any intention of spying, I idly noted that it was addressed to a girl named Marjory Walshire, at a very fashionable girls' school in New York state.

I saw that a letter from this girl lay beside the other one, and though it was an atrocious breach of manners, in my curiosity to know why a girl in a society school like that would be writing a prizefighter, I picked up the partially completed letter and glanced idly over it. The next moment I was reading it with fierce intensity, all scruples forgotten. Having finished it, I snatched up the other and ruthlessly tore it open.

I had scarcely finished reading this when Mike entered with Ganlon. His eyes blazed with sudden fury, but before he could say a word I launched an offensive of my own—for one of the few times in my life, wild with rage.

"You born fool!" I snarled. "So this is why you've been crucifying yourself!"

"What do you mean by getting into my private correspondence?" his voice was husky with fury.

I sneered. "I'm not going to enter into a discussion of etiquette. You can beat me up afterward, but just now I'm going to have my say.

"You've been keeping some girl in a ritzy finishing school

back East. Finishing school! It's nearly finished you! What kind of a girl is she, to let you go through this mill for her? I'd like for her to see your battered map now! While she's been lolling at ease in the most expensive school she could find, you've been flattening out the resin with your shoulders and soaking it down with your blood—"

"Shut up!" roared Brennon, white and shaking.

He leaned back against the table, gripping the edge so hard his knuckles whitened as he fought for control. At last he spoke more calmly.

"Yes, that's the incentive that's kept me going. That girl is the only girl I ever loved—the only thing I ever had to love.

"Listen, do you know how lonely a kid is when he has absolutely nobody in the world to love? The folks in the home were kind, but there were so many children—I got the beginnings of a good education. That's all.

"Out in the world it was worse. I worked, tramped, starved. I fought for everything I ever got. I have a better education than most, you say. I worked my way through high school, and read all the books in my spare time that I could beg, steal or borrow. Many a time I went hungry to buy a book.

"I drifted into the ring from fighting in carnivals and the like. I never got anywhere. After I whipped Mulcahy the night you talked to me, I quit. Drifted. Then in a little town on the Arizona desert I met Marjory Walshire.

"Poverty? She knew poverty! Working her fingers to the bone in a cafe. Good blood in her too, just as there is in me, somewhere. She should have been born to the satins and velvets—instead she was born to the greasy dishes and dirty tables of a second-class cafe. I loved her, and she loved me. She told me her dreams that she never believed would come true—of education—nice clothes—refined companions—everything that any girl wants.

"Where was I to turn? I could take her out of the cafe—only to introduce her to the drudgery of a laboring man's wife. So I went back into the ring. As soon as I could, I sent her to school. I've been sending her money enough to live as well as any girl there, and I've saved too, so when she gets out of school and I have to quit the ring, we can be married and start in business that won't mean drudgery and poverty.

"Poverty is the cause of more crimes, cruelty and suffering than anything else. Poverty kept me from having a home and people like other kids. You know how it is in the slums—

parents toiling for a living and too many children. They can't support them all. Mine left me on the door-step of the orphanage with a note: 'He's honest born. We love him, but we can't keep him. Call him Michael Brennon.'

"Poverty can be as cruel in a small town as in a city—Marjory, who'd never been out of the town where she was born—with her soul starved and her little white hands reddened and calloused—

"It's the thought of her that's kept me on my feet when the whole world was blind and red and the fists of my opponent were like hammers on my shattering brain—that's the thought that dragged me off the canvas when my body was without feeling and my arms hung like lead, to strike down the man I could no longer see. And as long as she's waiting for me at the end of the long trail, there's no man on earth can make me take the count!"

His voice crashed through the room like a clarion call of victory, but my old doubts returned.

"But how can she love you so much," I exclaimed, "when she's willing for you to go through all this for her?"

"What does she know of fighting? I made her believe boxing was more or less of a dancing and tapping affair. She'd heard of Corbett and Tunney, clever fellows who could step twenty rounds without a mark, and she supposed I was like them. She hasn't seen me in nearly four years—not since I left the town where she worked. I've put her off when she's wanted to come and see me, or for me to come to her. When she does see my battered face it'll be a terrible shock to her, but I was never very handsome anyway—"

"Do you mean to tell me," I broke in, "that she never tunes in on one of your fights, never reads an account of them, when the papers are full of your doings?"

"She don't know my real name. After I quit the game the first time, I went under the name of Mike Flynn to duck the two-by-four promoters I'd fought for, and who were always pestering me to fight for them again. The first time I saw Marjory I began to think of fighting again, and I never told her differently. The money I've sent has been in cashier's checks. To her, I'm simply Mike Flynn, a fighter she never hears of. She wouldn't recognize my picture in the papers."

"But her letters are addressed to Mike Brennon."

"You didn't look closely. They're addressed to Michael Flynn, care of Mike Brennon, this camp. She thinks Brennon is merely a friend of her Mike. Well, now you know why I've fought on and stinted myself. With Van Heeren, it was different. I'm responsible for his condition. I had to help him.

"These four fights now; one of them may be my last. I've got money, but I want more. I intend that Marjory shall never want again for anything. I'm to get a hundred grand for this fight. My third purse of that size. With good management, thanks to you, I've made more money than many champions. If I whip these four men, I'll fight on. If I'm knocked out, I'll have to quit. Let's drop the matter."

I haven't the heart to tell of the Brennon-Slade fight in detail. Even today the thought of the punishment Mike took that night takes the stiffening out of my knees. He had slipped even more than we had thought. The steel-spring legs, which had carried him through so many whirlwind battles, had slowed down. His sweeping haymakers crashed over with their old power, but they did not continually wing through the air as of old. Blows that should not have jarred him, staggered him. The squat sailor, wild with the thought of a knockout, threw caution to the winds. How many times he floored Mike I never dared try to remember, but Brennon was still Iron Mike. Again and again the gong saved him; in the fourteenth round Slade went to pieces, and the iron tiger he had punched into a red smear found him in the crimson mist and blindly blasted him into unconsciousness.

Brennon collapsed in his corner after Slade was counted out, and both men were carried senseless from the ring. I sat by Mike's side that night while he lay in a semi-conscious state, occasionally muttering brokenly as his bruised brain conjured up red visions. He lay, both eyes closed, his oft-broken nose a crushed ruin, cut and gashed all about the head and face, now and then stirring uneasily as the pain of three broken ribs stabbed him.

For the first time he spoke the name of the girl he loved, groping out his hands like a lost child. Again he fought over his fearful battles and his mighty fists clenched until the knuckles showed white and low bestial snarls tore through his battered lips.

In his delirium he raised himself painfully on one elbow, his burning, unseeing eyes gleaming like slits of flame between the battered lids; he spoke in a low voice as if answering and listening to the murmur of ghosts: "Joe Grim! Battling Nelson!

Mike Boden! Joe Goddard! Iron Mike Brennon!"

My flesh crawled. I cannot impart to you the uncanniness of hearing the roll call of those iron men of days gone by, muttered in the stillness of night through the pulped and delirious lips of the grimmest of them all.

At last he fell silent, and went into a natural slumber. As I went softly into the other room, Ganlon entered, his savage eyes blazing with fierce triumph. With him was a girl—a darling of high society she seemed, with her costly garments and air of culture, but she exhibited an elemental anxiety such as no pampered and sophisticated debutante would, or could have done.

"Where is he?" she cried desperately. "Where is Mike? I must see him!"

"He's asleep now," I said shortly, and added in my cruel bitterness: "You've done enough to him already. He wouldn't want you to see him like he is now."

She cringed as from a blow. "Oh, let me just look in from the door," she begged, twining her white hands together—and I thought of how often Mike's hands had been bathed in blood for her—"I won't wake him."

I hesitated and her eyes flamed; now she was the primal woman.

"Try to stop me and I'll kill you!" she cried, and rushed past me into the room.

CHAPTER VI

A Cinch to Win!

The girl stopped short on the threshold. Mike muttered restlessly in his sleep and turned his blind eyes toward the door, but did not waken. As the girl's eyes fell on that frightfully disfigured face, she swayed drunkenly; her hands went to her temples and a low whimper like an animal in pain escaped her. Then, her face corpse-white and her eyes set in a deathly stare, she stole to the bedside and with a heart-rending sob, sank to her knees, cradling that battered head in her arms.

Mike muttered, but still he did not waken. At last I drew her gently away and led her into the next room, closing the door behind us. There she burst into a torrent of weeping. "I didn't know!" she kept sobbing over and over. "I didn't know fighting was like that! He told me never to go to a fight, or listen to one over the radio, and I obeyed him. Why, how could I know—here's one of the few letters in which he even mentioned his fights. I've kept them all."

The date was over three years old. I read: "Last night I stopped Jack Maloney, a foremost contender. He scarcely laid a glove on me. Don't worry about me, darling, this game is a cinch."

I laughed bitterly, remembering the gory wreck Maloney had made of Mike before he went out.

"I've been doing you an injustice," I said. "I didn't think a man could keep a girl in such ignorance as to the real state of things, but it's true. You're O.K. Maybe you can persuade Mike to give up the game—we can't."

"Surely he can't be thinking of fighting again if he lives?" she cried.

I laughed. "He won't die. He'll be laid up a while, that's all. Now I'll take you to a hotel—"

"I'm going to stay here close to Mike," she answered passionately. "I could kill myself when I think how he's suffered for me. Tomorrow I'm going to marry him and take him away."

After she was settled in a spare room, I turned to Spike: "I guess you're responsible for this. You might have waited till Mike was out of bed. That was a terrible shock for her."

"I intended it should be," he snarled. "I wrote and told her did she know her boy Mike Flynn was really Mike Brennon which was swiftly bein' punched into the booby-hatch? And I gave her some graphic accounts of his battle. I wrote her in time for her to get here to see the fight, but she says she missed a train."

"Let him fight," Spike spat. "Costigan will kill him, if they fight. I've seen these iron men crack before. I was in Tom Berg's corner the night Jose Gonzales knocked him out, and he died while the referee was countin' over him. Some men you got to kill to stop. Mike Brennon's one of 'em. If the girl's got a spark of real womanhood in her, she'll persuade him to quit."

Morning found the battered iron man clear of mind, his super-human recuperative powers already asserting themselves. I brought Marjory to his bedside and before he could say anything, I left them alone. Later she came to me, her eyes red with weeping.

"I've argued and begged," she cried desperately, "but he won't give in!"

All of us surrounded Mike's bedside. "Mike," I said, "you're a fool. The punches have gone to your head. You can't mean you'll fight again!"

"I'm good for some more big purses," he replied with a grin.

Marjory cried out as if he had stabbed her. "Mike—oh, Mike! We have more money now than we'll ever use. You haven't been fair to me. I'd have rather gone in rags, and worked my fingers to the bone in the lowest kind of drudgery than to have you suffer!"

His face lighted with a rare smile. He reached out a hand, amazingly gentle, and took one of the girl's soft hands in his own.

"White little hands," he murmured. "Soft, as they were meant to be, now. Why, just looking at you repays me a thousand times for all I've got through. And what have I gone through? A few beatings. The old-timers took worse, and got little or nothing."

"But there's no reason for your crucifying yourself—and me—any longer."

He shook his head with that strange abnormal stubbornness which was the worst defect in his character.

"As long as I can draw down a hundred thousand dollars a fight, I'd be a fool to quit. I'm tougher than any of you think. A hundred thousand dollars!" His eyes gleamed with the old light. "The crowd roaring! And Iron Mike Brennon taking everything that's handed out, and finishing on his feet! No! No! I'll quit when I'm counted out—not before!"

"Mike!" the girl cried piercingly. "If you fight again, I'll swear I'll go away and never see you again!"

His gaze beat her eyes down, and her head sank on her breast. I never saw the human being—except one—who could stand the stare of Mike Brennon's magnetic eyes.

"Marjory," his deep voice vibrated with confidence, "you're just trying to bluff me into doing what you want me to do. But you're mine, and you always will be. You won't leave me, now. You can't!"

She hid her tear-blinded face in her hands and sobbed weakly. He stroked her bowed head tenderly. A failure in the ring perhaps, but outside of it Brennon had a power over those with whom he came in contact that none could overcome. The way he had beaten down the girl's weak pretense was almost brutal.

"Mike!" snarled Ganlon, speaking harshly and bitterly to hide his emotions; for a moment the hard-faced middleweight with his two hundred savage ring battles behind him, dominated the scene; "Mike, you're crazy! You got everything a man could want—things that most men work their lives out for and never get. You're on the border-line. You couldn't whip a second-rater.

"Costigan's as tough as you ever were. If I thought he'd flatten you with a punch or two, I'd say, go to it. But he won't. He'll knock you out, but it'll be after a smashin' that'll ruin you for life. You'll die, or you'll go to the bughouse. What good will your money, or Marjory's love do you then?"

Mike took his time about replying, and again his strange influence was felt like a cloud over the group.

"Costigan's over-rated. I'll show him up. He never saw the day he could take as much as I can, or hit as hard."

Spike made a despairing gesture, and turned away. Later he said to the girl and me: "No use arguin'. He thinks it's the money, but it ain't. The game's in his blood. And he's jealous of Mike Costigan. These iron men is terrible proud of their toughness. Remember how Van Heeren fought?"

"Win or lose, ten rounds with Costigan means Mike's finish. Each is too tough to be knocked out quick. It'll be a long, bloody grind, and it may finish Costigan, but it'll *sure* finish Mike. He'll end that fight dead, or punched nutty. At his best, Brennon would likely have wore Costigan down like he did Van Heeren. But Mike's gone away back, and Costigan is young—in his prime—which in a iron man is the same as sayin' you couldn't hurt him with a piledriver."

Mike Brennon trained conscientiously, as always. I discharged his sparring partners and had him punch the light bag for speed, and do a great deal of road work in a vain effort to recover some of the former steel spring quality of his weakening legs. But I knew it was useless. It was not a matter of conditioning—his trouble lay behind him in the thousands of cruel blows he had absorbed. A clever boxer may get out of condition, lose fights and come back; but when an iron man slips there is no comeback.

In the four months which preceded the Costigan fight, an air of gloom surrounded the camp which affected all but Mike himself. Marjory, after days of passionate pleading, sank into a sort of apathy. That he was being bitterly cruel to the girl never occurred to Mike, and we could not make him see it. He laughed at our fears as foolish, and insisted that he was practically in his prime. He swore that his fight with Slade, far from showing that he had slipped, proved that he was better than ever! For had he not beaten Slade, the most dangerous man in the ring? As for Costigan—a few rounds of savage slugging would send him down and out.

Mike was aware of his fistic faults; he frankly admitted that any second-rater who could avoid his swings could outpoint him; but he sincerely believed that he was still superior in ruggedness to any man that ever lived. And deep in his heart, I doubt if Mike really believed he would ever be knocked out.

One thing he insisted on; that Marjory should not see the fight. And she made one last plea for him to give it up.

"No use to start all that," he answered calmly. "Think, Marjory! My fourth hundred-thousand-dollar purse! That's a record few champions have set! One hundred thousand with Flash Sullivan—Gonzales—Slade—and now Costigan! Thousands of tickets sold in advance! I've got to go on now, anyhow. And I'm a cinch to win!"

CHAPTER VII

Framed

As if it were yesterday I visualize the scene; the ring bathed in the white glow above it; while the great crowd that filled the huge outside bowl swept away into the darkness of each side. A circle of white faces looked up from the ringside seats. Farther out only a twinkling army of glowing cigarettes evidenced the multitude, and a vast rippling undertone came from the soft darkness.

"Iron Mike Brennon, 190 pounds; in this corner, Iron Mike Costigan, 195!"

Brennon sat in his corner, head bowed, a contrast to the nervous, feline-like picture he had offered when he had paced the floor in his dressing-room. I wondered if he was still seeing the tear-stained face of Marjory as she kissed him in his dressing-room before he came into the ring.

When the men were called to the center of the ring for instructions, Mike, to my surprise, seemed apathetic. He walked with dragging feet. However, in front of his foe he came awake with fierce energy. Iron Mike Costigan was dark, with tousled black hair. Five feet eleven, and heavier than Brennon, what he lacked in lithe ranginess he made up in oak and iron massiveness.

The eyes of the two men burned into each other with savage

intensity. Volcanic blue for Costigan; cold steel gray for Brennon. Their sun-browned faces were set in unconscious snarls. But as they stood facing each other, Brennon's stare of concentrated cold ferocity wavered and fell momentarily before Costigan's savage blue eyes. I realized that this was the first man who had ever looked Mike down, and I thought of Corbett staring down Sullivan—of McGovern's eyes falling before Young Corbett's.

Then the men were back in their corners, and the seconds and handlers were climbing through the ropes. I hissed to Mike that I was going to throw in the sponge if the going got too rough, but he made no reply. He seemed to have sunk into that strange apathy again.

The gong!

Costigan hurtled from his corner, a compact bulk of fighting fury. Brennon came out more slowly. At my side Ganlon hissed: "What's the matter with Mike? He acts like he was drunk!"

The two Iron Mikes had met in the center of the ring. Costigan might have been slightly awed by the fame of the man he faced. At any rate he hesitated. Brennon walked toward his foe, but his feet dragged.

Then Costigan suddenly launched an attack, and shot a straight left to Brennon's face. As if the blow had roused him to his full tigerish fury, Mike went into action. The old sweeping haymakers began to thunder with all their ancient power. Costigan had, of course, no defense. A sweeping left-hander crashed under his heart with a sound like a caulking mallet striking a ship's side; a blasting right that whistled through the air, cannon-balled against his jaw. Costigan went down as though struck by a thunderbolt.

Then even as the crowd rose, he reeled up again. But I was watching Brennon. As though that sudden burst of action had taken all the strength out of him, he sagged against the ropes, limp, cloudy-eyed. Now sensing that his foe was up, he dragged himself forward with halting and uncertain motions.

Costigan, still dizzy from that terrific knockdown, was conscious of only one urge—the old instinct of the iron man—bore in and hit until somebody falls! Now he crashed through Brennon's groping arms and shot a right hook to the chin. Brennon swayed and fell, just as a drunken man falls when a prop against which he had been leaning is removed.

Over his motionless form the referee was counting: "Eight! Nine! Ten!" And the ring career of Iron Mike Brennon was at an end. A stunned silence reigned, and Iron Mike Costigan, new king of all iron men, leaned against the ropes, unable to believe his senses. *Mike Brennon had been knocked out!*

Around the ring the typewriters of the reporters were ticking out the fall of a king: "Evidently Mike Brennon's famous iron jaw has at last turned to crockery after years of incredible bombardings. . . ."

We carried Mike, still senseless, to his dressing-room. Ganlon was muttering under his breath, and as soon as we had Mike safe on a cot with a physician looking to him, the middleweight vanished. Marjory had been waiting for us and now she stood, whitefaced and silent, by the cot where her lover lay.

At last he opened his eyes, and instantly he leaped erect, hands up. Then he halted, swayed and rubbed his eyes. Marjory was at his side in an instant and gently forced him back on the cot.

"What happened? Did I win?" he asked dazedly.

"You were knocked out in the first round, Mike." I felt it better to answer him directly. His eyes widened with amazement.

"I? Knocked out? Impossible!"

"Yes, Mike, you were," I assured him, expecting him to do any of the things I have seen fighters do on learning of their first knock-out—weep terribly, faint, rave and curse, or rush out looking for the conqueror. But being Mike Brennon and a never-to-be-solved enigma, he did none of these things. He merely rubbed his chin and laughed cynically.

"Guess I'd gone farther back than I thought. I don't remember the punch that put me out; funny thing—I've come through my last fight without a mark."

"And now you'll quit!" cried Marjory. "This is the best thing that could have happened to you. You promised you'd quit if you were knocked out, Mike." Her voice was painful in its intensity.

"Why, I wouldn't draw half a house now," Mike was beginning ruefully, when Ganlon burst in, eyes blazing.

"Mike!" he snarled. "Steve! Don't you two boneheads see there's somethin' wrong here? Mike, when did you begin feelin' drowsy?"

Brennon started. "That's right. I'd forgotten. I began feeling queer when I climbed in the ring. I sort of woke up when the referee was talking to us, and I remember how Costigan's eyes blazed. Then when I went back to my corner I got dizzy and drunken. Then I knew I was moving out in the ring and I saw Costigan through a fog. He hit me a hummer and I woke up and started swinging and saw him go down. That's the last I remember until I came to here."

Ganlon laughed bitterly. "Sure. You was out on your feet before Costigan hit you. A girl coulda pushed you over, and that's all Costigan done!"

"Doped!" I cried. "Costigan's crowd—or the gambling ring—"

"Naw—Mike's been crossed by the last person you'd think of. I been doin' some detective work. Mike, just before you left your dressin'-room, you drunk a small cup of tea, didn't you? Kinda unusual preparation for a hard fight, eh? But you drunk it to please somebody—"

Marjory was cowering in the corner. Mike was troubled and puzzled.

"But Spike, Marjory made that tea herself—"

"Yeah, and she doped it herself! She framed you to lose!"

Our eyes turned on the shrinking girl—amazement in mine, anger in Ganlon's, and a deep hurt in Mike's.

"Marjory, why did you do that?" asked Mike, bewildered. "I might have won—"

"Yes, you might have won!" she cried in a sudden gust of desperate and despairing defiance. "After Costigan had battered you to a red ruin! Yes, I drugged the tea. It's my fault you were knocked out. You can't go back now, for you've lost your only attraction. You can't draw the crowds. I've gone through tortures since I first saw you lying on that cot after your fight with Slade—but you've only laughed at me. Now you'll have to quit. You're out of the game with a sound mind—that's all I care. I've saved you from your mad avarice and cruel pride in spite of yourself! And you can beat me now, or kill me—I don't care!"

For a moment she stood panting before us, her small fists clenched, then as no one spoke, all the fire went out of her. She wilted visibly and moved droopingly and forlornly toward the door. The wrap which enveloped her slender form, slid to the floor as she fumbled at the door-knob, revealing her in a cheap gingham dress. Mike, like a man awakening from a trance, started forward:

"Marjory! Where are you going? What are you doing in that rig?"

"It's the dress I was wearing when you first met me," she answered listlessly, "I wrote and got back my old job at the café."

He crossed the room with one stride, caught her slim shoulders and spun her around to face him, with unconsciously brutal force. "What do you mean?" he said.

She collapsed suddenly in a storm of weeping. "Don't you hate me for drugging you?" she sobbed. "I didn't think you'd ever want to see me again."

He crushed her to him hungrily. "Girl, I swear I didn't realize how it was hurting you. I thought you were foolish—willful. I couldn't see how you were suffering. But you've opened my eyes. I must have been insane! You're right—it was pride—senseless vanity—I couldn't see it then, but I do now. I didn't understand that I was ruining your happiness. And that's all that matters now, dear. We've got our life and love before us, and if it rests with me, you're going to be happy all the rest of your life."

Ganlon beckoned me and I followed him out. For the only time since I had known him, Mike's hard face had softened. The sentiment that lies at the base of the Irish nature, however deeply hidden sometimes, made his steely eyes almost tender.

"I had her down all wrong," Ganlon said softly. "I take back everything I might have said about her. She's a regular—and Mike—well, he's the only iron man I ever knew that got the right breaks at last."

They Always Come Back

"Three years ago you were the foremost heavyweight contender—now you're a whiskey-soaked tramp in a Mexican saloon!"

The voice was hard and rasping, with a bitter contempt that cut like a knife. The man to whom the words were addressed flinched and blinked his liquor-reddened eyes.

"And what business is that of yours?" he demanded roughly.

"Just the fact that I hate to see a man make a hog of himself—just because I hate to see a man with championship material in him lying around in a one-horse border village!"

They made a strange contrast, those two, and the loafers and Mexicans who lounged in the rear end of the 'dobe saloon eyed them curiously. The man who lolled half across the beer-stained table was young, and in spite of his ragged garments his athletic frame was evident. His face was not a bad face, in spite of the lines of wild dissipation. The face was surprisingly finely molded, with a thin-bridged regular nose that spoke of good blood. About the mouth there was a sign of weakness, at first glance. A second glance showed a keen observer that it was a sensitive mouth, rather than a weak one—an index to a certain flaw in the character that was erratic and unstable rather than bad.

The man who stood looking down on the other was a slender wiry man of more than middle age. His lips were thin and straight, his nose beak-like, his eyes hard and bitter. He was dressed in a manner costly but plain, and seemed out of place in this sordid dive.

"Three years ago," continued his inexorable voice, "you were touted for the next heavyweight champion. Jack Maloney—a classy boxer and a terrible puncher. The man with the mallet right! You slashed through opposition like a second Dempsey. Starting at eighteen, you cleaned up your division and at the age of twenty-one, you were beating at the doors of the title. Twenty-one! An age at which most men are fighting in the preliminaries for ten dollars a round. And you were drawing down the thousands. In three years you came up from nowhere. You were fast as a cat, keen, brainy and tough. You hit like the blow of a caulking mallet. You were wined, dined and petted as the favorite of society—the classy pride of the ring!

"Then what happened? You were matched with Iron Mike Brennon, then an unknown. He stopped you in three rounds. You went all to pieces. You lost your guts. You were knocked out in your next start by Soldier Handler, a hard-hitting second-rater. Then you quit the ring; disappeared. You went to the gutter. You'd lost your nerve; turned yellow—"

"That's a lie!" Maloney was stung out of his indifference.

"Alright, I won't say you were yellow. But you'd lost your guts. You took to booze fighting. Went to the gutter. Went broke. Now, in three years you've made a no-stop flight from Broadway to this dump."

Maloney's mighty fists clenched into iron knots on the table. His eyes flamed through the tousled mass of black hair.

"I ought to kill you," he said huskily, inflamed by the stuff he had been drinking. "Just because you've managed a few champions you think you can talk to a man any way. You don't manage me."

"I'm not in the habit of managing whiskeysoaks," sneered the other. "The men I managed may not have been as fast or as hard hitting as you were, but they were men. They didn't go all to pieces, just because somebody hung a k.o. sign on their chin."

Suddenly he changed his manner and sat down opposite the ex-fighter.

"You're still young, Maloney," said he slowly. "Why don't you try to come back?"

"Fight again?" Maloney shuddered as from a nightmare memory. "Ugh!"

"You've brooded over that knockout until it's become an obsession with you. Get yourself in shape again—"

"No! No! I couldn't. I don't want to try—to even think about it."

"Then you've no more guts than I thought," the bitter rasp had come back into the voice. "I thought—"

"Listen!" the other cried with a desperate note in his voice. "What do you know of my trouble? You never fought in your life."

"No," the other admitted, "but I know you fighters better than most of you know yourselves. And I know you could come back if you had the guts."

"Sit down," Maloney ordered huskily. "I'll tell you my side of it."

"Alright, I'll listen to your tale of woe—and buy you a drink, too," the older man added with a cutting sneer.

Maloney's eyes momentarily flashed, but he had sunk too low to be over resentful of anything beyond a direct insult. He motioned to the bartender, gulped down the fiery draught and said savagely:

"Guts! Bah! What do you know of a man who has the heart knocked out of him? Listen, I was all you said and more. Till I met Brennon. I thought I was invincible. I wore myself out punching him. I ruined myself—"

"And why?" broke in the other. "You mean you were ruined mentally. You came out of that fight with only one mark. A cut on your cheekbone and a few bruises. I've seen fights in which the winner was carried out of the ring. You took that defeat to heart. Just because you couldn't stop Brennon, you lost all your nerve, permanently.

"And why couldn't you stop him? Because he's a freak. An iron-jawed, steel-bellied gorilla that can't be knocked out! No man's ever turned the trick, and won't until he cracks from the continual punishment. Remember Joe Grim, what Gans, Fitzsimmons and Johnson failed to stop! But you punched yourself out and took the count. And you let it beat you! Bah! Your vanity couldn't stand the shock. You'd gotten to the point where you didn't believe any man could hurt you.

"If you'd had the stuff it takes to make a real man, that beating would have done you good—taken some of the conceit out of you. As it was, it ruined you."

"Listen!" there was fury and agony in Maloney's voice; he was drunk but his mind was lucid. "Listen! I'll try to tell you—

"I'd never met a man like Brennon. I didn't credit much those stories I'd heard of Grim, Goddard and Boden—those old-time iron men. I didn't believe the man lived who could stand up to my punches.

"Then I met Brennon at the Hopi A.C. in San Francisco. I'd heard he was tough—been knocking over a bunch of second-raters on the coast till Steve Amber took him over and began getting him good matches.

"At the first I was impressed by the ferocity of Brennon's face and the steady glare of his eyes. I half expected him to be awed by my name and k.o. record, but he glared at me as if I were one of the second-raters he had been pushing over. Or rather, as if he were a tiger and I a bison he was going to tear limb from limb. I tell you, the fellow isn't human! He's made of solid iron and there's room in his skull for only one thought—the killer instinct!

"At the gong he came out of his corner wide open; no defense at all. And he knew nothing about scientific hitting. He lifted his swings from the floor, in the old rough-house style. I went in to finish him quick. I expected to flatten him with the first rush, but when I landed my first blow, a left hook to the body, I got the surprize of my life. Brennon didn't even flinch; instead of sinking wrist deep into his body, my fist rebounded just as if I had struck a metal boiler instead of a human body!

"I tell you, he was almost as hard as steel. But I didn't stop to worry; I began throwing rights and lefts to the body and head with everything I had. I was the first first-class man Brennon had met, the papers said. That was his introduction into the first-rate ranks, and I gave him a baptism of fire and blood.

"I battered him all over the ring without a return. He didn't even know enough to duck or wrap his arms around his jaw. Blood spattered all over us; I closed one of his eyes nearly shut. But he wouldn't go down. And just before the gong, when I thought he must be weakening, he suddenly landed one of those wide sweeping left-handers under my heart. It felt for a second as if he had caved me in. Took my breath away. But it wasn't the blow that sent me to my corner so discouraged; it was the fact that for three solid minutes he'd taken everything I could hand out, and was apparently as strong as ever.

"Between rounds my manager and handlers urged me to go slow; they were getting afraid that I'd fight myself out. But my pride was stung. I'd trained perfectly, but I was beginning to feel fatigued. None of my fights had been at such a pace as this! Just imagine battering away, with all your power, for three minutes straight! And consider the fact that Brennon had taken every blow I started! I could scarcely believe it, but at the gong here he came with his wild beast eyes glaring in his bloody face.

"I threw caution to the winds. Mike Brennon must have gone through hell in that second round. Near the end of it his nose was smashed flat, both eyes closed to mere slits, his face one red mask of pulped flesh and blood. But through the slits of his eyelids his eyes still blazed with their old light—I tell you, you have to kill a man like Iron Mike Brennon to stop him! He's tougher than Battling Nelson was.

"I felt myself slipping. My blows were coming slower I knew. My arms seemed to be turning to lead; my legs were trembling, my chest heaving. I rallied with one more ferocious attack just before the gong, and crashed my right four times to his jaw. Think of that! And I'd knocked men out with one blow of that right many a time, to the side of the head or face. For the first time Brennon reeled. His knees buckled, but just as I thought 'he's going!' he straightened and glanced a right from my cheekbone. It opened a cut and for a second I was blinded by a flash of white light in my brain. Oh, I'd been hit before. Hit hard; knocked down. But never such blows as those; and what was worse was the knowledge that I couldn't hit Brennon hard enough to weaken him.

"My knees trembled as I walked back to my corner, and I looked over my shoulder to see if Brennon was showing the effects of his beating. I shouldn't have done that. When I saw him walk to his corner without a quiver, something went out of me. I had an all-gone feeling. As I sank onto my stool, I heard the crowd yelling: 'Hey, whatsa matter, Jack? Lost your punch? How come you ain't stopped this tramp? This boy must be made outa iron!'

"I began to wonder if I had lost my punch. My brain reeled. This was a nightmare! I, the hardest puncher since Dempsey's days, had pounded this wide-open dub for two solid rounds without even weakening him! Surely there must be some limit to his endurance! There must be an end even to his incredible vitality!

"My manager was begging me to box him, take my time.

Be content to outpoint him. I scarcely heard. I was in a panic. The factor that sent me out to kill or be killed wasn't so much wounded vanity as you think—it was more fear than anything else! Yes, fear! Just like a man penned in with a tiger who must kill or die!

"I gathered my waning powers and tore out for the third round like a wild man. Brennon with his longshoreman's style was easy to hit. He fought straight up and wide open. I fought like a man in a trance. Left, right! My left hand broke on his head, but I didn't notice it. I threw my right again and again, with a wild desperation. Every ounce of weight, power and fighting fury went behind that right hand at every blow. When it landed it sounded like the blows of a caulking mallet. And Brennon reeled, wavered—went down!

"When he fell, all my unnatural fury went out of me; I staggered back against the ropes, completely fought out—an exhausted shell of a man. The referee was counting. Then to my utter horror, Brennon shook his head and began to get his feet under him. I nearly fainted. I thought I'd finished him—I knew I was done. And he was getting up! The ring floated before my eyes.

"Then Brennon was up and coming for me. I tottered away from the ropes on buckling legs and lifted arms that were no stronger than a girl's. I was all gone—out on my feet. Even then he missed—missed—missed. At last he crashed a leaping left-hander to my head. There was a flash of white light again, I reeled and he smashed a terrible swing under my cheekbone. The lights went out. They said I came up again at the count of nine, and he floored me the second time before I was counted out. I don't know. I don't remember anything after that fearful right-hander that first dropped me."

A momentary silence fell. Maloney's blood-shot eyes burned unseeingly and when he continued he seemed to be talking more to himself than to his listener.

"That fight made Iron Mike Brennon," he said huskily, at last. "It broke me. My mind was in a chaotic whirl. I couldn't get down to training. I couldn't settle on anything. I stayed out of the ring for four months, then went back in against Soldier Handler. I was all at sea. I hit with my old force, but I had no timing or accuracy. Every time I started a blow the vision of Iron Mike Brennon's bloody and snarling face rose up before me. I was wild and awkward. Every time I saw a blow coming, the memory of Brennon's terrific knockout smashes made me flinch and back away. The crowd booed me, hissed me, called me yellow. At last, in the fifth round I went down and out from the swings of a man I should have stopped in the first rush. The sports writers said I quit. Maybe I did. I could hear the referee counting over me; I wasn't unconscious but I couldn't drag myself to my feet."

Grendon moved restlessly. His quick nervous energy made it impossible for him to keep still long at a time.

"It's the mind," said he. "Your superiority complex got a jolt. You should have recovered by this time. It wouldn't be impossible for you to get back in shape. I saw the Handler fight. You were like a man dazed or drugged. Even so he staggered every time you landed, and it took him five rounds to beat you down, in the condition you were in. You were not in shape, mentally or physically.

"As for Brennon," the harsh rasping note stole in again, "You said you were in shape for him. You weren't. You thought you'd trained. You'd been going through the motions, but your heart wasn't in your work. You were too sure of yourself. And that same conceit whipped you; you fought yourself out and when Brennon dropped you—as he might have dropped any man that ever lived—you didn't have the stuff to take it and come back.

"Once more I ask you: will you let me take you and put you back in the ring?"

Maloney's sole answer was to turn his back on his interrogator and reach for the bottle of tequila which the bartender had left on the table. He felt the cold eyes of Grendon on him for a few moments, then was vaguely aware that the manager had gone.

Maloney had been drinking hard three years. Today he plunged into his old vice with a sort of desperation, to drown the old ghosts which Grendon had conjured up. In a short time he was too muddled to even wonder why the bartender kept bringing the liquor for which he, Maloney, had no money to pay.

He swiftly passed into the hazy semi-consciousness of extreme intoxication and as he hovered on the borderline of complete oblivion, he was dimly aware of a commotion. There were shouts, a fall of chairs, the crash of broken bottles—something struck him a powerful blow and he struck back. Or at least that was his intention, but he was so far gone in drink that he never knew whether or not he put the thought into action.

Jack Maloney awoke with a thirst and a splitting headache. Neither particularly worried him, since the last few years this had been a common phenomenon on waking. But he at last realized that he was in strange surroundings. A pitcher of water close at hand first occupied his attention, then he looked about him. He was in a small room, walled, floored and roofed of 'dobe. There was one door which was closed; one small heavily-barred window.

The ex-fighter lurched and tried the door. It was locked. Slowly the truth dawned on him. He was in jail. A sort of panic struck him. He knew the horrors of these Mexican jails in whose vermin-ridden cells men die forgotten. He pounded on the door and shouted loudly.

Steps sounded outside in the corridor and presently the door swung open. Two heavy-faced Mexican soldiers, heavily armed, stood on either side of a third man.

"Grendon!" Maloney exclaimed. "What's all this mean?"

There was no sympathy in Grendon's cold eyes.

"Don't you remember last night?"

Maloney passed an uncertain hand over his throbbing brow.

"I don't remember anything after our talk."

"No," Grendon rasped, "you were drunk as a swine. Anyway, after I left, a row started in that joint where you were and when the police came in to stop it, one of them bumped into you and you knocked him stiff. It's a serious offense to strike an officer in this part of Mexico. You've been given a heavy fine."

"I haven't any money," said the ex-fighter. "Pay my fine and I'll pay you back."

"Pay out five hundred dollars, American money, for a rum-soaked ruin?" Grendon's voice was more bitter than Maloney had ever heard it.

"Five hundred dollars!" Maloney was dumbfounded.

"Sure. And if you can't pay it, you'll lay it out—and not in this cool cell either. These soldiers have come to take you to the bull pen, they tell me. You know what a few months there means."

Maloney shuddered. He had looked into these "bull pens" and had seen the men imprisoned there, the maundering wrecks that milled ceaselessly to and fro beneath the merciless sun.

For a Mexican bull pen is simply a jail with high walls and no roof. No breeze can blow upon the men there; only the semi-tropical sun beats down upon their defenseless bodies all day long. There is no shade; nowhere to sit or lie save on the hard flagstones or the packed dirt floor, in the broiling sunshine. Men go insane there.

"You won't leave a man of your own race for a fate like that?" the fighter cried desperately.

"No?" Grendon sneered. "Watch me!" Then seeing the utter despair on Maloney's face, he said:

"The alcalde happens to be a friend of mine. I'll do this much for you. There's a sort of one-horse fight club here, run by an American gambler, as you probably know. Alright. A Mexican heavyweight by the name of Diaz is in town looking for a match. They'll let you out of jail to fight him. You'll get nothing, of course, but I'll bet five hundred dollars on you *and you'll win!* If you don't, it's the bull pen."

Maloney cried out in horror: "Fight? After three years of idleness and dissipation? Why, I couldn't even spar a round! I've no wind, stamina or punch. A child could push me over."

"Alright," Grendon snapped, "suit yourself; maybe you'll have an easier time in the bull pen, anyhow." He turned away.

"Wait!" Maloney shouted in desperation. "I'll fight! But how can I expect to win?"

"A man can do anything he has to," Grendon answered grimly. "I'll go arrange things. They won't let you out of this cell till Diaz is in the ring. Till then you might while away the time thinking about the sun on the bare walls of the bull pen!"

Maloney lay face down on the dirt floor, his aching head forgotten. How could he even stand up to a fighter, even such a dub as this Mexican most undoubtedly was? Much less, how could he win? Then the vision of the bull pen rose up in his mind. The thought of the fight nauseated him; the thought of the prison crazed him.

Time passed. At last the door opened and two Mexican guards entered. They motioned him to precede them, and they followed close behind, their bayonets barely touching his back.

In the ring in the squalid little sheet iron fight stadium, Diaz lolled in his corner and awaited the coming of the dub he was to slaughter. Diaz was sure of himself; he had been told that they were taking an American out of the jail to meet him, and surely no fighter of any consequence could be in a jail in this tiny border town which owed its sole existence to the thirst of the white men across the river, and which even Diaz held in contempt. He had not even taken the trouble to learn the name of his opponent.

He glanced up languidly. A black-haired American was climbing unsteadily through the ropes, aided by a wiry man of late middle age whom Diaz, with a start, recognized as the great Grendon himself. Diaz' heart skipped a beat. What was the manager of champions doing here, and why was he seconding a fourth-rater? Something wrong here!

Diaz stole a look at the other fighter with quickened interest. He looked closer, with unbelief in his eyes. He blanched and spoke swiftly and passionately to his manager.

Jack Maloney felt an involuntary shudder go through him as he looked about at the old familiar sight—the ropes of the ring, the stained canvas, the shouting crowd. Again there rose dizzily a by-gone vision—a vaster, more pretentious ring, a huger throng—and a black-haired battler who writhed broken at the feet of a gory slugger. Then another vision blotted this out—a vision of a roofless Hades where men went staring crazy.

He glanced at his opponent, a second-rate Mexican he had never heard of. He saw recognition flare in Diaz' eyes, saw the pallor on the dark face. A faint pride stirred in him. As low as he had sunk, the very memory of his name was enough to frighten this second-rater. Bitterness flooded him at the thought of his past glory and his present degradation.

The referee called the men to the center of the ring and gave them the usual unheard instructions. Diaz was beginning to get back some of his confidence. His manager had told him that this man was the same one who had been lying about the saloons for months, and he himself knew that Maloney had not fought for three years. The lines of dissipation in the American's face and the lack of training evident in his whole frame cheered him; but he must be careful. Must take no chances and be sure that this man was harmless before risking anything. Diaz had once fought a preliminary to one of Maloney's fights and the memory was still fresh in his mind, of the sledge-like smashes that had flattened the man's opponent on that occasion.

The men went back to their corners and as Grendon climbed through the ropes he hissed one parting word: "I've sunk five hundred dollars on you! Win and you're a free man; lose and it's the bull pen!"

The gong sounded. Maloney rose and walked slowly toward

the middle of the ring. Diaz came out even more slowly and carefully. Maloney scarcely saw him; in his mind he saw a snarling blood-stained demon who rushed and smote like the very spirit of the primitive.

A moment the men circled each other. At last Diaz led halfheartedly; his left got home under Maloney's heart and the Mexican, awed by his own audacity, involuntarily closed his eyes, expecting to be blasted out of existence instantly. But Maloney made no attempt to return the blow. It had not been hard, but the feel of it brought back in a nauseating wave all his old fears; again in that instant he relived his nightmare battle with Brennon, his slaughter by Soldier Handler.

Finding himself still alive, the Mexican repeated his lead. This time Maloney countered with his own left and Diaz, shrinking away from it, was surprised to feel it glance lightly from his shoulder. No force there. Diaz' intelligence told him that the once great Maloney was only a shell of himself; but his instinctive fears kept him from rushing in to make a quick finish of it.

He attacked warily, jabbing at Maloney's face, then as the American retreated heavily, he followed up his advantage with a right to the body that carried force. Maloney felt as if a keen knife had cut off his breath for a fleeting instant. Already he was beginning to feel the effects of his lack of training. His knees were beginning to tremble, his breath to come in gasps. And the first round had scarcely progressed a minute.

Only Diaz' caution kept him from flattening his opponent in the first round. He kept a steady stream of straight lefts in Maloney's face, blows that cut and hurt but did not stun, and occasionally he drove his right hard to the body, knowing that Maloney was in no shape to take punishment there.

Maloney was already in a bad way. Those right-handers sank deep in his flabby midriff; sweat soaked his body, his gloves and trunks and it seemed his heart would burst with the exertions of his labored breathing. Worse than all, the blows that rained steadily upon him brought up the memories of those last two fights—

Diaz grew in confidence. So far his opponent had not laid a glove on him. The great Maloney was staggering before his blows! As this feeling grew, Diaz increased the savagery of his attack. Just before the gong Maloney went down, partly from the increasing force of the Mexican's blows, partly from his own exhaustion.

He came to himself in his corner. Grendon was working over him with all the skill of an old time handler, but Maloney gasped: "I'm through. I can't even get up off my stool."

Grendon reached for the sponge to toss it in. His eyes were bitter.

"All right, the bull pen for you. This fourth-rater's punched you right into it."

At that moment the gong sounded. From whence his renewal of strength came, Maloney never knew. He always secretly believed it was a flare of momentary insanity and perhaps he was right. But at Grendon's words, a fearful chaos of hatred flamed up in his brain; hatred for Grendon who was consigning him to a living death, hatred for the Mexican soldiers who stood about to see that he did not escape, hatred for Iron Mike Brennon who was the prime cause of all his trouble. And, naturally, all of his hate centered on the man in the ring with him.

Diaz came rushing from his corner like a great tiger. He was wild with the killer instinct, inflamed with the desire to stretch this once great battler at his feet. But he met a different man. Somehow Maloney heaved up off his stool, knocking the sponge out of Grendon's hand. His legs seemed dead, but he lurched forward and, as Diaz plunged savagely in, Maloney steadied him with a straight left to the face, and crashed his right under the heart with a force which even surprized himself.

Diaz staggered, whitened. For the first time in his life he had run full into the blow of a real hitter and the sensation left him weakened and nauseated. He felt as if he had been caved in; as if his heart had momentarily stopped. No longer did he dally with a desire to see the great Maloney stretched at his feet. He only desired to avoid utter destruction.

He commenced a hasty retreat and Maloney, realizing that his strength was swiftly fading, and with the bull pen before his eyes, lurched desperately after him. Diaz was still unmanned by that blow under the heart and on the ropes Maloney caught him. And there, holding the ropes with his left hand to keep him on his feet, Maloney crashed another right-hander over, this time to the jaw, and Diaz dropped for the full count.

As the referee said, "Ten!" Maloney dropped likewise, his fading thought being that he was going to die of fatigue.

He came to himself to see Grendon bending over him, and if the manager felt any satisfaction, his face did not show it.

"Alright, hustle out of it," he rapped harshly. "We're leaving town. I paid your fine."

"You can go to hell," snarled Maloney, sitting up, all his hatred of Grendon blazing in his eyes. "I fought my bout like you said and I'm grateful for what you did—getting me the fight. Otherwise I owe you nothing."

"You owe me five hundred dollars," Grendon retorted. "The stakeholder skipped with the money I bet on you. I paid your fine out of my own pocket. That way I've lost a thousand dollars on you, but we will just call it five hundred. And you're going to work it out for me."

"Work it out?"

"Fight it out, if you like the word better. That fight showed one thing; you're not as far gone as I thought. You still know how to hit and you've got more than a shadow of your old punch. Close, careful training will sweat the booze out of your system and get you back in shape. You'll never be much, maybe, but you can slap down a flock of pushovers and pay back my money."

"I won't do it," Maloney answered shortly. "I went through Hades last night. I won't do it again for anybody."

"Maloney," said Grendon, looking at him piercingly, "you hate me, don't you?"

"As much as one man could hate another," answered Maloney with his characteristic honesty.

Grendon seemed not displeased. In fact he grinned thinly.

"Alright, do you want to go through life knowing you're obligated to a man you hate?"

Maloney's black-crowned head jerked up and his eyes glinted into Grendon's hawk-like gaze.

"I'll do it," he said abruptly. "You ought to make your money back off me in one fight. Then we're through, understand."

Grendon's only answer was a wintry smile.

Thus came Jack Maloney, once a coming champion, now a has-been, to the managerial care of "Iceberg" Grendon. No words of love passed between them, their conversation was limited to short abrupt advice or requests on the part of the manager and shorter replies on the part of the fighter.

After the affair at the border town, they went directly to the coast and took ship for Australia, Grendon's native land. Maloney having no money, Grendon paid all expenses, and the fighter wondered that he should spend so much merely to assure himself of the payment of five hundred dollars. Grendon seemed not at all parsimonious except in this matter, and Maloney decided that the man hated him as much as he hated Grendon and was merely taking this revenge. He remembered that in his early career he had knocked out one of Grendon's proteges and though the Australian was not a man to harbor grudges, Maloney for lack of a better reason decided that Grendon had never forgiven him. He determined to pay back not only the five hundred that Grendon had spent paying his fine, but the five hundred which the crooked stakeholder had stolen. After that—Maloney's fists slowly clenched as the black tide of his hate surged through his brain.

Grendon had a training camp in the country back of Sydney and there Maloney plunged into the work of conditioning himself.

Grendon proved himself a first class trainer, whatever else his faults. He made Maloney go easy at first, start very gradually to building up his long abused body, and Maloney, realizing his manager's wisdom and experience, followed his instructions to the letter.

Months passed; slowly Maloney was rounding into shape. He was training harder now, and his muscles were vibrant with strength and life. He felt no craving for liquor. He had never been a natural sot, had drunk only to drown his dreams. He could do miles of roadwork now without discomfort and when he struck the heavy punching bag, it leaped and tossed like a ship on a windy sea. In the daily bouts with his sparring partners he felt that his timing and speed had come back to a remarkable extent. Speed and punch—the secret of his earlier successes—and now he strove to regain them. The punch that numbed and shocked the toughest fighter, the speed that carried him through the guard of cleverer men. Maloney had never been a really clever boxer in the fullest sense of the word. He had been more of the slugger; but his defense was not to be sniffed at and his shifty footwork would have done credit to many a more crafty boxer. Speed to catch his man and the punch to finish him!

At last when he believed he was ready to face a fairly good opponent, Grendon kept him at light training a month longer. In a way Maloney was eager to fight and get it over. His labor had been one of hatred, not love, and the sooner he could fling the money he owed into Grendon's face with a curse, the better it would suit him. But when he thought of entering the ring again, the old red ghost came back and left him weak and trembling.

Still, he was secretly grateful for one thing: he was no longer a whiskey-soaked hobo, but a man. Like all natural athletes, he reveled in the feel of his new strength and vibrancy—in the smooth flowing muscles and the work of the great clean lungs. He decided that he would never again sink into the gutter; he was still young, scarcely twenty-five years old. He would get some sort of a job and if he could not be a fighter, he would at least be a man.

Then at last Grendon announced that he had gotten Maloney a match.

"An American by the name of Leary," said Grendon. "You ought to draw a good crowd, if the fight fans down under remember you. And they always turn out to see a couple of Americans battle. I don't know what's the matter with Australia; she turns out so few fighters worthy of the name these days. I remember when Young Griffo, Hall, Murphy—"

Maloney gave him no heed. The vanished glories of Australia's fistic past was the one subject on which Grendon was prone to grow garrulous.

The old all-gone feeling came back when Maloney stood in the ring that night in Sydney. The crowd, some of them remembering him, had given him quite a hand, but he was remembering—

With an effort he jerked himself out of his crimson reveries and looked across at his opponent: a rangy red-headed fellow, taller than himself but lighter. The announcer was saying:

"—Jack Maloney, America, weight 195; Red Leary, also of America, weight 180—"

At the gong, Grendon hissed: "Remember my five hundred—and that you hate me!" And Maloney found time to wonder at the avariciousness of the man.

Leary, like Diaz, knew Maloney of old, and like the Mexican, he had no desire to serve as a stepping stone on the comeback road of a former great one. But differently from Diaz, he attacked instantly, though warily. Grendon had taught Maloney more of the real art of boxing than he had ever known before, and now as he blocked and side-stepped the rangy boxer's leads, Maloney realized that he was a better boxer than ever before. But the knowledge is not all—the heart must be in the game—

and with no horror of bull pens before his eyes, not even his hatred of Grendon could keep the old red memories from Maloney.

He retired on the defensive, flinched involuntarily from blows that did not hurt, and could not seem to untrack himself. The first round was slow; toward the end Leary drew first blood with a volley of straight lefts to the face. Maloney scarcely felt them, and retaliated with a whistling left hook which Leary cleverly blocked.

"Can't you untrack yourself?" rasped Grendon back in his corner. "You're in perfect shape; his best blows are not hurting you. You're hitting as hard as you ever did in your life. But you don't hit often enough. You've been on the run since the tap of the gong. This second-rater is going to outpoint you if you don't take a chance." Then as Maloney made no reply, Grendon snarled bitterly, "Bah! Your heart's not in your work. You're going to take a whipping just from pure lack of guts."

Maloney went out brooding over his manager's words and Leary, taking advantage of his abstraction, smashed a wicked left hook to the body and staggered his man with a sweeping right to the body. Stung out of his apathy, Maloney came back with a hard left hook to the ribs, knocking Leary into the ropes and bringing the crowd to its feet yelling. But the burst of action was brief. As Leary rebounded from the ropes, Maloney seemed to see Mike Brennon's shadow wavering between, and the heart went out of him. His reason told him that the blow he had dealt Leary had not landed solidly enough to knock down any trained man, but his blind unreasoning inhibitions clamored that here was the old tale all over again—a man whom his blows could not hurt.

Thus passed the second, third and fourth rounds, and the sixth and seventh rounds. Leary, boxing carefully, taking no chances, piling up an enormous lead, with Maloney defending in his half-hearted manner. Then came the eighth round.

Maloney came up as fresh as he had been at the first gong. He felt no fatigue whatever. But Leary saw only his cut and blood-stained features. He did not know that Maloney, tough and in perfect trim, had scarcely felt the jabs which had marked him. Leary believed that Maloney's lack of aggressiveness was from weakness. "They never come back!" And as he rushed out for the eighth, Leary suddenly discarded his former intention of winning on points and went savagely in for a knockout.

The crowd rose roaring; it was in hopes of this that they had sat so patiently through the fight. Maloney found himself the center of a whirlwind. Leary, though no match in hitting power for his opponent, carried a wicked punch and knew how to use it. Throwing caution to the winds, he battered Maloney all over the ring and floored him in a neutral corner.

Maloney took a count of nine, though he could have risen sooner. He was dizzy, not hurt. As he rose, Leary was on him, wild with the instinct of the kill. Maloney missed a vicious left, landed hard under the heart with the same hand and took a volley of lefts and rights to the head as he backed away, covering up.

Leary gave him no rest. He feinted him out of his position, ducked a venomous right and crashed his own right to Maloney's jaw. Again he landed. Maloney was dizzy; out on his feet. Suddenly it seemed that he was fighting, not Red Leary, but Iron Mike Brennon. Through the blood which veiled his eyes, he seemed to see Brennon's snarling face floating before him.

Suddenly Jack Maloney went crazy. He had suffered enough from this phantom. At last his instinct was fight, not run. He had forgotten all about Leary. Now he bunched himself into a solid cannonball of destruction and shot forward, blasting his terrible right hand full into the ghostly face which mocked him. And that blind smash found Red Leary's jaw.

Maloney, waking as from a nightmare, heard the referee counting and saw at his feet the limp form of his victim.

Grendon came to him in his dressing room.

"Here's your part of the purse; five hundred and fifty-five dollars."

Maloney snatched it from his hand. "Now then, here's your money, you—"

Grendon seemed not to notice him; he drew from his pocket a newspaper cutting. "Read this."

The date of the paper was a month old. The paper itself had been torn and was pasted together in a crude manner. Maloney read it and cried out incredulously: "Mike Brennon knocked out! Why, this can't be true! It says, 'Red Leary knocked out Iron Mike Brennon tonight in the first round of a scheduled fifteen frame go. It was Leary's last fight before leaving for Australia.' Why—"

He sat down, his brain reeling. He had whipped the man

who knocked out the terrible Mike Brennon. A wild feeling of exultation swept over him. He whirled on Grendon, his hatred of the man submerged in his new emotion.

"You'll keep on managing me! You'll get me some more fights! If I whipped the man who whipped Brennon, I can whip any of them! Including Brennon!"

"Handler's in England," said Grendon with a strange eager gleam in his cold eyes. "Do you think you can take him?"

Maloney laughed like a boy. A terrible load seemed lifted from his shoulders and only then did he realize how black and terrible it had been, distorting his entire viewpoint on life.

"I can take a roomful of him! Grendon, you're managing the next champion! First Handler! Then Brennon! Then whoever stands between me and the title! I'll flatten them all!"

"And, say," as Grendon started for the door, "here's your money."

"Keep it!" Grendon rapped. "I never accept money from my fighters. Keep it and pay me back by winning the title!"

Fight fans of London will remember the Maloney-Handler battle as long as they live, after the memories of longer, harder contested struggles have passed into oblivion. It was short, but it was sensational—the kind of fight which brings fans to their feet holding their breath and which sends them away babbling deliriously.

Before the gong sounded, Maloney sat in his corner, fresh and glowing with health after his long sea-trip, vibrant with fierce energy, which many took for nervousness. Across from him Handler sneered confidently. Had he not stopped this youth three years before? Maloney had been better then, surely. The burly Soldier had heard of his life since then. What if he had pushed over a couple of dubs since he started his come back? Handler laughed confidently; he himself was at the height of his career.

At the gong, Maloney shot from his corner like a thunderbolt. And like a thunderbolt he smote the astounded Soldier. Gone were all the red ghosts that once lurked in Maloney's brain, chaining his limbs. Again he was Jack Maloney, the Virginia Thunderbolt.

Handler had scarcely time to get out of his corner before the whirlwind struck. A sizzling straight left rocked his head back and as his jaw came up from behind the hunched and protecting shoulder, Maloney's fearful right crashed over. Only a born hitter can deliver a blow like that; the whole body working in unison, the mighty shoulder following the drive of the arm, the body pivoting at the waist, the feet thrusting powerfully upward and forward—and all done in the flash of a split second.

Handler dropped face down, nor did he move until he was brought to in his dressing room. His first words have come down the years with other ring classics:

"Baby!" caressing his chin, "That galoot don't hit! He explodes!"

Two more fights followed in England; to Maloney they were mere incidents, stepping-stones on his upward trail. His eventual goal was the title, he felt, but even that was subordinate to his desire to meet Iron Mike Brennon again. For this he lived.

Shortly after he knocked out Soldier Handler, he was matched with Tom Walshire, the champion of England. The clever Briton eluded the wrath to come for nine rounds, but Maloney was not to be denied, and in the tenth he cornered Walshire and smashed him to the canvas for the full count.

Gunboat Sloan followed. The Gunner was past his prime, but he still had his old time ring craft and a left hand as deadly as a crossbow bolt. Boxing superbly, he kept Maloney at bay for four rounds and in the fifth landed that terrible left flush to the jaw. Maloney's knees buckled, but even while the crowd held their breath expecting his fall, he lurched headlong into the Gunner and brought him down with an inside right under the heart.

It was a few days after this victory when Maloney rushed into Grendon's room. The relations of the two men had changed subtly. Grendon's manner had altered after Maloney's decision to continue in the ring, and Maloney's feeling had changed from hatred to a grudging admiration. He had stayed with Grendon because he realized that the man was one of the cleverest pilots in the game and could aid him in his climb. At last he had come to have a secret liking for the Australian and had often wondered if the man's cold hard attitude were not a mask to hide his real sensitive nature.

But now as he entered Grendon's room, his brain was in a turmoil.

"Look here!" he waved a newspaper in his manager's face. "Last night in America, Iron Mike Brennon was knocked out by a fellow they call Iron Mike Costigan! In the first round! And the paper says that's the first time Brennon has been flattened!"

Grendon nodded.

"But you told me," stammered the fighter, all at sea, "you told me that Red Leary, whom I whipped in Sydney, had knocked Brennon out! The knowledge that I'd whipped Leary has been what's holding me up!"

Grendon shook his head. "More than that, Jack. You needed something then to brace you. Now you're able to go on your own."

Maloney frowned and cogitated, then suddenly threw back his shoulders and grinned with the pleasant arrogance of youth.

"You're right; I'm over all that stuff. I realize that it was just mental—just an inhibition or complex or something that I'm rid of. I'll go on and fight—"

He halted, suddenly realizing something of which he had not thought before.

"Brennon must be terribly battered, or he couldn't have been knocked out."

"The last time I saw him," said Grendon, "months before I first met you in Mexico, he was a battered wreck. Nearly ready for the padded cell. Anybody could have pushed him over in this last fight. That's the way these iron men go; they seem invincible for years, then they crack suddenly."

Maloney shook his head pityingly. "I've hated him for three years. I don't hate him any longer and I don't want to fight him. Anyway, the paper says he's retiring. If he wasn't, I wouldn't push over a punch drunk ruin—say, get me Costigan, the fellow that knocked him out!"

"But Jack, he's an iron man too! Just a counterpart of the Brennon who knocked you out nearly four years ago."

"No matter—and Grendon, I want to say that at last I appreciate everything you've done for me. I was a hog and you made me a man against your will. What your original object was I don't know—"

"Why, Jack," Grendon's hard eyes were strangely soft, "years ago when you were just a hard slugging kid, I kept my eye on you; wanted to manage you but couldn't buy your contract. I've always liked you as a fighter; of late I've come to like you as a man.

"When I found you wasting your life in that little border town, I wanted to see if you were capable of getting out of the gutter, even with help. I told you that time that the alcalde in the town was my friend. He was and is. I framed the whole thing. You didn't sock an officer; you were too drunk to do anything, or remember anything. I didn't bet any money on you. There wasn't any fine to pay.

"I admit it was cruel sending you in against Diaz in your condition. But I wanted to find out if you had anything left. Even if he flattened you with the first punch, I didn't intend leaving you there to rot in those low class dives.

"But you showed me in that fight that you still had your super-human physical ability. I don't believe the man ever lived before who could have knocked out a fighter in good condition after having gone through what you'd been through! And I saw your heart was in the right place, too. Nothing wrong there. The same old fighting heart. But it was your mind. You needed a bracer.

"I was afraid to show you the paper about Leary and Brennon before the fight, and if you'd lost I'd never have used it. But you see the result."

"How'd you frame that?" Maloney asked.

Grendon smiled. "You noticed how the paper was torn. I simply tore out a few words and pasted the torn edges together. The original lines were: 'Red Leary *was knocked out by* Iron Mike Brennon in one round!'"

Maloney laughed. "It served the purpose. It made me regain my confidence. Now I'll never lose it again if I live to be a hundred. And now I want a match with Costigan!"

"Jack, you'll gain nothing by fighting this iron man; just now he's at his prime. Dempsey couldn't knock him out, neither could Fitzsimmons. If you beat him you'll gain considerable prestige, but if he beats you, you're ruined. These iron men are the worst opponents in the world for nervous sensitive fighters like you. Pass him up and take on a fast clever fellow like yourself."

Maloney shook his head. "I'm older now. I won't make a fool out of myself again. I won't punch myself out on Costigan as I did on Brennon, but I want to beat the man who beat the man who broke me. Till then I won't have regained my fullest self respect and self confidence."

This is an item which appeared in the newspapers a month later: "Jack Maloney, whose sensational rise and fall four years ago was the talk of the sporting world, rose another step on the fistic ladder which he is remounting when he outpointed

Iron Mike Costigan, the conqueror of Iron Mike Brennon. Maloney seems to have regained all the speed and punch which four years ago caused sports writers to christen him The Virginia Thunderbolt, and to predict his early accession to the heavyweight crown.

"This was Maloney's first battle in an American ring since he began his come back campaign. He held the upper hand throughout the bout, taking every round of the fifteen round go, and in the last frame, sent Costigan twice to the canvas for counts of nine. Only Mike's superhuman endurance and vitality saved him from the first knockout of his career, and it seemed that if it had gone a few more rounds, he would have taken the count in spite of his ruggedness, which is of a quality to make Joe Grim jealous. Maloney, though he did not score a knockout, deserves praise for superb work, and seems a cinch for the title."

Fists of the Desert

CHAPTER I

A small railroad station, its sunblistered paint cracking in the heat—across the tracks a scattering of adobe huts, a cluster of frame buildings—that was Yucca Junction, baking in the desert that stretched from horizon to distant horizon.

Up and down, in the scanty, breathless shade of the little station, Al Lyman paced restlessly, his patent-leather shoes grinding dryly in the cinders. A small man, Lyman, with narrow, stooped shoulders; cheap, flashy, a product of city slums. Predatory beak of a nose, gimlet eyes—tinhorn was written all over him.

His meal-ticket lumbered beside him—big Spike Sullivan, well know to the habitues of the Barbary Street A. C. Shoulders like an ox, big hands hanging low, half open like an ape's, matted with stiff black hair. A sullen face, jutting jaw, murky black eyes. He was as incongruous in his present setting as Lyman was. His real name sounded nothing like Sullivan.

He glared around him as he shuffled up and down with Lyman—both men walking because moving was more tolerable in that heat than keeping still. Sullivan scowled at the tiny town across the tracks, at the man just visible inside the waiting room, and at the mongrel dog under a bench beside the wall.

The dog mistook the man's glare. He stretched himself and came from under the bench, wagging his tail. Sullivan cursed him away stormily. At the impact of his angry rumble on the stillness, the man in the waiting room came to the door and surveyed the strangers impersonally.

He was as much a part of the scene as they were alien to it. He was as tall as Sullivan, though lacking something of the pugilist's bulk. But he was clean-cut, forged in a mold of sun and desert that had bronzed his skin and stripped all surplus weight from his lean-waisted, thick-chested frame. Tranquilly he folded his massive arms and stared off across the wastes to where, in the distance, the train for which all three were waiting was struggling up a long grade.

The dog trailed after the strangers, dejected, but still hopeful of a pat on the head. Sullivan reached the edge of the shade, turned suddenly and fell sprawling over the surprised canine, rasping his hands on the hot cinders. The dog yelped and scurried out of reach just as Sullivan scrambled up, launching a heavy foot after him. The boot grazed the dog's back and the animal darted under his bench and cowered there. Sullivan rushed at him, all the beast roused in him. He was hardly responsible for his actions—merely a slow-witted, evil-tempered brute who reacted unreasoningly to his chance environment.

"Easy, Spike!" whined Lyman anxiously. "Let the mutt be."

Sullivan paid no heed. Deliberately he drew back his foot to crush in the ribs of the shivering animal, when the man in the doorway took a hand in the game. With no appearance of haste he stepped between Sullivan and the bench, and pushed the man backward, not gently.

"Let that dog alone," he said.

"Is that your mutt?" the fighter snarled, balling his huge fists.

"No, it ain't," answered the desert man. "If it was, I'd throw a hunk of lead through you. As it is—"

Just then Sullivan let go with a right that had murder behind it. Sullivan could hit; any man who is a favorite in the Barbary Street A. C. must be a puncher. The desert man was caught flat-footed. Square on the jaw he took the full drive of Sullivan's murderous right. Lyman yelped and jumped back to let the victim fall clear.

But he did not fall. He reeled backward from the impact, with blood starting from the corner of his mouth. But he kept his feet, and Sullivan, instead of following up, gaped and half lowered his hands with the surprise of it. And that was Sullivan's mistake. The desert man's return was like the strike of a big cat.

Cinders spurted from under the balls of his feet as he hurtled in, and his left fist crunched savagely into Sullivan's ribs. He was wide open; Sullivan's fists slugged home. No man had ever stood up and outslugged him in the Barbary, where the toughest ham-and-eggers of the West Coast display their wares.

The stranger knew nothing of boxing. His blows were swings, but each carried behind it the weight of the broad shoulders and the drive of the muscular thighs. He seemed built of granite and steel. Sullivan's fists tore skin and brought blood, but the man shook them off, redoubling his fury. Desperation grew in Sullivan's eyes as his breath began to whistle between his teeth. No human could take what he was handing out—yet this man was taking it.

An agonized grunt burst from Sullivan as his opponent's left, smashing through his weakening guard, sank wrist-deep in his belly. Involuntarily his hands went down. And for the first time the stranger's mallet-like right exploded square in the prize-fighter's face. Sullivan's features vanished in a flood of crimson. With a groan he staggered, groping; and the stranger threw his right again, as a man throws a hammer.

At its impact Sullivan went down sidewise and lay where he fell. The mongrel crawled from under his bench, whimpering. Inside the click-click of the telegraph was the only sound. The station agent had not left his seat. Impassively he stared through the open window.

"W-Who-who are you?" whispered Al Lyman, tugging at his sweat-soaked collar as if it choked him.

"Kirby Karnes," answered the other briefly, turning to glance down at the shaking manager.

"Are you a fighter?" Lyman seemed to have forgotten Sullivan, lying there on the cinders. "What do you do for a living? Did you ever fight—in the ring, I mean?"

Karnes shook his head.

"I've been dressin' tools in the San Pedro oil field, lately, until they shut down. I'm lookin' for a job now."

"Listen!" urged Lyman excitedly, glancing toward the train, which was chugging up the last grade before it hit Yucca Junction. "You're wasting your talents in an oil field. You know what you've just done? You've flattened Spike Sullivan, one of the toughest eggs on the West Coast! You'd be a sensation in the ring."

"I've fought plenty with bare fists," said the other, unconsciously flexing his thick biceps. "I never thought of fightin' in the ring."

"Let me handle you!" urged Lyman. "You'll make more in a month in Frisco than you'll make in a year hammering drill bits. What do you say?"

Karnes glanced out across the aching emptiness of the desert before he replied.

"I've always wanted to see Frisco," he said at last. "I've got no job, and none in sight. Work's awful scarce now."

"Good!" Lyman almost capered in his delight. "Help me pack this egg into the waiting room." A few seconds later the still senseless Sullivan was stretched on a bench in the sweltering station. Flies buzzed about his bloody head.

"Come on!" Lyman grabbed Karnes' sleeve. "The train's pulling in, and it only stops a few minutes."

"What about him?" Karnes indicated the recumbent figure.

"Let him lay," yelled Lyman, pulling his find toward the door. "I'm through with the big palooka. Let him go back to the mines, where he belongs. Come on!"

The click of the wheels as they whirled westward was like the rattling clink of falling coins to the ears of Al Lyman. Easy money! The phrase beat a refrain to the clash and rumble of the wheels. A cheap skate de luxe, Al Lyman. Already he had worked out his frame for Kirby Karnes, and it was a typical Lyman set-up. And Karnes, unused to judging men, ignorant of Lyman's type, no more recognized the tinhorn brand than he could foresee the role for which Fate had already cast him.

CHAPTER II

Fall Guy

Lyman had no trouble getting Kirby Karnes a match at the Barbary. The promoter knew that Lyman's fighters always had *something*. Lyman knew how to cater to the mob. He took care that Karnes' first opponent was not dangerous—a fading veteran who never had much to begin with.

Barbary Street interest was roused, however cynically, for Lyman talked loudly of his "desert tiger's" ferocity and ruggedness.

"He don't know nothin', gents," Lyman proclaimed to the boys. "He don't have to know nothing. He's all rawhide and whalebone, see? Joe Grim was a sissy beside of him! You all seen Spike Sullivan fight. Spike was a bum, but you know he could punch. Well, Spike hits this boy on the button with all he's got, and the fellow don't even blink. I tell you, they can't knock him out!"

Not old Joe Harrigan, at least. Karnes plunged out of his corner at the gong like a desert sandstorm, wide open, fighting the only way he knew. He didn't suppose that ring-war was any different from the fights he had had in the bars and windblown streets of the desert towns. The lights, the noise of the crowd bothered him at first, but he forgot all that when the bell shot him out into the ring.

At his best Harrigan had never been much. Now his knuckles were knobs of brittle chalk, the muscles in his legs were rotten cords, and the jolt of a glove against his battered jaw sent waves of blackness across his brain.

For a round he evaded the swirling maulers of Kirby Karnes—jabbed at the brown, grim face before him, ducked the sweeping swings and tied up the desert man in the clinches.

But in the second round Karnes' right, swishing up from the floor, sank deep in Harrigan's midriff, and the old-timer went to his knees, green-faced and gagging, just as the bell ended his torment.

Lyman babbled praise in Karnes' ear, bade him hark to the roar of the fans. What the Barbary crowd wanted was always action—gloves smashing, blood, somebody writhing in the resin. Lyman smirked as they yelled; but in the first row, ringside, a slender man with silvered temples shook his head and muttered under his breath, twisting his lips as though he smelled something repugnant.

Harrigan came up for the third with his belly heaving spasmodically. Karnes rushed and threw his right like a hammer. Harrigan was too weary to duck, too sick to care. The weighted glove only grazed his jaw, but it was enough. Harrigan hit the resin, as he had in his last four fights, and the referee raised Kirby Karnes' arm. The crowd jeered and cheered—jeered because they knew old Joe Harrigan was washed up—but cheered because, after all, Karnes had done what it was his job to do.

"Great stuff, Kirby!" babbled Lyman, throwing a bathrobe about his man's shoulders. "I told you! Fight your natural style. Take all they got and wear 'em down. You don't have to box. Nobody can knock you out."

As the crowd moved out through the doors, one fan nudged another and indicated a slender, silver-templed man making his way toward the street. "See him? That's John Reynolds. Managed a dozen first-raters. Always hanging around these small clubs, looking for material."

The other, impressed, found himself pushed against the slender man in the crowd, and, admiring his own temerity, spoke: "Well, Mr. Reynolds, how did you like the fights?"

"They were rotten, as usual," answered Reynolds. "Lyman has a good man—but he'll ruin him, as he always does his fighters."

The truth of this prophecy was not at first apparent. Karnes became intensely popular at the Barbary. He could hit and he could take it. That was all Barbary Street asked.

Karnes' ignorance of the game was monumental. He followed Lyman's guidance unquestioningly. He never even knew how much Lyman cheated him when his manager gave him his cut of the purse. He lived in a cheap room not far from the arena, trained in a dingy gym that was built in an old stable. Between fights he worked behind the bar of a beer joint.

A broken-down veteran taught the desert man the simplest rudiments of the game. No more. Lyman did not want Karnes to learn anything. He was capitalizing on his ability to soak up punishment. The less he knew, the more punishment he must absorb, the more highly emphasized must appear his unusual stamina.

"Rush 'em and clout 'em," he instructed. "Nobody can hurt you."

Karnes won his first four or five fights by the k.o. route. Green youngsters and worn-out trail horses could not evade his ferocious charges with hurricane swings. Then they matched him with Jim Harper, who was neither a clumsy kid nor a washed-up ruin. He could box and he could hit. He outpointed Karnes in ten furious rounds. Karnes was not discouraged. Lyman assured him that such setbacks were inevitable to any fighter; all boxers lost fights. Loss of a decision hurt nobody. The main thing was that no knockout should be chalked up against him.

In a re-match, Karnes, pitting raw strength and iron jaw against Harper's superior skill, slugged out a draw by pure ferocity. In that fight the customers for the first time realized the desert man's full stamina and toughness. His ribs were like oak, his jaw like iron. Blows that crushed the bones of other men bounced harmlessly from his steely frame.

And so the exploitation of bone and nerve and muscle began in earnest. They matched him with the hardest hitters that could be persuaded to show their wares in the dingy old Barbary. He dropped decision after decision, his rough-house style futile against clever men. That did not matter—to the promoter and Al Lyman. His drawing power lay in his iron jaw. The fans did not expect him to win; they turned out to see whether he could weather the storm and finish on his feet. Occasionally he did score a k.o. when some opponent wearied and one of the desert man's hammer-like smashes crashed home.

They billed Kirby Karnes as the man who could not be knocked out. Night after night the roof of the Barbary echoed to the roar of the pack—and under the lights, Kirby Karnes, reeling before some hard-faced slugger with dynamite in his forearms, doggedly kept his feet and fighting back till the last gong ended his torment.

And night after night John Reynolds sat at the ringside, watching with inscrutable eyes.

At last Lyman, watching his man like a hawk, decided that the time had come to gather in the harvest. They matched Karnes against Jack Miller.

Miller was a better fighter than the general run of those who passed through the portals of the Barbary. Not a headliner, nor a man-killer, but a fair hitter, and clever. None doubted that he would win; the only question was whether he could supply the k.o. which Karnes had so far avoided. Plenty of money—for Barbary Street—was in sight; and considering Karnes' record and Miller's lack of real dynamite, the odds were about three to one that Karnes would finish on his feet.

Before the go, one Big John Lynch held conclave with Al Lyman.

"Remember, Lyman," rumbled Lynch in conclusion, "Karnes flops in the ninth or earlier."

"I'll see to it," promised Lyman. "I've got plenty of my own dough up. Karnes is about washed up. He's taken too many on the chin. Back to the desert for him. Miller might do the job without any help. But I'm taking no chances."

Lyman was shrewd enough to sense Karnes' innate honesty, and to say nothing about the set-up. He kept assuring Karnes that his chance would come, that his best bet was to keep on plugging and await the breaks. Karnes knew that in any job in life a man had to keep plugging. He never doubted his manager. But doubts of his own ability assailed him. He could not realize how ruthlessly he was being exploited.

When he sat in his corner that night, waiting for the bell, he stared idly around the ring at the faces that had grown familiar to him. He saw the lean, keen face of the man he knew vaguely as John Reynolds. He saw the swarthy, brutal face of Big John Lynch, flanked by his hard-jawed henchmen—Steinman, McGoorty and Zorelli. Lynch was a gambler, almost the boss of Barbary Street.

Across the ring, Jack Miller, lean, hard with corded muscles, a merciless face unmarked except for a dented nose. A man who would never reach the top himself, but over whose form an ambitious fighter must climb. By far the best man Karnes had ever faced.

Lyman fumbled with towels and bucket, glancing furtively toward Big John Lynch, chewing his cigar in the first row. Mechanically Karnes shuffled his feet in the resin dust. This was an old story, now. He despaired of beating Miller. But he would stay the limit. The idea was beginning to crystallize in his mind that that was all he had—an iron jaw. Each man has his niche in life; his was the role of the iron man, fighting not so much to win as to stay the limit. To finish on his feet constituted a victory for him. It was strange—but Lyman said it was so.

The life into which he had plunged was too complicated for the desert man. Blindly he had followed Lyman's guidance. He never even knew what his purse was. It seemed consistently small. He wondered dully about that now. Of late he had found it difficult to think straight. At times he seemed to be moving in a fog, and often there was a throbbing at the base of his brain. It was harder to shake off the numbing paralysis of squarely-landed blows than it had once been. He passed his gloved hand absently over his thickened ears. Already he was marked like a veteran. A revulsion shook him. A man must start at the bottom in any game—but he seemed fated to remain at the bottom. He shook himself and came erect at Lyman's quick warning.

The gong brought him out of his corner in a rush that carried him straight across the ring. The roar of the throng was a familiar thunder in his battered ears. Karnes! Karnes! Karnes! The man they can't knock out!

Miller smiled coldly. He'd met iron men before. He was more dangerous to them than a man-killer was. Wear him down with an endless stream of jabs and hooks. Make him miss and sweat. Don't kill yourself trying to knock off his block with one haymaker.

Miller backed away, stabbing. Karnes crowded in. Miller didn't make the mistake of trying to prop Karnes off with the left. He drifted before the onslaught, shooting his jab on the run. Karnes' swings looped around his neck; in close he hammered away at the slugger's body. Nobody had ever taught Karnes anything about infighting. He could only grab Miller awkwardly and hold on till the referee broke them. His belly muscles were like rigid steel cords under Miller's knuckles. Miller grunted. This boy would take a lot of wearing down.

Round after round Karnes surged in, his fighting spirit undimmed. When he landed Miller felt those lashing swings clear to the end of his toes. But few licks landed. Miller was fighting a heady fight, pouring a steady hail of lefts and rights to Karnes' head and body. Blood trickled from Karnes' nose; his face lacked some skin. Otherwise he was unmarked and breathing easily. He looked a cinch to finish on his feet, at the end of the seventh.

Big John Lynch took his cigar from his thick lips and nodded ponderously to Lyman. Lyman's hand snaked into his hip pocket, came out with a small flask. Karnes' stupid-faced second held a towel so it masked the fighter from the crowd. Under this cover Lyman fumbled for Karnes' lips.

"Drink this!" he hissed.

Karnes drank without question. It was his manager's orders. The liquid had an aromatic tang that was unpleasant. He grunted, spat, started to speak—the gong banged.

Karnes started up and was almost in Miller's corner before he realized that something was amiss. The lights seemed to waver, and while he blinked, puzzled at this phenomenon, Miller's left hook swished to his jaw.

Karnes reeled back into the ropes—rebounded from them and waded in. He kept shaking his head, feeling as if a glove were still jammed against his jaw. His feet dragged. His arms lacked their spring. His brain was clouded. Dumbly he groped for understanding. That punch had been hard, but no harder than many he had shaken off. There was something the matter with him.

He was wilder than ever. To the crowd this seemed merely the result of Miller's cleverness, but Karnes knew better. Something ailed him—something that tied up his muscles and misted his vision. Miller sensed the change in his foe, but was wary. This might be a trick. He took no chances. He worked his long, sharp-shooting left hand in Karnes' face like a piston, but kept his right cocked. Karnes was on his feet at the bell.

Back in his corner, Lyman glanced toward Big John Lynch, glowering and chewing his cigar savagely. Lyman bent over the fighter.

"How do you feel, Kirby?"

"Queer," muttered Karnes. "What was that you gave me to drink?"

"Just a little brandy and water," lied Lyman. "You looked wilted. Must of been something you ate."

"I'll stay the limit!" Karnes lurched to his feet. "They can't knock me out—"

They can't knock me out—the thought beat in Karnes' numb brain as he reeled and staggered, bloody and battered, before merciless fists. Miller, sensing his condition at last, unleashed his full fury. They can't knock me out. The crowd thundered the refrain to the roof; louder than their roar it cried out in his dizzy brain. He must stay the limit. It was his one bid for glory in a life bitter with failure. He must keep his feet, though those agonizing fists that rained ceaselessly upon him tore his brain loose from his skull, though the very roof crashed down on him—he must finish on his feet.

Back in his corner, limp on his stool, he saw Al Lyman's face, white in the arc-lights.

"Quit, Karnes, quit!" Lyman begged over and over, his voice sounding as if from far away. "For God's sake, take it on the chin and flop!"

It would do no good to throw in the sponge. Bets were laid on a ten-count k.o. The referee would not stop the fight, knowing Karnes' reputation. Lyman was caught in his own trap.

"I'm all right," mumbled Karnes through bloody lips. "I'll stay the limit. They can't knock me out."

Clang of the gong and thunder of the crowd. Crunch of knuckle-loaded leather, sweat in pain-misted eyes. And Kirby Karnes, keeping his feet in spite of hell and high water.

Karnes had but one defense. In his extremity he simply wrapped his arms about his head, crouching. It was pitifully inadequate. Miller knifed uppercuts between his arms, looped smashes over his ears. When he unwound with swiping swings they cut empty air and Miller's leather-guarded knuckles were like knives against his flesh. The gong found him on the floor, fighting frantically for his feet.

His handlers dragged him to his corner, dumped him onto his stool. Lyman was wild with rage and fright. But the second shook his head.

"He can't last half a round," said he. "Nobody could."

"They can't knock me out," mumbled Karnes. The crowd's roar was a distant echo. The light of the ring was a bloody mist. Jack Miller was a white blur, armed with weighted bludgeons. The gong was a faint tinkle, somewhere on the other side of the universe.

Drunkenly he lurched up, rolled out into the ring. Miller was on him like a panther, afire for the kill.

Karnes, bent in a half crouch, fighting back spasmodically, felt Miller's blows only as dull impacts that no longer hurt his frozen nerves. He had reached that dangerous point where a man must be killed to be stopped—and where he wavers perilously close to the deadline. A few more rounds and the career of Kirby Karnes might have ended forever.

But it was only a ten round bout. And when the gong ended it, a disheveled, bloody figure swayed upright in the center of the ring—beaten and yet invincible. Karnes collapsed in his corner as the crowd filed out, cheering him to the last echo, booing the disgusted, exhausted Miller, as crowds will.

Kirby Karnes seemed floating in a gray mist. Faintly he remembered staggering to his dressing room, supported by his seconds. He lay on the rubbing table while somebody looked for the club physician, who was out of the way somewhere, as was usual in the Barbary.

But his incredible vitality was already asserting itself. He wondered dully why Al Lyman shivered as if with an ague. Lyman started convulsively as the door lurched inward under the impact of a heavy boot. Big John Lynch shouldered in, followed by his henchmen, and Big John's face was like a thunder cloud.

"Scram!" he mouthed at the hangers-on, and they scurried out in stumbling haste. Lyman made as if to follow them, but Big John's beam-like arm barred his way.

"You dirty, double-crossin' rat!" he said, and Lyman shriveled. "You'd fix it! Yes, you fixed it! And I lose three grand! You—"

"Don't John!" screamed Lyman. "I tried to make him quit! Honest to God, I did! Didn't I, Karnes? Didn't I keep telling you to quit?"

"Yes, you did," mumbled Karnes, his muddled brain not understanding.

"You see?" chattered Lyman. "I gave him the dope, too. You saw me give it to him. It just wouldn't work on him. He ain't human—"

An open-handed slap sent him staggering across the room. Karnes painfully hauled himself to his feet. He didn't know what this was all about. His head whirled and the lights wavered. But nobody could knock his manager around that way. Nobody—

"So you was the smart boy that crossed us!"

Big John struck out unexpectedly. The blow was clumsy, but heavy. Karnes reeled back against the table, and Zorelli struck him from behind with a blackjack. Karnes sagged, trying to fight back. To his dizzy brain it seemed that he was in the ring again, trying to stave off the rushing tide of blackness. But this time it would not be denied. Blackjacks, fists and gun-barrels beat down upon him. Big John's furious voice bellowed orders. A back door crashed back against the wall. Through it a bleeding, senseless form was hurled, to lie motionless in the dust of the alley.

CHAPTER III

Law of the Desert

John Reynolds sat beside the dingy bed in the drab little room where Kirby Karnes lay. A week had passed since the night of the Miller fight, and Karnes' face was still scarcely recognizable. Only a man of rawhide and steel could have recovered from the double beating he had received.

"Lyman been around to see you?" asked Reynolds casually.

A scornful grunt was his only answer.

"I thought not." Reynolds was silent for a while, and then he said, abruptly: "I've been watching you for months. It was none of my business, but I hate to see a good man ruined. Lyman's a cheap crook, and a fool. All he could see in you was a chance to make a few dirty dollars."

"And what do you see in me?" asked Karnes cynically.

"Everything. Speed, guts, punch. You could learn. You do everything wrong now. Lyman taught you nothing."

"He taught me one thing," Karnes answered grimly. "He taught me what kind of a game this is."

"You can't judge a whole profession by a few rats hanging around the fringe. You've never met the real men of the ring. Let me handle you! You've got a future before you."

Karnes' laugh was not pleasant to hear.

"That's what Lyman was always tellin' me. Then he doped me and sold me out to Lynch. I was so dizzy after the fight it took me days to dope it out, but I got it at last. I never had anything but an iron jaw. Lyman built me a reputation on that, just so he could make a haul by framin' me for a k.o."

"That sounds like Lyman. But you've got more than an iron jaw. It was Lyman's fault that you never got anywhere."

"It'll be my fault if I stay in this racket," growled Karnes. "I'm goin' back to the desert, where I belong—after I've settled this score."

Reynolds paled at the red glare of Karnes' eyes.

"Don't try that!" he begged. "They're not worth getting into trouble over. Come in with me. I'll make something out of you."

"A bigger sap than Lyman made out of me," answered Karnes roughly. "Get out of here. I don't want to talk to anybody that looks like a fight manager. What I do is my own business."

Reynolds started to speak, then rose and left the room silently. Karnes rose and dressed himself, moving stiffly. From among his scanty belongings he took a blue-barreled .45. This he thrust into the waistband of his pants, under his coat. His battered face was grim as that of a carven image, his eyes bleak.

A few moments later he emerged into the dingy street. He walked hurriedly down it a few blocks, then turned into an alley. The slink of a stalking panther was in his walk now. At the other end of that alley there was the back door of a speakeasy where Big John Lynch and his mob hung out.

But as he stepped into the alley, a figure moved out from the wall and confronted him. It was Reynolds.

"I thought you'd come this way," said Reynolds. "I've seen the killer look in men's eyes before. Give it up, Karnes. You'll only land in the chair. I tell you, it's not worth it."

"Where I come from," said Karnes somberly, "there's only one answer to the deal they gave me. Get out of my way."

Karnes threw out an arm to brush him aside, but Reynolds grabbed it and hung on with surprising strength. Karnes tried to shake him off, unwilling to hurt him. In the scuffle his coat fell back, revealing the ivory stock of the gun. Reynolds caught at it, dragged it from Karnes' belt, tried to throw it over the board fence. Karnes grabbed at it, swearing, twisted it out of Reynolds' clinging fingers. Somebody's thumb slid over the hammer, unavoidably, pulling the fanged head back. There was a crashing report, a burst of smoke, and then Karnes stared stupidly at Reynolds on the ground, white-faced, blood gushing from his leg.

A policeman ran into the alley, shouting. Reynolds reached up and jerked the gun from Karnes' hand before the cop saw.

"What is this?" demanded the officer. "What happened?"

"An accident," panted Reynolds. "I was showing Karnes my gun and I shot myself in the leg."

Karnes opened his mouth—closed it at the look Reynolds gave him. He dropped beside the wounded man and made a tourniquet of his belt, while the cop ran to a phone-box.

Days later Karnes sat beside the bed where John Reynolds lay. Karnes fumbled his hat, glancing sidewise at Reynolds' right leg, which ended in a bandaged stump. The heavy bullet, crashing downward through the thigh, had severed arteries, splintered the bone beyond repair. To save John Reynolds' life they had taken off his leg above the knee.

Reynolds stared at the ceiling, his thin face tranquil. There was no tremor in his hands when he moved them on the sheets.

"What are you goin' to do?" Karnes blurted out, his voice like a physical impact on the silence of the little hospital room.

"I've saved a little," answered Reynolds.

"Not very much. I've been findin' out about you. You're square. You ain't like Lyman. I might've known. You've managed a lot of good men, but you ain't got nothin' to show for it. You gave away all your dough. And now—I'm responsible for this. I don't know how to repay."

"If you want to do anything for me, forget Lynch and Lyman," responded Reynolds. "You wouldn't bother hating a rat because it bit you, would you?"

"All right, I won't touch 'em. But that ain't nothin'. If you still want to manage me—well, you don't need a—a leg to manage a fighter. I'd like to fight for you, if you still want me to. I don't want a cent, except just what it takes to live on. You can have all the rest I make. I'm no boxer, but they can't knock me out—"

A rare smile lit Reynolds' pain-lined face. His hand reached out, closed on bronze fingers.

CHAPTER IV

Rungs of the Ladder

Seven months later John Reynolds, walking a little awkwardly on his artificial leg, came to the matchmaker of the Golden Glove.

"As a favor, Bill," he said, "match my boy Kirby Karnes with Jack Miller."

"Karnes?" scowled Bill Hopkins. "Isn't he that palooka that Lyman used to feed to the lions every week down at the Barbary? Why, John, that fellow is no good."

"He is now," answered Reynolds. "I knew he had the stuff from the start. All he needed was proper coaching. I sat in a wheel chair in my gym and taught him the game from the ground up, with some first class sparring partners. He never knew there was that much science in boxing, and Lyman had made him believe he couldn't learn anything. Learn? He took to it like a duck to water.

"He was nearly punch-drunk when I got him, but he's sound as a steel bolt now. He's ready for anything. A bit green, yes; but all he needs now is experience. He's fast. He can box. He can hit. He's what I've dreamed of for years. None of my other boys quite made the grade. But at last I've got a champion in the making. As a favor to me, put him on."

"All right, John." Bill's voice was gentle as he reached for a phone. He didn't look toward Reynolds' leg, but it wasn't difficult to guess what he was thinking. Hard lines for a man to just miss his goal, all his life, and then be crippled as old age approached. That fight with Miller would be in the nature of a benefit for John Reynolds.

Miller did not particularly relish the match. His failure to stop Karnes still rankled. This time, he swore, he would walk in from the first bell and trade swats with the punch-drunk tramp. Why John Reynolds, a wise hombre, wanted to pick an also-ran like Karnes out of the ash-heap was more than Miller could understand, and he said so, vindictively.

The Golden Glove, with its clean, modern dressing rooms, was like a dream to Kirby Karnes, used to the dingy, musty-smelling dens of the Barbary. There was a subtle difference about everything. It wasn't merely that the crowd was bigger. It seemed cleaner. Men and women of prominence and prosperity occupied the ringside. Kirby Karnes breathed deeply, feeling like a man coming into his own at last.

Reynolds, leaning against the corner of the ring, patted his glove.

"The first rung on the ladder, boy!" he said. Karnes smiled faintly. It was the first time anyone in Frisco had ever seen him smile. Across the ring Miller scowled and sneered. The gong!

Karnes came swiftly out of his corner, not in a wide-open rush, but sliding smoothly in a half-crouch. Miller came at him like a hornet, then hesitated, backed up. There was a change in Karnes that puzzled him—a dynamic certitude. Memory of that silver-templed man in Karnes' corner roused caution in Miller's wary mind.

Karnes glided in, perfectly poised. Miller poked out a long left. Karnes exploded into breath-taking action. In a blur of speed he was inside that extended arm and his right ripped under Miller's heart. The impact of the blow brought the crowd to its feet. Miller gasped, stiffened. Karnes' left swished up to his jaw, loaded with dynamite. The desert man was not swinging, now; his punches were short hooks, blinding in speed, explosive in effect.

Miller swayed forward, his knees buckling, but before he could fall a right hook to the chin pitched him backward to the canvas, out cold. In their clamorous acclaim the crowd hardly noticed the main event that followed.

It was the boxing world's introduction to Kirby Karnes, the new star cast in an old-time mold. Into a dizzy world of jazz, cocktails, and fallen idols had come a breath out of the past, a fighting man who believed his proper business was fighting.

Turn back the years and look at him. Kirby Karnes! A bronze barbarian from the desert, surcharged with the speed of a panther and the devastating fury of a sandstorm.

Kirby Karnes was John Reynolds' masterpiece. Into his making went all the hard-won experience of the old master. Shades of old-time champions stalked with Karnes across the resined ring—shades of the days when boxing was an art, not a burlesque show.

Emerging from obscurity, Karnes blazed like a meteor across the fistic heavens. Sports writers hailed him as a fighting man who *fought*. While the heavyweight champion was enacting the role of a Broadway butterfly, Kirby Karnes was battling his way up the long, hard trail that leads through the resin dust rings under the blazing white lights.

He was known no longer as an iron man—not that he was less rugged than of old, but because he no longer need depend on his toughness. Under John Reynolds' coaching he had become a boxer. Illusive as a ghost, quick as a cat, with T.N.T. in either hand, Kirby Karnes was the fighter of which managers have dreamed in vain since the days of Jem Figg.

Within a year from the night he knocked out Jack Miller, he had fought his way up through the ranks—eighteen fights, eighteen knockouts, and not a setup among them!—and only one man stood between him and the champion. Diego Lopez. A caveman, this giant from Honduras. Not clever, but strong as a bull, with a right fist like a lead-weighted club. While Karnes was mowing them down on the West Coast, Lopez was clubbing the best men of the East into senseless pulps.

That the two should meet was inevitable. The cartoon by Ledgren, the dean of sports' writers, presented the situation well: Karnes and Lopez each standing amidst a heap of senseless figures that represented the foremost contenders, glaring at one another across the continent.

The go was looked upon almost as a title fight. The champion must meet the winner, and everybody knew that either man was more than a match for the titleholder, who, since winning the crown, had done his training in night clubs.

The big clubs of Chicago and New York bid for the match, but it went to a smaller one—the Golden Glove, which was John Reynolds' way of repaying Bill Hopkins for a favor.

The papers headlined the match, and down in the dingy alleys that flank Barbary Street, certain tinhorns put their heads together and muttered beneath their breath, like rattlers, coiling and hissing together among the weeds.

CHAPTER V

Ghosts of the Past

It was the evening of the fight. The boxers had weighed in that afternoon—Karnes 196, Lopez 210. Physicians had pronounced them in perfect shape.

Now, in the lull before the fight, Karnes sat alone in a back room of his training quarters, reading. He and Reynolds had plenty of money now, but their tastes were simple. He still trained in a gym a few blocks from the Golden Glove. And he liked to relax a few hours before the fight. Up in the front part of the building his handlers and seconds and sparring partners were shooting craps or clowning for the reporters. Reynolds was due any minute from the club.

A knock sounded at the back door.

"Come in," Karnes called, frowning slightly. That would not be Reynolds.

A figure entered hesitantly—a slight figure in cheaply flashy garb. Karnes stared in silence, memories of a sordid past oozing over him sickeningly.

"Well?" he demanded harshly. "What do you want?"

Al Lyman licked his lips. A green pallor underlay his pasty skin.

"Big John Lynch sent me," he stammered.

"Well?"

"They've got Reynolds!" blurted Lynch, bringing it all out in a rush. "They snatched him off the street an hour ago!"

"What?" Karnes was on his feet.

"Wait, Kirby!" begged Lyman, dodging away. "It wasn't my idea. Lynch had got me in a spot. He's gone clean bad in the last year. If I squawked he'd bump me off. Lynch is sinking all his dough on Lopez, and he's working for a ring of big gamblers, who want to see Lopez go in there against the champion next fall.

"So Lynch says for you to take a dive in the fifth, or they'll bump Reynolds off. They'll do it, too, Kirby. If you spill it to the cops, they'll take it out on Reynolds. If you do like they say, they'll send Reynolds back O.K. after the mill. They know you won't squeal to the cops then. That'd be to admit that you took a dive."

Karnes stood silent. This was like a foul, evil breath out of the past. He had not forgotten Lynch and the score against him. His memory was that of the desert, which never forgets and never forgives. But for John Reynolds he had put his smoldering hate aside. Rage surged up in Kirby Karnes so deep and hot that it did not show in his eyes, nor sound in his voice.

"Could I come and talk this over with Lynch?" he asked.

"Sure," Lyman agreed. "Lynch said you could come, alone. He figured you might want to. Don't hold it against me, Kirby. I don't even know where they've got Reynolds. Honest I don't. Come on. My car's outside."

By back streets and alleys they came to that speak where Lynch hung out, in the alley of which a bullet had wrecked John Reynolds' leg. Karnes' big hands clenched into knobby mallets, the skin over the knuckles showing white. He did not speak as he followed Lyman into a back room.

Big John Lynch sat in a chair near a desk, dark, gross as ever, chewing the inevitable cigar. Behind him stood Zorelli, his right hand in his coat pocket. Lyman mopped his forehead with a shaky hand.

"Here he is, John," he offered.

"I can see that, you fool," grunted Lynch. "Shut that door."

"Where's Reynolds?" Karnes demanded.

"You don't see him, do you?" asked Lynch sardonically.

Karnes shook his head, sweeping the room with his eyes. He fumbled his hat, turning it round and round in his hands. His eyes crossed the floor, lingered briefly on the rug upon which stood the legs of Lynch's chair.

"He's where you nor the cops won't ever find him," said Lynch, pointing his cigar at Karnes. "Don't try no funny stuff.

Zorelli's got a rod trained on you right now. Lyman gave you the lowdown. Are you going to play ball with us?"

"Looks like I'll have to," muttered Karnes. Lynch exhaled gustily in satisfaction and tilted back his chair on its hind legs, feeling in his vest pocket for a cigar. Karnes dropped his hat. It fell on the rug. Karnes bent, reached for it—gripped the edge of the rug and heaved. Lynch went over backward with a bellow, catapulting into Zorelli, bearing him down with him. Karnes was into the heap instantly, with the silent fury of a berserk tiger.

Zorelli heaved up, tugging at the gun which had stuck in the lining of his pocket. He fired once through the cloth as Karnes plunged on him, then threw up his right arm as a guard, and lunged low with a knife in his left hand.

Karnes felt a stinging pain above the groin, and then his mallet fists beat down the Italian's guard, smashed him senseless to the floor.

Lyman had bolted out down the alley. Lynch floundered up, waving a pistol. It had been years since Lynch had done his own fighting. He was slow, awkward. Before his fumbling thumb could find the safety catch of the automatic, Karnes gripped his thick hairy wrist and twisted it savagely, a cold grin of hate writhing his thin lips.

Something snapped like a breaking stick, and Lynch bellowed. The pistol clattered on the floor. Lynch turned green; he retched, sagging in Karnes' merciless grip.

Voices sounded outside the door.

"What's the row, boss? Are you O.K.?"

"Tell 'em to scram," Karnes muttered. "Tell 'em, before I twist your arm off."

"Beat it!" howled Lynch, his eyes bloodshot with the pain of his broken bone. "Get away from that door, damn it!"

The voices receded, muttering.

"Where's Reynolds?" demanded Karnes.

All the fight had gone out of Big John Lynch.

"McGoorty and Steinman have got him," he groaned.

Karnes dragged Lynch up, slammed him down in a chair by the desk where the phone stood.

"Get McGoorty, quick!"

Sobbing with pain, Lynch dialed a number with a shaky finger.

The voice that came back over the phone was audible to Karnes, stooping close.

"Tell him to bring Reynolds back to the gym," muttered Karnes. "Tell him to put him out at the door, unharmed."

Lynch cringed away from the wrath in Karnes' eyes.

"McGoorty!" he bawled into the mouth-piece. "The snatch is off! Take Reynolds back to his gym and let him go. Yes, I know what I'm talking about. Damn you, don't you argue with me!"

"O.K.," the voice came plain to Kirby Karnes, puzzled, disgusted but resigned. "I'll do it. Right now."

Karnes dialed the gym. To a surprised sparring partner he spoke briefly: "When Reynolds gets there, all of you go on to the Golden Glove. I'll be there right away. Yes, Reynolds is on his way to the gym now."

He looked down for a moment at the great, gross figure moaning in the chair, and then without a word he turned and went into the alley.

Blood was trickling down his leg. In the light of an arc, inside the alley mouth, he investigated. Zorelli's bullet had missed, but not his knife. Karnes' trousers and underwear were soaked with blood which oozed from a gash just above where the groin meets the belly. It looked deep—felt deep. With each step he took the wound gaped and more blood spilled.

Turning, he walked quickly and with purpose through the alley and into a little, dimly-lighted side street. There he knocked on a certain door. A voice answered him.

"Doc Allister!" he called. "Let me in, quick!"

The physician stared at Karnes, surprised at his presence, not at his wound. Such things were common on Barbary Street.

"Don't waste time," said Karnes hurriedly, throwing off his blood-soaked clothes. "Get busy. I'm due in the ring within the hour."

"Why man, you can't fight with a gash like that in your body!" Allister expostulated.

"I want to borrow some of your clothes, too," said Karnes. "I'd have every reporter in town on his ear if I showed up in these bloody rags."

CHAPTER VI

Showdown

Reynolds was fidgeting with nervousness in the dressing rooms of the Golden Glove when Karnes entered.

"You're all right? They didn't hurt you?"

"No, no!" exclaimed Reynolds, impatiently brushing aside his own experience, which was still a mystery to him. "What about you? Where have you been? What happened? You look pale."

"I was worried about you," answered Karnes, beginning to shuck his shoes. "I'll give you the whole yarn later. Chase everybody out of here till I get dressed. Get out there and chin with the reporters. We don't want a scandal."

With the room to himself, Karnes hurriedly got into his togs, noticing with relief that his trunks hid the neat bandage Doc Allister had strapped over his wound. Donning his bathrobe, he opened the door. Handlers, seconds and newspaper men swarmed in. Karnes hardly heard their babble. He sat like an image, hoping that the time would pass swiftly. He felt Reynolds' gaze on him, with a curious hunger. The old master was nearer to his dream of a title now than he had ever been. He wondered what would prevent it this time. Repeated failure had instilled fatalism in him.

A newspaper man blurted out: "Odds are four to three on Karnes. The boys are banking on his footwork. He'll outstep Lopez."

Reynolds nodded. "His footwork will win the title for us."

Karnes bent his head; under the bandage that none could see the raw wound ached. The door flew open. Somebody yelled: "All right, Karnes! Let's go!"

Karnes moved up the aisle between the yelling human masses, stepping slow and leisurely. He did not bound into the ring as Lopez did. He crawled carefully through the ropes.

Lopez was already in the ring, a giant of bone and muscle. A great hairy chest, heavy brows which overhung small glittering black eyes; a shock of tangled black hair. He looked the caveman, all right. While the referee instructed them in the center of the ring, he glared at Karnes like a wild man. Back in their corners again, and the crowd tense, waiting.

"Box him, boy!" Reynolds' voice was urgent in Karnes' ear. "Keep stepping. Fight as we planned it."

Karnes did not reply, remembering long hours spent in planning this fight, with carefully chosen sparring partners and moving pictures of Lopez' fights.

The gong! Lopez roared across the ring like a hurricane, right hand ready.

The crowd roared in amazement. Karnes did not glide out to meet the attack in his swift, easy illusive stance. He took a few steps forward, crouched—met the hurting onslaught squarely.

All the experts looked to see him sidestep, spring in again like a panther to rip lefts and rights into a man off-balance. He did nothing of the sort. He ducked under the downward flailing right, edged in close and began to smash away at the Honduran's midsection. This was meat for Lopez. A roaring rumble of gratification rose from his throat. At last, a man who would stand up to him. His ponderous right began to whirl like a flail, crashing and thundering.

Behind his corner, Reynolds stood frozen, unable to believe what his senses told him. He had drilled into Karnes that his footwork was his best bet against the ponderous Honduran. And now Karnes had abandoned any attempt at footwork, was standing still and trading punches with the foremost man-killer of the age.

Not that he was fighting wide open. With superlative skill he was ducking, blocking, riding with the punches. But they showered on him so thickly and terrifically that he could not avoid all of them. Blood trickled from his nose, oozed from cuts on his scalp. At the gong the delirious broadcaster shouted to radio listeners all over the continent that Lopez had taken that round by a wide margin, that Karnes had apparently gone crazy.

In Karnes' corner Reynolds was pleading frantically, a bewildered, grief-stricken man who looked suddenly old.

"Kirby, for God's sake, box him! Fight as we planned!"

Karnes sank his face in his gloves to shut out the pain in Reynolds' stare.

Back in the ring again, he ducked his head, crouched and smashed away at the huge, hairy torso before him. Lopez' matted muscles were like ridges of iron. Karnes' murderous left hooking up from below, rocked the Honduran's head back.

But Diego Lopez was not to be felled by one blow from any man. He roared and came lashing back like a typhoon. His right was a constant threat of destruction. He whirled it like a war-club, threw it like a hammer. Its thunderous impact against Karnes' head or body resounded all over the house, and John Reynolds winced with each impact. Between rounds he worked over Karnes. His lips moved soundlessly; his face was ashen. Why was this fighter taking punishment he could avoid so easily?

Karnes could not change his tactics. He had fought this far along the ladder according to Reynolds' instructions; this fight he must fight in his own way.

Blood was in his eyes, the salt of blood in his mouth. He staggered to the impact of that thunderous right hand, but all the time he was slashing back, and he could see pain growing in the eyes of the giant. A fierce joy surged in him. Again he was the iron man, fighting his old fight, pitting his toughness against dynamite in loaded gloves. Blood was oozing through his trunks, but there was so much blood on both men that no one noticed.

Before the gong opened the fifth, Reynolds made a last desperate appeal.

"Kirby, for God's sake, snap out of it! Are you throwing me down?"

Karnes lowered his head. The crowd groaned to see him shuffle out and resume his crouching stance. The torturing grind began once more.

That destruction-weighted right had reduced the side of Karnes' face and head to a pulp. He knew he had at least one broken rib, that his left side was raw beef. But he had not been merely taking it; he had been handing it out—savage, slashing hooks that ripped and crushed.

Smash, smash, smash! Four gloves flashing past each other, ripping savagely into quivering flesh. The experts said no man could stand up and trade punches with Diego Lopez. What did the experts know of the Barbary, and the man who served his apprenticeship there? Time rolled back to Kirby Karnes, to a smokier, dingier ring, a fiercer crowd. Again he was the iron man, staking all on his granite jaw, his oaken ribs. They can't knock him out! It seemed the rafters shook with the roar.

And now Karnes saw, through the blood and mist, a look growing in the eyes of Lopez—the same desperate look he had seen so often in the eyes of the men he had fought in the Barbary. Lowering his head, he slugged away with full body-drive behind each punch, iron fists sinking deeper and deeper in the Honduran's flesh. Lopez reeled back, spattering blood and roaring—rallied and flailed back. Karnes straightened from his crouch, hooking for the head, and missed. That clubbing right ripped in, low. Karnes distinctly felt the tearing of his own flesh. Blood cascaded down his thigh and a gasp of amazed horror rose from the crowd. The dumfounded referee sprang forward, but before he could interpose, Karnes sprang like a panther. Caution to the winds now, everything staked on one blasting plunge.

He did not heed the knifing agony in his side. He did not heed the bludgeoning right, falling weaker and weaker upon him. He fought as he fought of old, like a wild man, with fury and destruction behind every smashing blow. Dazed by the whirlwind he had loosed, the giant reeled backward, his eyes glazing, his knees buckling, vainly striving to fight back.

Left to the head, right to the head—left, right—in a constant stream, and each loaded with dynamite—and one last terrible hook ripping up from Karnes' right hip, with every nerve and sinew and muscle behind it—and there was Diego Lopez motionless on the canvas, his shaggy head in a pool of blood.

Time rolled back again to the Barbary and a gory, terrible figure fighting to keep his feet—"Ten!" tolled out the referee, and Kirby Karnes toppled headlong across the body of the man he had conquered.

The first voice he heard was that of Reynolds, and it shook with horror: "Good God, that wound! It's been sewed up, and that body blow Lopez landed tore out the stitches. Kirby! Kirby! Why didn't you tell me?"

The battered lips grinned.

"You wouldn't have let the fight go on. That's why I stood still and slugged; had to crouch to protect that wound, and was afraid if I stepped around too brisk, I'd tear it open again. I'm all right. Don't look so sick. You're goin' to manage a champion yet. They can't knock me out!"

THE INCREDIBLE ADVENTURES OF DENNIS DORGAN

INTRODUCTION

"Conan the Barbarian" has become Robert E. Howard's most famous character, but he also invented many other colorful ones. Among these was "Sailor" Dennis Dorgan.

Robert E. Howard had found *Weird Tales* to be his most dependable market. When a companion magazine, *Oriental Stories*, was begun in 1931, he began to tailor stories to its special specifications.

By the early 1930's Howard's markets had begun to expand. In addition to *Weird Tales* he had sold stories to *Strange Detective Stories, Jack Dempsey's Fight Magazine, Strange Tales, Top Notch, Argosy, Fight Stories, Action Stories*, and others.

One of Howard's most popular characters was a fighting sailor named Steve Costigan. Most of the Sailor Steve Costigan stories had appeared in *Action Stories* and *Fight Stories*. In fact, Howard had written so many of these stories that they were stacking up faster than he could submit them. He had a bright idea. Why not re-write some of these stories and start another series?

He changed the name of the leading character to Sailor Dennis Dorgan. The white bulldog Mike became Spike. Costigan's ship *The Sea Girl* became *The Python*. Other necessary changes were made. He would set these stories in exotic settings like Hong Kong, Singapore, Shanghai and other Oriental ports. They would fit nicely into *Oriental Stories*. And why not a new name? His market was expanding so rapidly he could well use a pseudonym or two.

Farnsworth Wright bought Howard's first Dennis Dorgan story, "Alleys of Darkness." In the meantime, the title of *Oriental Stories* was changed to *Magic Carpet Magazine*. The story appeared in the January 1934 issue of *Magic Carpet Magazine* under the Patrick Ervin pseudonym.

Howard sold three more Sailor Dennis Dorgan stories to *Magic Carpet Magazine*: "Dennis Dorgan and the Jade Monkey," "Dennis Dorgan and the Yellow Cobra," and "Dennis Dorgan and the Turkish Menace." *Magic Carpet Magazine* folded before any of these stories were published. However, these stories as well as other unpublished Dennis Dorgan manuscripts were unearthed by that legendary literary sleuth, Glenn Lord. Now, a wholly new generation of readers and fans of Robert E. Howard have the opportunity of reading these exciting and humorous yarns.

I have edited, retitled and arranged these stories in chronological order for publication. Here is a brief literary history of the Dennis Dorgan stories.

• • •

"The Alleys of Singapore"

was originally published in *Magic Carpet Magazine* in the January 1934 issue under the title, "Alleys of Darkness." The story was published under the Howard pseudonym: Patrick Ervin.

"The Jade Monkey"

was scheduled to appear in *Magic Carpet Magazine* but was never published because the magazine folded with the January 1934 issue. The original title was "Sailor Dorgan and the Jade Monkey" and it appeared under this title in *The Howard Collector*, Spring 1971, using the Patrick Ervin Pseudonym.

"The Mandarin Ruby"

was never sold professionally but was published under its original title, "Alleys of Treachery," in the Summer 1966, *The Howard Collector*, using the Patrick Ervin pseudonym.

"The Yellow Cobra"

was sold to *Magic Carpet Magazine* but was never published. The title on the original manuscript was "Sailor Dorgan and the Yellow Cobra" by Patrick Ervin.

"In High Society"

was originally titled "Cultured Cauliflowers" by Patrick Ervin, and is one of several unpublished manuscripts found after Howard's death.

"Playing Journalist"

was originally titled "A New Game for Dorgan" by Patrick

Ervin, and is another unpublished manuscript discovered years after Howard's death.

"The Destiny Gorilla"

was originally titled "Sailor Dorgan and the Destiny Gorilla" by Patrick "Dorgan." (Later, Howard crossed out "Dorgan" and wrote in the word "Ervin.") This is another unpublished manuscript.

"A Knight of the Round Table"

was originally titled "Iron-Clad Fists" by Robert E. Howard. Apparently Howard never noticed that he had forgotten to use the "Patrick Ervin" pseudonym on this unpublished Dennis Dorgan yarn.

"Playing Santa Claus"

was originally titled "A Two-Fisted Santa Claus" by Patrick Ervin, and is another unpublished manuscript found many years after the death of Howard.

"The Turkish Menace"

was originally titled "Sailor Dorgan and the Turkish Menace" by Patrick Ervin. This story was accepted by *Magic Carpet Magazine* but was never published. When a copy of the manuscript was discovered a few years ago, ten pages were missing from the middle of the 21-page manuscript. Page 3 and page 21 were also missing. Darrell C. Richardson has completed the story, writing the missing page 3, the missing middle part of the story, and the ending of the tale.

The Alleys of Singapore

When the gong ended my fight with Kid Leary in the Sweet Dreams Fight Club, Singapore, I was tired but contented. The first seven rounds had been close, but the last three I'd plastered the Kid all over the ring, though I hadn't knocked him out like I'd did in Shanghai some months before, when I flattened him in the twelfth round. The scrap in Singapore was just for ten; another round and I'd had him.

But anyway, I'd shaded him so thoroughly I knowed I'd justified the experts which had made me a three to one favorite. The crowd was applauding wildly, the referee was approaching, and I stepped forward and held out my glove hand—when to my utter dumfoundment, he brushed past me and lifted the glove of the groggy and bloody Kid Leary!

A instant's silence reigned, shattered by a nerve-racking scream from the ringside. The referee, Jed Whithers, released Leary, who collapsed into the rosin, and Whithers ducked through the ropes like a rabbit. The crowd riz bellowing, and recovering my frozen wits, I gave vent to lurid langwidge and plunged outa the ring in pursuit of Whithers. The fans was screaming mad, smashing benches, tearing the ropes offa the ring and demanding the whereabouts of Whithers, so's they could hang him to the rafters. But he had disappeared, and the maddened crowd raged in vain.

I found my way dazedly to my dressing-room, where I set

down on a table and tried to recover from the shock. Bill O'Brien and the rest of the crew was there, frothing at the mouth, each having sunk his entire wad on me. I considered going into Leary's dressing-room and beating him up again, but decided he'd had nothing to do with the crooked decision. He was just as surprised as me when Whithers declared him winner.

Whilst I was trying to pull on my clothes, hindered more'n helped by my raging shipmates, whose langwidge was getting more appalling every instant, a stocky bewhiskered figger come busting through the mob, and done a fantastic dance in front of me. It was the Old Man, with licker on his breath and tears in his eyes.

"I'm rooint!" he howled. "I'm a doomed man! Oh, to think as I've warmed a sarpint in my boozum! Dennis Dorgan, this here's the last straw!"

"Aw, pipe down!" snarled Bill O'Brien. "It wasn't Denny's fault. It was that dashety triple-blank thief of a referee—"

"To think of goin' on the beach at my age!" screamed the Old Man, wringing the salt water outa his whiskers. He fell down on a bench and wept at the top of his voice. "A thousand bucks I lost—every cent I could rake, scrape and borrer!" he bawled.

"Aw, well, you still got your ship," somebody said impatiently.

"That's just it!" the Old Man wailed. "That thousand bucks was dough I owed them old pirates, McGregor, McClune & McKile. Part of what I owe, I mean. They agreed to accept a thousand as part payment, and gimme more time to raise the rest. Now it's gone, and they'll take the ship! They'll take the *Python!* All I got in the world! Them old sharks ain't got no more heart than a Malay pirate. I'm rooint!"

The crew fell silent at that, and I said: "Why'd you bet all that dough?"

"I was lickered up," he wept. "I got no sense when I'm full. Old Cap'n Donnelly, and McVey and them got to raggin' me, and the first thing I knowed, I'd bet 'em the thousand, givin' heavy odds. Now I'm rooint!"

He throwed back his head and bellered like a walrus with the belly-ache.

I just give a dismal groan and sunk my head in my hands, too despondent to say nothing. The crew bust forth in curses against Whithers, and sallied forth to search further for him, hauling the Old Man along with them, still voicing his woes in a voice like a steamboat whistle.

Presently I riz with a sigh and hauled on my duds. They was no sound outside. Apparently I was alone in the building except for Spike, my white bulldog. All at once I noticed him smelling of a closed locker. He whined, scratched at it, and growled. With a sudden suspicion I strode over and jerked open the door. Inside I seen a huddled figger. I jerked it rudely forth and set it upright. It was Jed Whithers. He was pale and shaking, and he had cobwebs in his hair. He kinda cringed, evidently expecting me to bust into loud cusses. For once I was too mad for that. I was probably as pale as he was, and his eyes dilated like he seen murder in mine.

"Jed Whithers," I said, shoving him up against the wall with one hand whilst I knotted the other'n into a mallet, "this is one time in my life when I'm in the mood for killin'."

"For God's sake, Dorgan," he gurgled; "you can't murder me!"

"Can you think of any reason why I shouldn't put you in a wheel-chair for the rest of your life?" I demanded. "You've rooint my friends and all the fans which bet on me, lost my skipper his ship—"

"Don't hit me, Dorgan!" he begged, grabbing my wrist with shaking fingers. "I had to do it; honest to God, Sailor, I *had* to do it! I know you won—won by a mile. But it was the only thing I *could* do!"

"What you mean?" I demanded suspiciously.

"Lemme sit down!" he gasped.

I reluctantly let go of him, and he slumped down onto a near-by bench. He sat there and shook, and mopped the sweat offa his face. He was trembling all over.

"Are the customers all gone?" he asked.

"Ain't nobody here but me and my man-eatin' bulldog," I answered grimly, standing over him. "Go on—spill what you got to say before I start varnishin' the floor with you."

"I was forced to do it, Dennis," he said. "There's a man who has a hold on me."

"What you mean, a hold?" I asked suspiciously.

"I mean, he's got me in a spot," he said. "I have to do like he says. It ain't myself I have to think of—Dorgan, I'm goin' to trust you. You got the name of bein' a square shooter. I'm goin' to tell you the whole thing.

"Sailor, I got a sister named Constance, a beautiful girl, innocent as newborn lamb. She trusted a man, Dorgan, a dirty, slimy snake in human form. He tricked her into signin' a document—Dorgan, that paper was a confession of a crime he'd committed himself!"

Whithers here broke down and sobbed with his face in his hands. I shuffled my feet uncertainly, beginning to realize they was always more'n one side to any question.

He raised up suddenly and said: "Since then, that man's been holdin' that faked confession over me and her like a club. He's forced me to do his filthy biddin' time and again. I'm a honest man by nature, Sailor, but to protect my little sister"—he kinda choked for a instant—"I've stopped to low deeds. Like this tonight. This man was bettin' heavy on Leary, gettin' big odds—"

"Somebody sure was," I muttered. "Lots of Leary money in sight."

"Sure!" exclaimed Whithers eagerly. "That was it; he made me throw the fight to Leary, the dirty rat, to protect his bets."

I begun to feel new wrath rise in my gigantic breast.

"You mean this low-down polecat has been blackmailin' you on account of the hold he's got over your sister?" I demanded.

"Exactly," he said, dropped his face in his hands. "With that paper he can send Constance to prison, if he takes the notion."

"I never heered of such infermy," I growled. "Whyn't you bust him on the jaw and take that confession away from him?"

"I ain't no fightin' man," said Whithers. "He's too big for me. I wouldn't have a chance."

"Well, *I* would," I said. "Listen, Whithers, buck up and quit cryin'. I'm goin' to help you."

His head jerked up and he stared at me kinda wild-eyed.

"You mean you'll help me get that paper?"

"You bet!" I retorted. "I ain't the man to stand by and let no innercent girl be persecuted. Besides, this mess tonight is his fault."

Whithers just set there for a second, and I thought I seen a slow smile start to spread over his lips, but I mighta been mistook, because he wasn't grinning when he held out his hand and said tremulously: "Dorgan, you're all they say you are!"

A remark like that ain't necessarily a compliment; some of

the things said about me ain't flattering; but I took it in the spirit in which it seemed to be give, and I said: "Now tell me, who is this rat?"

He glanced nervously around, then whispered: "Ace Bissett!"

I grunted in surprise. "The devil you say! I'd never of thought it."

"He's a fiend in human form," said Whithers bitterly. "What's your plan?"

"Why," I said, "I'll go to his Diamond Palace and demand the confession. If he don't give it to me, I'll maul him and take it away from him."

"You'll get shot up," said Whithers. "Bissett is a bad man to fool with. Listen, I got a plan. If we can get him to a certain house I know about, we can search him for the paper. He carries it around with him, though I don't know just where. Here's my plan—"

I listened attentively, and as a result, perhaps a hour later I was heading through the narrer streets with Spike, driving a closed car which Whithers had produced kinda mysteriously. Whithers wasn't with me; he was gone to prepare the place where I was to bring Bissett to.

I driv up the alley behind Ace's big new saloon and gambling-hall, the Diamond Palace, and stopped the car near the back door. It was a very high-class joint. Bissett was friends with wealthy sportsmen, officials, and other swells. He was what they call a soldier of fortune, and he'd been everything, everywhere—aviator, explorer, big game hunter, officer in the armies of South America and China—and what have you.

A native employee stopped me at the door, and asked me what was my business, and I told him I wanted to see Ace. He showed me into the room which opened on the alley, and went after Bissett—which could not of suited my plan better.

Purty soon a door opened, and Bissett strode in—a tall, broad-shouldered young fellow, with steely eyes and wavy blond hair. He was in a dress suit, and altogether looked like he'd stepped right outa the social register. And as I looked at him, so calm and self-assured, and thought of poor Whithers being driv to crime by him, and the Old Man losing his ship on account of his crookedness, I seen red.

"Well, Dorgan, what can I do for you?" he asked.

I said nothing. I stepped in and hooked my right to his jaw. It caught him flat-footed, with his hands down. He hit the floor full length, and he didn't twitch.

I bent over him, run my hands through his clothes, found his six-shooter and throwed it aside. Music and the sounds of revelry reached me through the walls, but evidently nobody had seen or heard me slug Bissett. I lifted him and histed him onto my shoulders—no easy job, because he was as big as me, and limp as a rag.

But I done it, and started for the alley. I got through the door all right, which I was forced to leave open, account of having both hands full, and just as I was dumping Ace into the back part of the car, I heered a scream. Wheeling, I seen a girl had just come into the room I'd left, and was standing frozen, staring wildly at me. The light from the open door shone on me and my captive. The girl was Glory O'Dale, Ace Bissett's sweetheart. I hurriedly slammed the car door shut and jumped to the wheel, and as I roared off down the alley, I was vaguely aware that Glory had rushed out of the building after me, screaming blue murder.

It was purty late, and the route I took they wasn't many people abroad. Behind me I begun to hear Bissett stir and groan, and I pushed Spike over in the back seat to watch him. But he hadn't fully come to when I drawed up in the shadows beside the place Whithers had told me about—a ramshackle old building down by a old rotting, deserted wharf. Nobody seemed to live anywheres close around, or if they did, they was outa sight. As I clum outa the car, a door opened a crack, and I seen Whithers' white face staring at me.

"Did you get him, Dennis?" he whispered.

For answer I jerked open the back door, and Bissett tumbled out on his ear and laid their groaning dimly. Whithers started back with a cry.

"Is he dead?" he asked fearfully.

"Would he holler like that if he was?" I asked impatiently. "Help me carry him in, and we'll search him."

"Wait'll I tie him up," said Whithers, producing some cords, and to my disgust, he bound the unconscious critter hand and foot.

"It's safer this way," Whithers said. "He's a devil, and we can't afford to take chances."

We then picked him up and carried him through the door, into a very dimly lighted room, across that 'un, and into another'n which was better lit—the winders being covered so the light couldn't be seen from the outside. And I got the surprise of my life. There was five men in that room. I wheeled on Whithers. "What's the idee?" I demanded.

"Now, now, Dennis," said Whithers, arranging Bissett on the bench where we'd laid him. "These are just friends of mine. They know about Bissett and my sister."

I heered what sounded like a snicker, and I turned to glare at the assembled "friends." My gaze centered on a fat, flashy-dressed bird smoking a big black cigar; diamonds shone all over his fingers, and in his stickpin. The others was just muggs.

"A fine lot of friends you pick out!" I said irritably to Whithers. "Diamond Joe Galt is been mixed up in every shady deal that's been pulled in the past three years. And if you'd raked the Seven Seas you couldn't found four dirtier thugs than Limey Teak, Bill Reynolds, Dutch Steinmann, and Red Partland."

"Hey, you—" Red Partland riz, clenching his fists, but Galt grabbed his arm.

"Stop it, Red," he advised. "Easy does it, Dennis," he addressed me with a broad smile which I liked less'n I'd liked a scowl, "they's no use in abuse. We're here to help our pal Whithers get justice. That's all. You've done your part. You can go now, with our thanks."

"Not so fast," I growled, and just then Whithers hollered: "Bissett's come to!"

We all turned around and seen that Bissett's eyes was open, and blazing.

"Well, you dirty rats," he greeted us all and sundry, "you've got me at last, have you?" He fixed his gaze on me, and said: "Dorgan, I thought you were a man. If I'd had any idea you were mixed up in this racket, you'd have never got a chance to slug me as you did."

"Aw, shut up," I snarled. "A fine nerve you've got, talkin' about men, after what you've did!"

Galt pushed past me and stood looking down at Bissett, and I seen his fat hands clenched, and the veins swell in his temples.

"Bissett," he said, "we've got you cold and you know it. Kick in—where's that paper?"

"You cursed fools!" Bissett raved, struggling at his cords till the veins stood out on his temples too. "I tell you, the paper's worthless."

"Then why do you object to givin' it to us?" demanded Whithers.

"Because I haven't got it!" raged Bissett. "I destroyed it, just as I've told you before."

"He's lyin'," snarled Red Partland. "He wouldn't never destroy such a thing as that. It means millions. Here, I'll make him talk—"

He shouldered forward and grabbed Bissett by the throat. I grabbed Red in turn, and tore him away.

"Belay!" I gritted. "He's a rat, but just the same I ain't goin' to stand by and watch no helpless man be tortured."

"Why, you—" Red bellered, and swung for my jaw.

I ducked and sunk my left to the wrist in his belly and he dropped like his legs had been cut out from under him. The others started forward, rumbling, and I wheeled towards 'em, seething with fight. But Galt got between us and shoved his gorillas back.

"Here," he snapped. "No fightin' amongst ourselves! Get up, Red.—Now, Dennis," he begun to pat my sleeves in his soothing way, which I always despises beyond words, "there ain't no need for hard feelin's. I know just how you feel. But we got to have that paper. You know that, Dorgan—"

Suddenly a faint sound made itself evident.

"What's that?" gasped Limey, going pale.

"It's Spike," I said. "I left him in the car, and he's got tired of settin' out there, and is scratchin' at the front door. I'm goin' to go get him, but I'll be right back, and if anybody lays a hand on Bissett whilst I'm gone, I'll bust him into pieces. We'll get that paper, but they ain't goin' to be no torturin'."

I strode out, scornful of the black looks cast my way. As I shut the door behind me, a clamor of conversation bust out, so many talking at wunst I couldn't understand much, but every now and then Ace Bissett's voice riz above the din in accents of anger and not pain, so I knowed they wasn't doing nothing to him. I crossed the dim outer room, opened the door and let Spike in, and then, forgetting to bolt it—I ain't used to secrecy and such—I started back for the inner room.

Before I reached the other door, I heered a quick patter of feet outside, I wheeled—the outer door bust violently open, and into the room rushed Glory O'Dale. She was panting hard, her dress was tore, her black locks damp, and her dark eyes was wet and bright as black jewels after a rain. And she had Ace's six-shooter in her hand.

"You filthy dog!" she cried, throwing down on me.

I looked right into the muzzle of that .45 as she jerked the trigger. The hammer snapped on a faulty cartridge, and before she could try again, Spike launched hisself from the floor at her. I'd taught him never to bite a woman. He didn't bite Glory. He throwed hisself bodily against her so hard he knocked her down and the gun flew outa her hand.

I picked it up and stuck it into my hip pocket. Then I started to help her up, but she hit my hand aside and jumped up, tears of fury running down her cheeks. Golly, she was a beauty!

"You beast!" she raged. "What have you done with Ace? I'll kill you if you've harmed him! Is he in that room?"

"Yeah, and he ain't harmed," I said, "but he oughta be hung—"

She screamed like a siren. "Don't you dare! Don't you touch a hair of his head! Oh, Ace!"

She then slapped my face, jerked out a handful of hair, and kicked both my shins.

"What I can't understand is," I said, escaping her clutches, "is why a fine girl like you ties up with a low-down rat like Bissett. With your looks, Glory—"

"To the devil with my looks!" she wept, stamping on the door. "Let me past; I know Ace is in that room—I heard his voice as I came in."

They wasn't no noise in the inner room now. Evidently all of them was listening to what was going on out here, Ace included.

"You can't go in there," I said. "We got to search Ace for the incriminatin' evidence he's holdin' against Jed Whithers' sister—"

"You're mad as a March hare," she said. "Let me by!"

And without no warning she back-heeled me and pushed me with both hands. It was so unexpected I ignominiously crashed to the floor, and she darted past me and throwed open the inner door. Spike dove for her, and this time he was red-eyed, but I grabbed him as he went by.

Glory halted an instant on the threshold with a cry of mingled triumph, fear and rage. I riz, cussing beneath my breath and dusting off my britches. Glory ran across the room, eluding the grasping paws of Joe Galt, and throwed herself with passionate abandon on the prostrate form of Ace Bissett. I noticed that Ace, which hadn't till then showed the slightest sign of fear, was suddenly pale and his jaw was grim set.

"It was madness for you to come, Glory," he muttered.

"I saw Dorgan throw you into the car," she whimpered,

throwing her arms around him, and tugging vainly at his cords. "I jumped in another and followed—blew out a tire a short distance from here—lost sight of the car I was following and wandered around in the dark alleys on foot for a while, till I saw the car standing outside. I came on in—"

"Alone? My God!" groaned Ace.

"Alone?" echoed Galt, with a sigh of relief. He flicked some dust from his lapel, stuck his cigar back in his mouth at a cocky angle, and said: "Well, now, we'll have a little talk. Come here, Glory."

She clung closer to Ace, and Ace said in a low voice, almost a whisper: "Let her alone, Galt." His eyes was like fires burning under the ice.

Galt's muggs was grinning evilly and muttering to theirselves. Whithers was nervous and kept mopping perspiration. The air was tense. I was nervous and impatient; something was wrong, and I didn't know what. So when Galt started to say something, I took matters into my own hands.

"Bissett," I said, striding across the room and glaring down at him, "if they's a ounce of manhood in you, this here girl's devotion oughta touch even your snakish soul. Why don't you try to redeem yourself a little, anyway? Kick in with that paper! A man which is loved by a woman like Glory O'Dale loves you, oughta be above holdin' a forged confession over a innocent girl's head."

Bissett's mouth fell open. "What's he talking about?" he demanded from the world at large.

"I don't know," said Glory uneasily, snuggling closer to him. "He talked that way out in the other room. I think he's punch-drunk."

"Dorgan," said Bissett, "you don't belong in this crowd. Are you suffering from some sort of an hallucination?"

"Don't hand me no such guff, you snake!" I roared. "You know why I brung you here—to get the confession you gypped outa Whithers' sister, and blackmailed him with—just like you made him throw my fight tonight."

Bissett just looked dizzy, but Glory leaped up and faced me.

"You mean you think Ace made Whithers turn in that rotten decision?" she jerked out.

"I don't think," I answered sullenly. "I know. Whithers said so."

She jumped like she was galvanized.

"Why, you idiot!" she hollered, "they've made a fool of you! Jed Whithers hasn't any sister! He lied! Ace had nothing to do with it! Whithers was hired to throw the fight to Leary! Look at him!" Her voice rose to a shriek of triumph, as she pointed a accusing finger at Jed Whithers. "Look at him! Look how pale he is! He's scared witless!"

"It's a lie!" gulped Whithers, sweating and tearing at his crumpled collar like it was choking him.

"It's not a lie!" Glory was nearly hysterical by this time. "He was paid to throw the fight! And there's the man who paid him!" And she dramatically pointed her finger at Diamond Joe Galt!

Galt was on his feet, his small eyes glinting savagely, his jaws grinding his cigar to a pulp.

"What about it, Galt?" I demanded, all at sea and bewildered.

He dashed down his cigar with a oath. His face was dark and convulsed.

"What of it?" he snarled. "What you goin' to do about it? I've stood all the guff out of you I'm goin' to!"

His hand snaked inside his coat and out, and I was looking into the black muzzle of a wicked stumpy automatic.

"You can't slug this like you did Red, you dumb gorilla," he smirked viciously. "Sure, the dame's tellin' the truth. Whithers took you in like a sucklin' lamb.

"When you caught him in your dressin'-room, he told you the first lie that come to him, knowin' you for a soft sap where women's concerned. Then when you fell for it, and offered to help him, he thought fast and roped you into this deal. We been tryin' to get hold of Bissett for a long time. He's got somethin' we want. But he was too smart and too tough for us. Now, thanks to you, we got him, *and* the girl. Now we're goin' to sweat what we want out of him, and you're goin' to keep your trap shut, see?"

"You mean they ain't no Constance Whithers, and no confession?" I said slowly, trying to get things straight. A raucous roar of mirth greeted the remark.

"No, sucker," taunted Galt; "you just been took in, you sap."

A wave of red swept across my line of vision. With a maddened roar, I plunged recklessly at Galt, gun and all. Everything happened at once. Galt closed his finger on the trigger just as Spike, standing beside him all this time, closed his jaws on Galt's leg. Galt screamed and leaped convulsively; the gun exploded in the air, missing me so close the powder singed my hair, and my right mauler crunched into Galt's face, flattening his nose, knocking out all his front teeth, and fracturing his jaw-bone. As he hit the floor Spike was right on top of him.

The next instant Galt's thugs was on top of me. We rolled across the room in a wild tangle of arms and legs, casually shattering tables and chairs on the way. Spike, finding Galt was out cold, abandoned him and charged to my aid. I heered Red Partland howl as Spike's iron fangs locked in his britches. But I had my hands full. Fists and hobnails was glancing off my carcass, and a thumb was feeling for my eye. I set my teeth in this thumb and was rewarded by a squeal of anguish, but the action didn't slow up any.

It was while strangling Limey Teak beneath me, whilst the other three was trying to stomp my ribs in and kick my head off, that I realized that another element had entered into the fray. There was the impact of a chair-leg on a human skull, and Jed Whithers give up the ghost with a whistling sigh. Glory O'Dale was taking a hand.

Dutch Steinmann next gave a ear-piercing howl, and Bill Reynolds abandoned me to settle her. Feeling Limey go limp beneath me, I riz, shaking Steinmann offa my shoulders, just in time to see Reynolds duck Glory's chair-leg and smack her down. Bissett gave a most awful yell of rage, but he wasn't no madder than me. I left the floor in a flying tackle that carried Reynolds off his feet with a violence which nearly busted his skull against the floor. Too crazy-mad for reason, I set to work to hammer him to death, and though he was already senseless, I would probably of continued indefinite, had not Dutch Steinmann distracted my attention by smashing a chair over my head.

I riz through the splinters and caught him with a left hook that tore his ear nearly off and stood him on his neck in a corner. I then looked for Red Partland and seen him crawling out a winder which he'd tore the shutters off of. He was a rooin; his clothes was nearly all tore offa him, and he was bleeding like a stuck hawg and bawling like one, and Spike didn't show no intentions of abandoning the fray. His jaws was locked in what was left of Red's britches, and he had his feet braced against the wall below the sill. As I looked, Red gave a desperate wrench and tumbled through the winder, and I heered his lamentations fading into the night.

Shaking the blood and sweat outa my eyes, I glared about at the battlefield, strewn with the dead and dying—at least with the unconscious, some of which was groaning loudly, whilst others slumbered in silence.

Glory was just getting up, dizzy and wobbly. Spike was smelling each of the victims in turn, and Ace was begging somebody to let him loose. Glory wobbled over to where he'd rolled offa the bench, and I followed her, kinda stiffly. At least one of my ribs had been broke by a boot-heel. My scalp was cut open, and blood was trickling down my side, where Limey Teak had made a ill-advised effort to knife me. I also thought one of them rats had hit me from behind with a club, till I discovered that sometime in the fray I'd fell on something hard in my hip pocket. This, I found, was Ace Bissett's pistol, which I'd clean forgot all about. I throwed it aside with disgust; them things is a trap and a snare.

I blinked at Ace with my one good eye, whilst Glory worked his cords offa him.

"I see I misjudged you," I said, lending her a hand. "I apolergize, and if you want satisfaction, right here and now is good enough for me."

"Good Lord, man," he said, with his arms full of Glory. "I don't want to fight you. I still don't know just what it was all about, but I'm beginning to understand."

I set down somewhat groggily on a bench which wasn't clean busted.

"What I want to know is," I said, "what that paper was they was talkin' about."

"Well," he said, "about a year ago I befriended a half-cracked Russian scientist, and he tried in his crazy way to repay me. He told me, in Galt's presence, that he was going to give me a formula that would make me the richest man on earth. He got blown up in an explosion in his laboratory shortly afterward, and an envelope was found in his room addressed to me, and containing a formula. Galt found out about it, and he's been hounding me ever since, trying to get it. He thought it was all the Russian claimed. In reality it was merely the disconnected scribblings of a disordered mind—good Lord, it claimed to be a process for the manufacture of diamonds! Utter insanity—but Galt never would believe it."

"And he thought I was dumb," I cogitated. "But hey, Glory, how'd you know it was Galt hired Whithers to throw my fight to Leary?"

"I didn't," she admitted. "I just accused Galt of it to start you fellows fighting among yourselves."

"Well, I'll be derned," I said, and just then one of the victims which had evidently come to while we was talking, riz stealthily to his all fours and started crawling towards the winder. It was Jed Whithers. I strode after him and hauled him to his feet.

"How much did Galt pay you for throwin' the bout to Leary?" I demanded.

"A thousand dollars," he stuttered.

"Gimme it," I ordered, and with shaking hands he hauled out a fold of bills. I fluttered 'em and saw they was intact.

"Turn around and look out the winder at the stars," I commanded.

"I don't see no stars," he muttered.

"You will," I promised, as I swung my foot and histed him clean over the sill.

As his wails faded up the alley, I turned to Ace and Glory, and said: "Galt must of cleaned up plenty on this deal, payin' so high for his dirty work. This here dough, though, is goin' to be put to a good cause. The Old Man lost all his money account of Whither's crooked decision. This thousand bucks will save his ship. Now let's go. I wanta get hold of the promoter of the Sweet Dreams, and get another match tomorrer night with Kid Leary—this time with a honest referee."

The Jade Monkey

I hadn't been in Hong Kong more'n a hour and a half when somebody hit me over the head with a bottle. I wasn't particularly surprized—the Asiatic ports is full of people which has grudges against Dennis Dorgan, A.B., on account of the careless habits I have with my fists—but I was irritated.

I was going down a dark alley, minding my own business, when somebody said, "Hsss!" and when I turned and said, "Huh?"—bang! come the bottle. I was so exasperated that I sot on my unseen assailant and we grappled and rolled around in the dark awhile, and it was music to my ears the way he grunted and gasped when I sunk my big fists into his lubberly carcass. At last, close-clinched, we staggered out of the alley under a dim street lamp, where I broke loose and crashed him with a right hook which the only reason it didn't knock his brains out was because I pulled it at the last second. And the reason I pulled it was because I rekernized, not a enemy, but a shipmate—that blot on the *Python*'s repertation, Jim Rogers, to be exack.

I bent over to see if they was any signs of life in him—because stopping one of my right hooks with the jaw, even if it is pulled at the last second, is no light matter—and after awhile his eyelids fluttered open, and he looked up dizzily and said: "That last sea must have carried away everything above decks!"

"You ain't aboard ship, dope," I answered irritably. "Get

up and explain why you assault a shipmate, when they is a whole portfull of heathing Chineses you couldst bust bottles on just as well."

"I wanted money, Dennis," he said shamefacedly.

"Well, what's that got to do with it?" I demanded. I detests this beating around the brush.

"You got fifty dollars," he accused. "But I bet you wouldn't lend it to me to buy a jade monkey with, now would you?"

"Lissen, Jim," I said, "it ain't nothin' to worry about. Onst I hit a Dutch rassler just like I hit you, and for weeks he thought he was the emperor of Chiner, and wore his shirt-tail outside of his pants. But he got all right, and so will you. It ain't likely your brain is addled permanent."

"I ain't ravin', dern it!" he said angrily. "I met a girl which has a jade monkey which is worth a fortune. She'll take fifty for it. I knowed you had fifty bucks, and I—well, I kinda hated to ask you for it, when it was all you had, and you on shore-leave, and all, so I was just goin' to kinda tap you on the head and borrer it—I was goin' to pay it back, honest I was, Dennis."

I glared at him more in sorrer than in anger.

"To think," I mourned, "that my repertation is so faint and feeble that a shipmate imagines he could flatten me with a mere bottle, like I was a ordinary longshoreman. Me, the bully of the toughest ship afloat! Besides, I ain't got no fifty dollars. Right after I left you on the dock, I lost it all in a fan-tan game."

He moaned, and said, "Woe is me! Whenever I gets a chance to make some big dough, Fate sneaks up behind me with a kick aft with a number twelve cowhide boot. And her such a purty gal!"

"Who?" I demanded, coming to life suddenly.

"Miss Betty Chisom, the gal which owns the jade monkey," mourned he. "Dennis, it irks me to the bone to see beauty in distress. She's forced to sell her jade monkey to get passage to Australia or Shanghai or somewheres, I've forgot. Anyway, she can get there on fifty bucks."

"Where at is she?" I demanded.

"What do you care?" he retorted. "You ain't got no fifty bucks."

"I got a conscience," I frowned. "I can't see no white girl langrish in a furrin land amongst heathing Chineses."

"Well," he said, "I left her in the back room of the American Bar, whilst I went to raise the dough. I guess she's still there waitin' for me to show up. I didn't tell her how I figgered on raisin' it."

"I'm goin' and talk to her," I said. "I don't want her jade ape, but maybe I can help her."

"You craves that monkey," he accused.

"I craves nothin' except a proper respeck from a yegg which has just tried to hi-jack me!" I growled. "If I shouldst profit by this here business, I'll see that you gets half of what I get. Now take your ungainly carcass elsewheres whilst I strolls down to the American Bar and aids this monkey-ownin' beauty in distress."

So I went to the saloon in question, and in the back room I found a girl patiently waiting. She was a nice-looking girl, refined and all, and not the type I expected to find. I was took aback, and pulled off my cap and stood there embarrassed-like, whilst she looked at me curiously.

"Your friend Jim couldn't come back, Miss Chisom," I finally stuttered, "so I come instead."

"Oh, dear, that's too bad!" she said. "About Mr. Rogers, I mean. He—he was going to raise some money to buy something of mine—"

"Yeah, he was goin' to raise it offa me," I said. "But I didn't have none, which no more I ain't got none now. But he said as how you was in trouble, and maybe—well, I thought—that is—"

I floundered around like a fool and perspired and wisht I was fighting a gang of squareheads in a forecastle or something easy.

"You mean you want to help me?" she asked.

"That's it," I agreed. "I ain't got no money, but—"

"Please sit down," she requested. And when I had, she rested her elbows on the table, and her chin on her hands, and said, "Why do you want to help me?"

"Well, gee whiz," I said, "no white man likes to see a girl stranded amongst a lot of Chineses. This ain't no place for you. If I wasn't broke—"

"I appreciate your kindness," she said, "but I couldn't accept charity from anyone. We Chisoms are proud, in our way. But I have something which I will sell, which is worth many times what I asked Mr. Rogers. It's no use boring you with how I came to be stranded here. But if I had fifty dollars I could get away and get back to somebody who—who cares for me. Look!" She set something on the table in front of me. It was a green glassy-looking monkey about four inches high.

"Do you know what that is?" she asked; then in a kind of hushed, awed voice, she said: "That is the monkey of the Yih Hee Yih!"

"You don't say?" I said vaguely. "How did he get that way?"

"It is the secret of the Mandarin Tang Wu," she said. "For thousands of years it embodied the power of Imperial China. It was the symbol of the Manchus, and before them, the fetish of Genghis Khan, the only god he ever worshipped. Its intrinsic value alone represents thousands of dollars; as a museum piece the owner could name his own price; as a symbol of China, it is priceless. Of course you've heard of the Mandarin Tang Wu, the war-lord of Canton?"

I hadn't but didn't say anything, not wanting to appear ignorant.

"Well," she said, "he had it in his keeping. With it carried at the head of his troops, lashed to his royal standard, his armies swept all before them—it was the psychology, you know. Then it was stolen. The standard-bearer fell, and before the standard could be raised, a Manchurian bandit slashed it off and ran with it.

"The bandit was executed by the Japanese, and they took the jade monkey off him. An Indian babu stole it, and sold it to my brother as a curio, neither of them knowing its real value. My brother sent it to me, and I recognized it as the jade monkey of the Yih Hee Yih! I was going to take it to Tang Wu myself—I have ways of knowing he's offered ten thousand dollars for its recovery—but with this war and all, I haven't dared. And now I've *got* to get back to Australia as quick as I can. So I'll sell the monkey for a pittance."

"But gee whiz," I protested, my head swimming at the thought of ten thousand bucks, "but it ain't right for you to get just a ornery fifty, when the egg that bought it gets ten thousand."

"Well," she said, "if I don't get fifty, I'll never need the ten thousand. Please, can't you help me?"

She leaned towards me, her white fingers clasping nervously, and the look weak womens gets in their eyes when they appeals to a strong, red-blooded, he-fisted man. Right then I would of dived off a main-mast to of helped her.

"If I warn't sailin' with the lowest-lifed lubbers which ever roamed the high seas," I said bitterly. "Does they save their dough so's they can sucker beauty in distress? Not them! They squanders it on fan-tan and craps, the dirty bunk-lice. And now, when we has a chance to get ten thousand from old Bang Jew, they fails us. Dern 'em! If I only had a match with some mugg—hey, wait! I got a idee!"

Turning to her, I said: "Wait right here! Don't go no place else for a hour and a half! By that time I'll be back with the dough!"

And turning, I fled out of the saloon, and down the street.

I was headed for the Quiet Hour Arena, a fight club run in the toughest part of the waterfront by a mutt named Spagoni. I arriv at the ticket window breathless. Inside was noises like gladiators being ate by lions. The ticket-seller was a red-headed Englishman with shoulders like capstans.

"Is the main event over?" I asked.

"It's on now," he snarled.

"I ain't got no money," I begun.

"Well, what do you want me to do about it?" he sneered brutally.

"I want you to let me in there, you pig-faced, knock-kneed, flat-headed son of a limey baboon," I answered, controlling my righteous indignation.

"On your way, you wind-jammin' gorilla," he sneered, and maddened beyond endurance, I let fly a right through the ticket window and tagged him square on the button, and he went to sleep with a sickly smile on his unshaven lips, as the poets says.

Finding that the ticket-taker had the door fastened on the inside, so he could watch the fight without interruption, I was forced to bust it in. The noise brung the ticket-taker, a half-caste, and he was rude enough to pull a knife on me. Beginning to feel that I wasn't welcome around there, I dissembled my resentment and, handing the half-caste a bust that left him standing on his neck in the corner, I strode down the aisle and halted near the ringside.

In the ring, a couple of fancy tap-dancers was making threatening motions at each other, and the crowd was muttering. The fans which frequented the Quiet Hour didn't give a dang about classy science; what they wanted was gore by the gallons. Unless one of the fighters left the ring on a shutter and the other'n had to be carried by his seconds, they figgered the bout was framed, and started in to wreck the joint.

They was some reason for their irritation in that case. I knowed both the eggs waltzing through the main event—a couple of clever tappers which wasn't fond of getting their gore split. Spagoni had been foolish enough to pay 'em in advance, and they wasn't putting no enthusiasm in their gestures. The crowd was beginning to talk to itself and move around restless.

Immediately I got to the ringside, where I stood up, obstructing people's view and adding to their irritation, I begun to holler: "What kind of a cake-walk is this? Make 'em fight or throw 'em out! O, what a couple of bums! Why don't you kiss and make up?"

All a dissatisfied crowd needs is a leader with a strong voice. Instantly the fans begun to holler and yell and cuss, and the alleged fighters quit waving their fists at each other, and looked around to see who started the rumpus. I am a man which stands out in any crowd, and they quickly spotted me.

"It's that plug-ugly Dorgan," said one of 'em.

"What are you tryin' to do, start somethin'?" the other'n demanded.

"I starts nothin' I can't finish!" I bellered, promptly climbing through the ropes. They started towards me, with war-like intent, but just then the crowd begun to throw things. The air was full of rotten eggs, defunct cabbages, and extinct cats, and the tap-dancers and referee run for cover, pursued by the missiles and expurgations of the maddened fans.

I waded through the carpet of rotten vegetables, ducked some more, and standing up in the middle of the ring, addressed the throng in a voice which has been used in times past for a foghorn.

The crowd, being in a mean mood, tried to howl me down, but quickly realizing the futility of pitting their feeble vocal cords against mine, and having throwed away all their ammunition, they quieted down and lemme have my say.

"You all have just witnessed a travesty on the art of boxin'," I bellered. "Are you all satisfied?"

"No!" they hollered.

"Then set still, you tinhorn, four-flushin' gutter-rats," I roared, "and I'll give you a chance to see some real action. I got fifty bucks which says I can lick any man in the house, here in this ring, right now!"

There was silence for a second, whilst buckoes all over the house was hastily counting their money—the egotism and ignerance of men is surprizing—then up riz a gigantic figger which I rekernized as "Swordfish" Connolly, the toughest A.B. that ever shipped aboard of a blackbirder.

"I got fifty that says you're a liar!" he bellered, waving a handful of greenbacks.

"Put up and climb in!" I roared, beginning to peel my duds. I often wears my ring togs under my regular clothes when in port, so as to be always ready to go into the ring at a second's notice.

"Put up yourself," he snarled. "I'm goin' to the dressin'-room and see can I find me some togs. When I get back, we puts up our dough with Spagoni."

The crowd was whooping joyously by this time, knowing us both by repertation. Connolly swaggered off to the kennels which served for dressing-rooms, and I called Spagoni over to me. He was rubbing his hands with glee, because it was a break for him—a show the fans would go hysterical over, and wouldn't cost him nothing.

So I got him in a corner and I said, "Spagoni, I'm doin' you a big favor, fightin' Connolly in your club for nothin'. Now, Spagoni, when Swordfish comes back here and gives you his fifty to hold, you tell him I done put up my fifty."

"But you ain't put up nothin'," he protested. "You wanta I should lie?"

"Spagoni," I said, putting my arm around his shoulders and smiling gently in his face so his hair stood right straight up, "I loves you like a brother. You and me is always been pals. I wouldn't ask you to do nothin' dishonest, and you know it. So when Connolly comes back, you just tell him you got my fifty, unless you want to spend the rest of your life in a wheel-chair."

"If you win, nobody knows," he sputtered, shuddering slightly. "But suppose-a you lose?"

"Me lose?" I snorted. "Ain't you got no sense? Anyway, Connolly couldn't do nothin' but bust you on the nose, and he couldn't bust you half as hard as I'll bust you, if you tries to go back on me."

So here come Connolly striding through the crowd, accompanied by three or four thugs from his ship. He clumb into the ring and shoved a bunch of bills into Spagoni's hands.

"There's my half," he rumbled. "Put up your dough, Dorgan."

"Oh, Spagoni's already got all he's goin' to get from me," I assured him. "Ain'tcha, Spaggi, old pal?" I asked, gently waggling my enormous fist under his pallid schnozzle.

"Oh, sure-a," he agreed. "Posicertainsolutely!"

"Well, le's get started," grunted Connolly, turning to his corner.

I set down in my corner, attended by a half-caste that worked for Spagoni, and Spagoni raised his hands for silence. He got it, also a empty beer bottle on the side of the head.

He staggered slightly, smiled gently, and begun: "Gents and ladeez, excuse, no ladeez here. In-a this corner, Swordfish Connolly of the *Indignation*, 195 pounds. in-a this corner, Sailor Dorgan of the *Python*, 190 pounds. You all-a know—"

"Yeah, we know 'em!" rose a maddened yell. "Set down and let things start, before we lunches you, you @†%¢&*!"

Spagoni ducked, the bell whanged, and the slaughter was on.

Me and Swordfish was of the same mind. We rushed from our corners, each intent on wiping the other'n clean out of existence with the first punch. As a result, and from over-eagerness, we both missed and sprawled on the canvas, to the hilarious delight of the crowd.

We riz, our tempers not improved by the accident, and Connolly tried to improve the shining hour with a right hook that made me look right down on my own spine. I retaliated by sinking my left mitt to the wrist in his midriff, and he turned a remarkable green. I might of finished him there, but I stopped to ask him sarcastically if he was sea-sick, which maddened him so that he banged me square in the mouth so hard it wedged my upper lip between my two front teeth, and set me down flat on the canvas.

Irritated by this mischance, I ariz and waded into him with both fists pumping and he met me, nothing loath. We traded smashes in the center of the ring till the lights seemed to be swimming in a red fog, and the ring rolled and rocked under our feet like a ship's deck in a squall. Neither of us heard the gong, and our seconds had to pull us apart; during the process one of Connolly's handlers give me a vi'lent kick in the belly, and I replied with a clout under the chin which knocked him through the ropes and under the first-row seats, where he slumbered peacefully throughout the rest of the fight.

My second was dousing me with water and slapping the back of my neck with a wet towel, but I told him irritably to try to work loose the bit of skin of my lip which was jammed between my teeth. He couldn't do it, and just as the gong sounded, in response to my urgent request, he whipped out his knife and cut it loose. I was instantly flooded with blood, but

I felt a lot better as I come out for the second round.

The crowd, however, seeing the blood gushing outa my mouth and down my chin, set up a yell of excitement, thinking I'd ruptured a vein or something, and Connolly, not knowing the reason and thinking I was in a worse fix than I was, rushed in for the kill, wild and wide open.

I caught him coming in with a blasting left hook to the jaw that turned him a full somersault, to the hysterical joy of the crowd. If he hadn't been made outa solid iron, it would of broke his neck. As it was, he took the count of nine, and riz glassy-eyed. I come in quick, but he backed away, groggy and crouching and covering up. I follered him around the ring, trying to work him into a opening, and hammering away at his arms and the top of his head, which was all I could see.

At last, in a rage, I crashed an overhand right to the back of his neck, which stretched him out flat on his face. I turned to go back to my corner, sure the go was over, when splash! one of his seconds dumped a bucket full of ice-water over him, and Connolly come to life with a frenzied yell. He come up wild-eyed and howling, and evidently blaming me for the ice-water, he rushed madly at me—I set myself to crash him—my foot slipped on the wet canvas—my left hook swished over his head, and he torpedoed me with an awful right to the solar plexus. As I went down I swung a wild overhand right to his jaw, and the round ended with both of us on the canvas.

Our seconds dragged us to our corners and propped us on our stools. I distinctly seen Connolly fall off of his three times whilst they was trying to hold the smelling-salts to his schnozzle. I was all doubled in a knot and couldn't neither get my breath nor straighten up. Finally my second put his knee in the middle of my back and grabbed my shoulders and kind of straightened me out by main force, and I began to feel better.

I seen Connolly's seconds jerk off his right glove and work over his hand, but I was too sick at my stummick to say anything to the referee. Anyway, the referees at the Quiet Hour don't bother theirselves much with what goes on between rounds—or during rounds either, for that matter. They're plumb broad-minded about such things as fouls and the like.

I always recuperates quick, and I felt purty good as I come out for the third. I went in eager to start in slugging again, but Connolly come out slow, and backed away as I advanced.

He fiddled with his left, and kept his right cocked, and the crowd yelled for me to go in and finish him. I done so, not because I cared what they was yelling, but because I ain't got the patience to fool around in a fight.

I plunged, missed a left hook as he ducked, started my right over—bang! I was on my back in the middle of the ring, feeling like my skull was busted, and the crowd was going crazy away off yonder some place in the universe. Through a swimming haze I heard the referee counting, and seen Connolly, dimly, leaning on the ropes and grinning wickedly down at me. I knowed! He had about a pound of lead in his right glove! I could tell by the feel of it.

I tried to get up and kill Connolly, but all the strength had went out of my legs. "Five!" said the referee. "Ten thousand bucks!" I groaned, beginning to drag myself towards the ropes. "Six!" said the referee. Them ropes seemed a thosand miles away. I grabbed for 'em, missed and fell on my face in the rosin. "Seven!" said the referee. I grabbed again, caught, and began to haul myself up. "Eight!" said the referee. "Beauty in distress!" I gurgled, on one knee. "Nine!" said the referee. And I was up, weaving and rolling, but hanging on to the ropes.

Connolly come pelting in to finish me, and threw his loaded right like a man throwing a hammer. But I seen it coming a mile, and as it swished ponderously through the air, I ducked, letting go of the ropes and falling forward on Connolly. My right almost carried him off his feet, and he had to grab a rope to keep from going down.

I hung on like a grizzly, whilst the crowd screamed, Connolly cussed and heaved, and the referee tried in vain to haul me loose. But each second the strength was rushing back into my dead legs, and when I finally broke free, I was a man again.

Connolly rushed like a wild man, swinging that weighted right, and nearly throwing hisself off his feet as he missed. And I realized he was my meat. His k.o. hand was always his right. And now he had so blame much lead in his glove, he couldn't shoot his punches. He had to swing his right like a club—heavy and slow.

Seeing this, I laughed a fiendish laugh, and waded in to him. I paid no heed to his left. I circled to his left all the time, away from his right, meanwhile slashing away with both maulers. He telegraphed that right every time, and I rolled with the punch or ducked. He couldn't land. He sweated and grunted and puffed and swung and missed—and meanwhile I was ripping away with both hands at his midsection. He battered me with his left, starting the claret in streams, but that hand didn't pack the dynamite. At last, in desperation, he let go again with the right; I stepped inside of it and crashed my left to his jaw, with all my beef behind it. That punch started at my hip, and would of dropped an ox. Connolly went down with a crash, and he didn't even quiver whilst he was being counted out.

The clamor of the throng was still ringing in the welkin when I grabbed the vanquished warrior's fifty out of Spagoni's unwilling hands, snatched on my street clothes, and raced out the arena. As I ran down the street, people got out of my way, evidently thinking I was drunk or crazy, but it made no difference to me.

Sure enough, Miss Chisom was still waiting in the back of the American Bar. They seemed to be quite a lot of empty glasses on the table, but I paid no heed. Miss Chisom give a kind of gasp as she seen my disheveled condition. Both my eyes was black, my face was bruised and skinned, and I hadn't washed off the dried blood.

"Heavens above!" she said. "What's happened?"

"Here's the dough," I gasped, cramming it into her fingers. "Gimme the monk!"

She placed it in my hands, and I grasped it firmly but reverently, feeling like I was holding ten thousand dollars.

"Gimme your address," I requested. "I'm leavin' for Canton tonight, if I have to walk or swim. And I want to split the money with you I get from Tang Wu."

"I'll send you my address," she said. "Now I must go—and thank you!"

And she left in a hurry which surprized me. I just stood there with my mouth open. Then I set down to get my breath, and examine the monkey. As I was doing this, the bartender come in.

"Say, Dorgan," said he, "that dame which just beat it out of here said you'd settle for all the drinks she's had since you left before. By golly, she had a thirst like a fish—"

"Huh?" I said in some surprize. "Well, say, Joe, you been to Canton—do you know a mandarin by the name of Tang Wu?"

"Tang Wu?" he said. "They ain't no mandarin in China by that name—"

At that instant I discovered a bit of paper glued on the under part of the monkey, and as I read what was on it, I was struck speechless, and then give a shriek that made the barkeep's hair stand up.

My howl was echoed from without, and Jim Rogers rushed wildly in.

At the sight of the monkey he give a squall.

"So you got it!" he hollered. "I knowed you'd double-cross me! You said you'd gimme half of what you got! I demands my share! I'll call a cop—"

"If I give you half of what I've got tonight," I grunted, "you wouldn't no ways survive it; but here's about one-tenth of one percent!"

And I give it to him free and generous—smack on the button. I laid the jade monkey of the Yih Hee Yih on his bosom, and strode broodingly forth. What was stamped on the bit of paper pasted on the monkey was: "Made in Bridgeport, Connecticut—15¢."

The Mandarin Ruby

I'll never forget the night I fit Butch Corrigan in the Peaceful Haven A. C. on the Hong Kong waterfront. Butch looked more like a gorilla than he did a human, and he fit the same way. It was a rough night for a sailor, even for Dennis Dorgan, Able Seaman. In the third frame he biffed me so hard on the jaw I stuck my nose to the hilt in the resin and was still trying to pry it out when the bell saved me. In the fourth he knocked my head so far back betweenst my shoulders I could count the freckles on my own spine. In the fifth he throwed me through the ropes and one of his pals busted a bottle over my head as I clumb back into the ring. It was the bottle which made me lose my temper; and Butch being the nearest to me, I stuck my left mauler up to the elbow in his hairy belly and then cracked a meat-axe right on his ear whilst he was trying to get back his wind. He was alread groggy from hammering my iron jaw and rock-ribbed belly, and that last clout which I unwound from my right heel, so plumb demoralized him that he fell down and forgot to get up till his henchmen dragged him outa the ring feet-first and throwed him into a horse trough to revive him.

Having been informed by the referee that the massacre was over, I groped my way to my dressing room, and after I had mopped the blood and sweat outa the eye that wasn't closed, I struggled into my clothes without the aid of my handlers which had decamped to join a crap game which was going on in the back alley. Then I headed for the office of Dutchy

Tatterkin, the promoter of the Peaceful Haven, to get my dough, and as I emerged into the hallway who should I meet but Corrigan's manager, and he was frothing at the mouth.

"Where's Dutchy?" I ast him, and he let out a laugh like a hyener with his tail in a wolf-trap.

"Where's Dutchy?" he hollered sourcastically. "I wish I knowed! He's skipped! Gone! Took a lam with the gate receipts!"

"What?" I bellered convulsively.

"Yeah! After all I've did for him!"

"But he can't do this to me!" I hollered desperately. "He owes me fifty bucks for lickin' your tramp tonight!"

"*Your* fifty!" said the manager fiercely. "What about me? Me, that's worked and slaved for my fighter, and spilt his blood in every third-rate arener from here to—"

I left him telling his woes to the world and I run into the cubby-hole Dutchy'd used as a office. He wasn't there. What's more, it was plumb empty, didn't even have a desk or chair in it. It was so. Dutchy had pulled out for good whilst the fight was going on, leaving us suckers holding the bag. Me and Butch was each out fifty dollars. I accepted Butch's loss philosophically, but when I thought of my fifty I seen red. I run out on the street to look for Dutchy, though I knowed in all probability he'd already left on the night boat. But I was so mad I was ready to *swim* after him.

As I charged into the street I fell over a native boy and when I got up and started to cuss him out for being there, I seen it was a Malay which mopped floors and did odd jobs around the Peaceful Haven. He had a welt on his dome like somebody had socked him with a chair-laig.

"Where's Tatterkin?" I roared, laying hold of his collar.

"He gone," he said sullenly. "He no pay my wages; he say he give me chairs and desk in office to sell. But when I go find man to buyum, Tatterkin sellum heself. Hit me with club when I settumup holler."

"Well, where'd he go?" I yelled, unconsciously heaving him into the air and waving him like a flag.

"I tell you, he kill me," he said.

"You no tell me," I assured him, "I kick your pants up around your neck."

"He thief," he agreed. "I show you. You sockum, hey?"

Being too overcome by emotion for words, I merely ground my teeth, which seemed to satisfy him, because when I sot him down he started off at a run, and I follered him through a flock of twisty stinking dark alleys full of rats and smells, till he stopped behind a corner and pointed at a house right on the water-front which looked deserted till I seen a gleam of light through the shutters that covered a winder.

"Tatterkin there," he said. "You sockum. Me go."

And he did, light and quick as a ghost. I stayed there at the corner looking at that house.

My enemies says my brains is all in my fists, but none of them smart sissies could of done any quicker thinking than what I done right then. I knowed Tatterkin could of got out of port already if he'd wanted to. The fact that he hadn't showed he had some reason for staying; and the only reasons he ever had was crooked ones. The light glinting through them shutters was the only light anywhere around. The old tumble-down houses on all sides looked like they was plumb deserted. It was a peach of a setting for a murder.

So instead of following my natural instinks and tearing down that alley like the bull of Basher to bust down the door, I snuck down slow along the side of a old ware-house and then ducked across the alley and crouched beside the winder. The shutters was over the winder, but the sash itself was up, as I could see through the cracks. Inside they was a oil lantern hanging from the ceiling, and I seen five men setting around a table drinking licker and talking with their heads together—five dark, ugly, scarred faces leaning clost to each other. I knowed 'em: one was the man I was looking for; the others was his pals—scum like infests any sea-port in the Orient. They was Tom Kells, Jack Frankley, Bill McCoy, and a Chinaman named Ti Ying which I knowed dern well to be a river-pirate.

McCoy was saying: "You suppose Yut Ling would try to double-cross us?"

Frankley said: "What you mean, cross us? How could he?"

"Ten grand is a lot of dough," said McCoy. "He might bring a gang of hatchet-men and take the body without payin' us nothin'."

"Well," said Tom Kells, "Mike Grogan's prowlin' around out in the alleys. If he sees Yut Ling's bringin' a mob, he'll give us the signal and we'll be ready for 'em. Don't get jumpy. Yut Ling ain't due for a hour yet."

"Well," said Tatterkin, "me, I'll be glad when we're safe at sea. I pulled me a little chob tonight mineself which giffs me a hundred dollars, but it ain't worth a hundred to get busted on the chaw by such gorillas like Dennis Dorgan or Butch Corrigan. I was ready to close up mine fight club, and thought I might as well make a little extra profit for the last card, but I don't want to meet dem fellers."

"Aw, forget 'em," snorted McCoy. "Even if they knowed where you'd went, what could they do against all of us? What's botherin' me is that derned English dick, Sir Cecil Clayton. He's still in Hong Kong, lookin' for the Mandarin Ruby. You know when they arrested that Chinaman which stole it, they didn't get the ruby back. It's still lost. Clayton's tryin' to recover it. The Chinaman wouldn't tell where he'd hid it."

"What I want to know," said Tatterkin, "is how you got so easy this feller in the back room. He looks like a smart vun."

"Aw," boasted Frankley, "that was easy. Just a little slick double-crossin'. When he offered to pay us to help him get Yut Ling, we made like we'd do it, whilst we secretly sent word to Yut Ling. Then we grabbed this fellow when he wasn't expectin' it, and tied him up, and there you are! Yut Ling offered more for his carcass than he was offerin' for Yut Ling's."

"Well, I wish it was done and we was gone," said Tatterkin, pouring hisself a drink. "I don't like these old houses with nobody in 'em."

"Forget it," said Kells. "In an hour Yut Ling'll be here. We hands him that feller in the back room, he hands us ten grand, and then we're on our way to Australia with old Cap'n Sullivan. His old tub sails within an hour and a—"

I was leaning with my ear against a crack to hear better, when wham! something butted into me from behind so hard my head went smash through the shutters and everybody in the room let out a startled yell and jumped up, and I heard Mike Grogan's voice hollering: "I got him, boys! It's this here cussed Dennis Dorgan!"

They bust into loud and terrible oaths and hollered: "Hold him, while we slam the winder on his neck!"

Which they done, three or four of them together, so enthusiastic the wooden frame busted all to pieces and bits of glass flew all over the floor. Now if they is anything that makes me mad it's to have a winder slammed down on my neck. I give a outraged beller and tore loose with pieces of winder-frame hanging around my neck, and hit Mike Grogan so hard on the jaw his shoe-laces busted. Then I clamped one arm around his neck and hauled him with me as I come surging through the winder disregarding the efforts of the defendants with beer bottles and chair-laigs. Their langwidge was something terrible.

Having arrived in their midst I let Grogan fall to the floor where he lay limply and was trompled on, and I commenced committing mayhem. And committing mayhem is the best thing I do. For a few minutes it was a kind of a whirlwind of fists and boots and bottles and chair-laigs, and the table splintering when the whole mob rolled onto it, all tangled up in a knot.

Presently I ariz out of the melee like Atrocious rising from the deep, with Dutchy Tatterkin by the neck.

"You rat!" I roared in righteous wrath, spitting out a mouthful of blood and fixing my good eye on him with a awful glare. "Where at is my fifty bucks?"

"Tom!" he bellered. "Bill! Ti Ying! Mike! Jack! Help!"

Ti Ying and Grogan was in no condition to answer his squawk, being out cold. But McCoy responded to the call of the clan by rising suddenly behind me and smashing a table laig over my head. Tatterkin tripped me at the same time and I went down into the heap, but dragged Dutchy with me and the kick McCoy aimed at me caught him in the ribs and curled him up like a eel with the belly ache. Kells was felling for my eye and he give a awful holler when I sunk my fangs to the hilt in his thumb, and then I riz with a tremenjus heave just in time to kick McCoy in the belly, and then Frankley come for me with a chair, and I ducked and butted him in the midriff so hard he crashed down on the floor with me on top of him, and Kells fell over us both.

And then the old rotten floor give way and we all crashed together into the cellar—me, and the gang, and pieces of the floor and the ruins of the chairs and table and bottles and everything. I was lucky enough to land on top of two or three other birds, and that cushioned my fall, because we fell about ten feet. I struggled up before the rest of them eggs was up, because some of them had got their wind knocked out, or had hit their heads on something.

The light was still shining from the lantern hanging from the ceiling and I seen that if they had ever been any stairs in that cellar they had fell down long ago. The floor had give way on the side next to the door that led into the back room, and the only way to get out was to jump and grab the sill of that door and climb out that way.

Well, they was a scramble of human beings right under that door, and Bill McCoy was just getting to his feet, and still bent over. So I give a run and jump and landed in the middle of his back, and he couldn't give way under me because he was wedged in by the other fellers which was tangled up under him.

So I give another big spring and caught the door sill and pulled myself up. McCoy was hollering something awful, and the others was moaning and cussing and yelling: "Help! Murder! I'm killed! My back is broke! What the hell is this anyway, a earthquake?"

I found me a chair near the door, and broke me a laig off, and whilst I was doing this, the gang discovered where they was, and they says: "†%&@* the %†@* luck! The *&$%† floor has busted and we have fell right into the †%&@* cellar."

Tom Kells said: "Where is that cussed sailor? He must have fell in with us. I want to kill him before I die. He chawed my thumb nearly off."

"Blast your thumb," said Frankley. "He has busted all my ribs with his head, and before that he knocked out three of my teeth."

"You devils ain't hurt," groaned McCoy, lying on his belly in the mud. "Look at me! He jumped on my back just now, and nearly busted me in half. He ain't here. He got out."

"Help!" hollered Tatterkin. "A snake chust bit me!"

"That ain't no snake," snarled Frankley. "It ain't nothin' but rats. This old cellar is full of 'em."

"I want outa here!" Dutchy began to clamor. "It's wet and muddy. I bet water seeps in here. I bet it's full of water at high tide. I bets these rats has all got bubonic plague! Help!"

"Aw, shut up," said Frankley. "I'll stoop over and Tom can get on my shoulders and grab that door sill up there and climb out, and then get a rope and help us out. Good thing we got a light."

So they did, and just when Kells had hold of the sill I reached out and hit his fingers a awful swat with the chair-laig and he hollered bloody murder and fell back into the cellar on top of Frankley, and Frankley hollered: "Are you crazy, you †@%$* fool?"

"Shut up!" howled Kells, sucking his fingers. "That cussed sailor is up there with a club! He just broke all my fingers!"

Then they begun to holler and cuss something terrible, and I leaned over the sill and said: "Shut up, you †%&@*'s! I'm sick of listenin' to that there &†@$%-x*' profanity."

"Let us out, Dorgan," they said.

So I said: "Not till Dutchy there gives me that hundred bucks he held out on me and Corrigan."

Kells wiped the blood and mud and sweat offa his face and says to Dutchy, "Give it to him, for God's sake."

"I ain't got it!" Dutchy howled. "I've lost it!"

"You're a liar, you stubborn Dutch monkey," snarled Frankley. "Give it to him. You want us to lose ten grand by your stubbornness?"

But Tatterkin swore his roll must of fell outa his pocket when the floor give way, and they cussed him some more, and got to fighting amongst themselves, and Kells and Frankley beat Tatterkin into a jelly and tore most of his clothes off, looking for the dough, and when they didn't find it on him, they decided he must be telling the truth, and they started looking for it in the mud, and I sot beside the door-sill with my chair-laig waiting for them to find it.

Grogan come to and helped McCoy groan and them two done a noble job of it, and purty soon Ti Ying come to also, but he was still so dizzy he didn't seem to know where he was or what was going on. I had clouted him with a beautiful right hook on the button before the floor caved in.

Well, as I sot there listening to the impassioned langwidge going on in the cellar, I was aware of a bumping noise behind me, and turned around quick. They was three doors in that room: the door I was setting in; a side door that opened onto a alley; and a door which opened into a back room. The noise was coming from the back room. I seen that the thungs in the cellar was too busy to notice what I was doing, so I got up and went and opened that door. They was a man in that room, tied up and gagged, and he was bumping his head on the floor like he was trying to attract my attention.

I untied him, and it was a Chinaman. Not no ordinary coolie, neither. He was a slender, keen-looking sort of a bird.

"Who the heck are you?" I demanded.

He said: "I am Soo Ong, a detective. I am working with Sir Cecil Clayton. Some months ago a valuable jewel known as the Mandarin's Ruby was stolen from a collection of rare stones. An innocent man, Ki Yang, was arrested and convicted on false evidence. I am trying to clear him and catch the real thief—Yut Ling. These men promised to aid me, then they betrayed me, and intend selling me to Yut Ling, who will murder me because he knows I am the only man in the world who knows he is the real thief."

"You got no cause to be scared now," I assured him. "I'll help you!"

"Hey, Dorgan!" bawled Frankley from the cellar. "We can't find that cussed roll!"

"Keep lookin'!" I roared back.

Soo Ong was looking through a back winder into the alley behind the house. He beckoned to me. "You say you will aid me?" he said.

"I'll help anybody which is tryin' to catch a thief," I said.

"I need your help desperately now," he said. "Look through the crack here in the shutters. Do you see that man?"

It was dark in the alley, but I seen a man sneaking towards the house.

"He is a spy for Yut Ling," said Soo Ong, "come to see that everything is safe, before Yut Ling ventures here. He is too strong for me, and I have no weapon. Will you capture him for me? Do not injure him, but tie and gag him and leave him here in the back room. I will watch the cellar."

I said I would, and he went to the door sill, and when them thugs seen him they shut up sudden, like their throats was cut, only I could hear Tatterkin breathing like he was fixing to have the hystericals.

The man in the alley come straight to the winder I was watching at, and I'd already unfastened the shutters. He pulled 'em open easy-like and was just climbing over the sill when I grabbed his neck with my left and socked him on the jaw with my right. Before he come to I had him tied and gagged with the cords they'd had on Soo Ong. He was a white man, but dressed rough, and dirty and grimy like a waterfront tramp.

I went back to the sill, and nodded to Soo Ong, and he said to me, under his breath: "These vermin are not worth catching. If they are here when Yut Ling comes, their noise will frighten him away. Let us let them go."

"They can't go till they gimme a hundred bucks," I said stubbornly.

Frankley heard me and he said fiercely: "We can't find Dutchy's roll, blast you, and that was all the dough any of us had."

Soo Ong thought for a little, and then he said: "Ti Ying can come up."

So they boosted Ti Ying up, and I taken his knife away from him, and Soo Ong looked at Ti Ying, and Ti Ying started shivering. And Soo Ong said: "Give to this white man the bank-roll you took from Tatterkin's pocket."

Ti Ying turned green, but he hauled a wad out of his pants and give it to Soo Ong, and when them fellers in the cellar seen it, you oughta heard the holler they sent up.

"How come you didn't gimme this and get out sooner?" I demanded, and he shrugged his shoulders and said: "White men are fools. I knew you would let us out anyway, when you knew they could not find the money."

"When I get my hands on you—" promised Tom Kells blood-thirstily.

Soo Ong peeled off a hundred and give it to me, and give the rest, about three or four hundred dollars, back to Ti Ying.

"Let me go before the white devils get out!" begged Ti Ying, grabbing the dough, and Soo Ong said: "Go the back way!" and Ti Ying went like a jackrabbit.

Them in the cellar was frothing at the mouth. "Let us out!" they clamored. "You got the dough, and that dirty thief Ti Ying is gettin' away with all we got!"

"You can catch him, perhaps, if you are quick," said Soo Ong. "He went down the back alley."

So we let 'em out, one at a time, and they was no more fight in 'em, though Soo Ong was ready with Ti Ying's knife, and I had my chair laig. Each man, as we let him out, went tearing through the back room without even seeing the feller tied up in the corner, and legged it down the alley in the direction Ti Ying had run. The last man out was Dutchy Tatterkin. I hauled him out myself and frog-marched him to the door and lifted him through it on the toe of my boot.

"How come you knowed Ti Ying had picked Dutchy's pocket?" I ast.

"I know Ti Ying," said Soo Ong.

"But how come you give their dough back to him?" I ast further.

"So they would pursue him, and get themselves out of the way," he said. "Each man will try to catch Ti Ying and take the money from him before any of the others can get there—and none will catch him. But none will be here to upset our plans when Yut Ling comes. He will be here soon. I overheard them talking."

Soo Ong said he'd come up the alley that run past the side

door, from a direction different from the way Ti Ying and the others had run. He told me to wait in the back room, and he sot down cross-legged in front of the side-door, with Ti Ying's long slim ivory-handled knife in his hand.

We'd hardly got settled when I heard somebody stepping soft and easy out in the alley, and then come a cautious rap on the door. Soo Ong riz and pulled the door open and stepped back into its shadder as he done so. A fat, smirking, sleek Chinaman come in at the door. He stopped short when Soo Ong stepped out from the shadders. He didn't move; his face just turned the collor of a fish's belly. Soo Ong said: "Traitor!"—and he sunk that knife to the hilt under Yut Ling's heart.

I come out all in a sweat. I hadn't expected nothing like that.

"What the hell! I said. "That ain't the way detectives does things! Leastways, in America—"

"Different methods for different lands," said Soo Ong. "But death to a traitor in any land." He stooped over and took a small leather case out of a inside pocket of Yut Ling's clothes. "I knew he would never trust it out of his own possession," muttered Soo Ong. "Even when coming among thieves who half-suspected his guilt." He took out a piece of paper and a pencil and scribbled on it in English, and wrapped the paper around the case and give it to me.

"Give this to the white man in the back room, and untie him," he said, and before I could say a word, he was gone into the night, and I was standing there alone with a Chinese corpse and a tied-up thug.

I begun to get a vague feeling that something was wrong about this deal. I got the jitters every time I looked at Yut Ling laying there with the knife hilt still standing up from his bosom. Finally I went into the back room and dragged the tied-up fellow out where they was more light, and pulled off the gag. And the first thing he said nearly knocked me down.

"You rotter!" he said. "You'll get life for this!"

"What?" I said. And my hair riz straight up, because I recognized him, under his make-up of old clothes and grime.

"Cecil Clayton!" I gulped. "The limey dick!"

"Sir Cecil Clayton to you," he snarled. "Dargan, I never thought I'd find you mixed up in a murder!"

"I never killed that Chinee!" I growled.

"I know," he said. "I heard what was going on. But you—"

"But I nothin'!" I grunted, untying him. "I was just helpin' that detective, Soo Ong—"

"Detective?" he sneered. "Do you take me for a fool? Are you pretending you don't know that was Ki Yang, the man who stole the Mandarin Ruby?"

"What?" I hollered. "But he said Yut Ling stole it—"

"That's what he said at the trial," snapped Sir Cecil. "He swore Yut Ling was the real thief, and had framed him, but there was nothing to back up his accusations. Yut Ling was a sort of stool-pigeon for the police—unsavory character, but necessary. If he knew Ki Yang was here, it's a wonder he hadn't tipped me off. I've been looking for Ki Yang ever since he escaped from prison a week ago. Just struck his trail tonight. He might have gotten clean away, but it was characteristic that he should lurk around to get revenge on Yut Ling, poor devil."

"Yut Ling didn't wanta tip you off," I said. "He was goin' to give a gang of white thugs ten grand for capturin' Ki Yang and handin' him over to him, so he could bump him off."

"You're either crazy or drunk," said Sir Cecil getting up.

"I ain't neither," I said, nettled. "Suppose Yut Ling was the man which stole the ruby? It's worth a lot more'n ten grand. Suppose Yut Ling knowed Ki Yang knowed he stole it? Maybe he'd figure it was worth ten grand to have Ki Yang outa the way for good."

"Ridiculous," snorted Sir Cecil. "You can't make a fool out of me with any such nightmare-story. The fact remains that Ki Yang murdered Yut Ling, and you were an accomplice. You'll have to—"

"You ain't goin' to arrest me," I roared. "Don't reach for your gun. I taken it offa you when I socked you. I ain't goin' to the jug just because I made a mistake. I thought Ki Yang was a detective, and that I was aidin' the law. Maybe I been made a fool of, but I ain't goin' to do time, you hear me? I'm goin' out that door and I don't want you to try to stop me. Before I go, though, here's somethin' Ki Yang said give you. He taken it offa Yut Ling after he killed him. There's a note, too."

Sir Cecil grabbed it, and read the note out loud. It said: "Sir Cecil Clayton: An innocent man can not prove his innocence in prison. Guile must be fought with guile. I can not prove that Yut Ling stole the ruby; but the gem can speak for itself. This white man, whom I tricked into helping me, thinking I was a detective, can attest the fact that it came from the pockets of Yut Ling. Your obedient servant, Ki Yang."

"Well, I'll be damned!" said Sir Cecil, and he ripped open the leather case, and a flaming red stone as big as a pigeon egg rolled into his hand. "Then Yut Ling *was* the thief! The rat! Well—his killing is one homicide that will never be brought into the courts, if I can help it. Dorgan, I apologize. It's evident that you did make merely an honest mistake, and in so doing aided justice. The case is at an end; the jewel will go back to the owner, the real thief has been punished—if illegally—and an innocent man vindicated. You've done a good night's work!"

"Aw," I said modestly. "that ain't nothin'. But I got to go and find Butch Corrigan now. I got fifty dollars which belongs to him, and if it hadn't been for me, he wouldn't never of got it. Butch ain't smart like me!"

The Yellow Cobra

When the *Python* docked at Fusan, I was all set for a quiet shore leave, because I didn't think they was a single fight club in Korea. But me and my white bull dog Spike had hardly found a decent bar, where we was lapping up some porter ale, when Bill O'Brien come in and he said, said he: "Great stuff, Dennis! You know Dutchy Grober of Nagasaki? Well, he's got a saloon here now, and in order to raise enough dough to pay off what he owes on it, he's puttin' on a fight show. I got you matched with a tough Englishman offa the *Ashanti*. Let's celebrate with a 'rickshaw ride."

"Get outa my sight," I said annoyedly. "I was plannin' on rest and quiet. Go celebrate by yourself, if you wanta—but take Spike. He likes to ride them 'rickshaws."

So Bill and Spike went off, and I started looking for a place to take a nap, because I knowed I was in for a tough scrap that night. As I passed the open door of the back room, I seen a man setting at a table inside with his head on his arms. He looked familiar and I went in and looked closer. Sure enough, I knowed him—Jack Randal, a mining engineer. I slapped him on the back and yelled: "Hello Jack!"

The next instant he was on his feet and had a blue steel barrel boring into my belly. He was kinda haggard and unkempt-looking.

"Oh, it's you Dorgan!" said he with a sigh of relief. "You gave me a scare. I must have fallen asleep in my chair—haven't slept any too regularly lately. Sit down and I'll order some drinks."

"Well, Jack," I said as we sipped our licker, "it looks like you been through a tough grind."

"I have," he said. "I've just got back from northern Manchuria. I can't give you all the details—but I went up there in the employ of a Chinese company no one knew anything about, but they seemed to have plenty of money. When I got on the ground I found they were nothing but a gang of bandits, working secret mines by slave labor. You wouldn't believe me if I told you some of the things I saw. I bolted, and they dogged me all the way to the Korean border. They put a secret society of Oriental fanatics on my trail—the Yellow Cobras, they call themselves, and there are branches of the cult all over the East."

"Whyn't you go to the cops?" I asked.

"I don't dare trust anybody," he said. "There are Yellow Cobras in unsuspected high places. I've got a hangout where no one would ever suspect a white man to hide—a deserted native hut down on the docks in the district called the Alley of Rotting Houses. I registered at a European hotel, just as a blind—in case I'm still being shadowed. At dawn I'll go aboard a steamer bound for Japan. My only chance is to hide and run. Those devils have murdered victims in locked rooms, and right under the noses of the cops."

"You think you've throwed 'em off?" I asked.

"I don't know," he said. "Their most persistent spy was a tall lean Eurasian with a long horse face and a scar running from his left ear down the rim of his jaw. I haven't seen him in Fusan, but—"

"Whyn't you go aboard the *Python* and stay till morning?" I asked.

"If they're here they'll be watching the docks for just such a move," he said. "They'd see me go aboard, have me spotted, and all night to figure out their next move. They wouldn't stop at blowing up the ship with all hands. No, my best bet is to hide tonight, and grab the steamer in the morning, just before she sails. Maybe I can steal a march on them."

I offered to stay with him all night and pertect him, but he said he could hide himself better alone. I'll admit a man of my build and habits ain't easy to conceal. I went with him to his hotel, where he shook hands with me, and said so-long out loud, and then whispered. "I'll go up to my room openly, then when it's dark I'll sneak out a side entrance and make for my hangout. If I'm lucky I'll see you on the wharf at dawn—for about five seconds!"

He went up, and I santered out to put in the time till it was time for the fight. I shot craps with some French sailors in a bar for a hour or so, and then headed for a eating-joint. I had plenty of time, because the show started kinda late. A heavy meal ain't good for a man just before a tough fight, but I never could see that I was done any harm by a light snack like a porterhouse steak with onions, and a quart of beer. I was crossing the street, when zip! a car whizzed around the corner and nearly run me down. I leaped back with a roar of wrath, shaking my huge fist at the driver and giving vent to a few choice remarks which drawed the admiring attention of the passers-by. I seen the face of the man setting beside the driver plainly in the light of a street lamp, and it caused a kinda vague stir in my mind, as I stalked into a eating-joint and with dignity ordered grub.

Whilst waiting for it, I tried to remember what that face in the street light had reminded me of. It had been a yellowish face, long, with a great scar on the left jaw. And suddenly it come to me with a blaze of light! I leaped up with a yell that caused one of the customers to swaller a whole potater. A horse face with a scar! It was the Eurasian spy Jack Randal hadst described to me!

Paying no heed to the screams of the proprietor which urged me to return and pay for the food I hadn't et, I bolted outa the door and up the street. I had a premonishun. I knowed something had happened, or was going to happen to Jack Randal.

I made straight for the hangout in the Alley of Rotting Houses—a low-class native districk close to the water front—rickety shacks all jumbled up together, sagging out over the water. Everything was still as death; they was no street lights, and no moon. I heered the water lapping at the rotten piles, and it give me the shudders, thinking how many corpses has been dumped into them waters.

Jack had told me how to get to his hide-out, but at that I had the heck of a time finding it. And when I did, my hair prickled; the bamboo door sagged open, and they wasn't a sound from inside which was as black as the belly of a cat. I stole inside, expecting a knife in my back, and struck a match. They was nobody there—just a busted cot and a shattered chair, and a pool of blood on the floor. Jack Randal was gone, and they was no trace to show where he'd went; and all the time

I heered them black waters lapping at the piles below.

I hate to have to depend on my brains. Gimme a problem which can be solved by busting somebody on the jaw. When I'm up against something I can't batter with my huge maulers, I'm all at sea. I stood there, and the more I tried to figger out what to do, the dizzier I got.

At last I decided they wasn't but one thing to do—get the crew and take Fusan apart, piece by piece, till we found Jack or his remainders. I set out at a run for Dutchy's arener, where I found Bill in a frenzy.

"Where you been?" he howled. "You kept the crowd waitin' for over a hour! Bull Richardson, your opponent, has been in the ring for—"

"Aw, shut up," I panted. "Dutchy, we gotta postpone the fight."

Dutchy gave a scream.

"I can't!" he howled, tearing his hair. "The crowd will want their money back, and I can't give it back! I've already give it to the man I owed, and he's gone with it! He was waitin' at the box office to get it! I'll be ruined! Please, Dennis! Think of all I've did for you!" He commenced to cry.

"Alright!" I yelled, going slightly offa my nut. "I'll give you your blasted fight, but I ain't goin' to be in that ring more'n fifteen seconds. Bill, tell the crew to be ready to jump the instant I flatten that mutt. Every minute counts!" I said, tearing off my street clothes, jerking on my trunks, and yanking on a pair of old gloves I found in a locker. "Let's go!"

And so saying I charged out of the dressing-room and up the aisle, not stopping to put on my bathrobe, and giving no heed to the crowd's enraged comments. I seen my opponent standing in his corner, glaring down at me, and I yelled: "Get off that robe and put up your mitts! Hit that bell! We ain't botherin' with ceremony tonight!"

Though bewildered at my lack of conventions, the timekeeper hit the gong as I bounded through the ropes, and throwing off his bathrobe, Richardson rushed at me. The crowd yelled with surprise, but they was no sticklers for etiket.

But I'd made a mistake. Richardson was already gloved, the pair of gloves intended for me laying in the center of the ring. The referee kicked 'em out as I come through the ropes. But my mistake was in having the bell hit before I was properly in the ring. Before I could get my hands up, Richardson crashed me back half-way through the ropes with a terrible right to the head. Rebounding, I staggered him with a left hook under the heart, and brought up a hurricane right for his jaw, but luck wasn't with me. My foot slipped and I fell into one of the hardest punches I ever took in my life.

I heered somebody counting, and realized that I was on my back in the middle of the ring.

Instantly the thought flashed through my mind that probably Jack Randal was getting tortured and murdered whilst I laid there—if he wasn't already. I scrambled up in a panic, and instantly perceived the truth of the statement that fighting requires concentration. If I hadst not been thinking about Jack Randal as I riz, I would of blocked the left hook Richardson greeted me with. As it was, he tagged me smack on the chin with all his beef behind it, and I shot backwards, turned in mid air and crashed face down on the canvas, amidst the appalling howls of the *Python*'s crew, and the admiring screams of all the limeys present.

They say when a man falls face first he's through. I've fell that way plenty and I have yet to be counted out. Still, it ain't no picnic. I tried to summon my remarkable vitality to aid me to get up and kill Bull Richardson, but as it happened, something outside myself brung me to. I was lying on my belly with my head under the bottom rope, and half supported by my elbows, whilst I stared blearily out into a blur of jeering faces. Then as my sight cleared a little, I was aware of one particular face which seemed to float at me outa the fog—a long yeller face, sneering, hateful, with a scar running down the jaw.

Instantly I come to myself with a incredulous beller! It was a lanky Eurasian setting on the first row ringside, and I was glaring right into his face. As I looked, he ariz with a sneer, made a insulting gesture at me and started up the aisle towards a exit like he was so disgusted at my rotten exhibition he wasn't going to stay no longer.

The referee hadn't got to "Ten" but I dunno just where he was counting. To tell the truth, I'd clean forgot about the referee and Bull Richardson too. I bounded to my feet and to the delirious amazement of the crowd, I started over the ropes.

"He's yeller!" howled the maddened fans. "He's tryin' to escape! Grab him! Sock him, Bull!"

I was just shoving my foot through the ropes, when some instink of self-preservation caused me to turn just in time to stop Richardson's left with my mouth. I crashed back into the ropes, and realized that I would have to stiffen this pest of a limey before I'd be allowed to leave the ring. Rebounding from the ropes with a maddened roar, I crashed my terrible right mauler under his jaw with every ounce of iron muscle I had behind it. Bull Richardson left the canvas bodily, shot back half-way across the ring, hit the canvas on his shoulders, turned a somersault and disappeared through the ropes on the other side. Counting him out was a needless affectation.

I didn't stop. I ripped off the gloves and leaped down outa the ring, throwing my admirers right and left when they swarmed around me.

"Foller me!" I bellered, because half a dozen fights had already started between the *Python* men and the thugs from the *Ashanti*. "Round up the crew, Bill, and get the cops! Come on, Spike!"

And busting through the ranks of both friends and foes, heedless of the aimless fists which bounced from my iron skull, I raced down the aisle towards the exit through which the scar-faced Eurasian hadst vanished. I plunged into the street, clad only in my fighting togs.

The Eurasian was just hailing some kind of a horse-drawn vehickle, one of them kind where the driver sets up on a kind of a monkey seat.

"Stand by to go about, you yeller-starned lubber!" I bellered, setting sail for him. "I got words to say to you!"

He could hardly of knowed what I was after him for, but he had a guilty conscience. He turned pale, leaped into the carriage or whatever they call it, screeched at the driver who begun to lash his horse, and the vehickle started off at break-neck speed. But with a maddened roar, I left the curb in a flying leap which landed me in the carriage right on top of the Eurasian which I instantly grabbed by the throat. He give a scream and flashed out a knife, but I had his wrist in a iron grip, and the battle was on. The horse was clean crazy with all the racket, and running for all he was worth with the bit in his teeth, and the lines flying. The native on the box hadst lost all control of the critter and was just holding on and yelling blue murder. A fleeting glimpse showed me Spike racing along behind.

And in the seat me and the Eurasian was locked in a death-tussle. The carriage rocked and bounded and careened like a life boat in a hurricane, and we was throwed so violently from one side to the other that our breath was knocked out, and I thought all my ribs was busted. It was a wild tangle of arms and legs, the Eurasian gurgling and trying to knife me, whilst I kept the knife at bay with one hand, and with the other'n alternated between hammering him to a pulp and choking him till he was black in the face.

The wheels knocked fire outa the cobble stones, and the natives run every whichaway yelling blue murder, and then we rounded a corner so sharp that the Korean sailed off the driver's box all spread-eagled like a flying bat, and me and the Eurasian was hurled violently to the floor together, our heads coming in contact with a *bop!* which musta been heard for blocks. The Eurasian went limp, and I tore the knife outa his nerveless hand, and knelt astraddle of him with my iron fingers sunk into his neck.

"What'd you do with Jack Randal?" I gasped, retaining my position with difficulty; the flying wheels was just hitting the high spots. "Tell me, or I'll tear out your neck cords!"

He was blue-faced and gagging, his clothes hanging in tatters, his face beat to a pulp.

"I'll tell!" he gasped, between the jouncing of the wheels and the lurching of the runaway carriage. "We took him—to Tao Tsang's warehouse—on Dock Number 7—ow, you're strangling me—"

Crash! The blamed horse hadst swept around another corner, and the wheel hit the edge of a stone wall. The carriage flew into kindling wood. The air was fulla spokes and nuts and bolts and splinters of wood, and then the horse went tearing down the streets, with strips of snapped harness flying, and I riz dazedly from amongst the ruins and felt myself to sey was I still alive. I seemed to be intact, outside of the places where some hide was missing, and some bruises and cuts here and there. The Eurasian was laying among the splinters, out cold, with a three-inch gash in his scalp. I didn't stop to give him no first aid.

Spike come up and set down with his tongue hanging out about a foot. He ain't built for long distance running. I looked dizzily around, wondering where we was, and my heart give a leap. Luck was with me at last. Or rather, I reckon the Eurasian had give the driver orders to take him to Tao Tsang's warehouse, and the horse just kept on in that direction after he started running away. Anyway, I realized that I wasn't far from the vicinity of Dock No. 7. And noticing a crowd of natives was beginning to gather and gawp, evidently taking me for a lunatick in my torn ring togs, I hastily beat it down a alley, follered by Spike.

Nobody tried to stop me, and purty soon their chatter faded out behind me, and next I saw Tao Tsang's warehouse looming up big and silent ahead of me.

Nobody was in sight, no sound except the everlasting water lapping at the piles. They was no lights; even the street lamps, dim and old-fashioned as they was, wasn't lit. I was as alone apparently, as if I was the only man in Fusan. But I felt that Tao Tsang wasn't the man to leave his property unguarded. He was a Canton Chinee, and had the name of a bad actor, though nothing hadn't never been proved on him.

But I believed the Eurasian had told the truth, and I was going to investigate, even if I had to commit burglary. I kept listening for sounds which might inform that the crew was hastening to my assistance. I believed they'd foller the runaway, and the natives would tell 'em which way I went. When I heard 'em yelling and shouting like they generally do, I was going to hail 'em. But they didn't come, and I couldn't wait.

I found a winder which looked like the bars on it wasn't too firm, and very cautious I laid hold of one and begun to work it loose. I braced my legs and slowly exerted my enormous strength, till the veins stood out on my temples, and purty soon one end come loose with a crash that made my heart jump into my throat. I waited, expecting anything, but nothing happened. So I worked the bar loose at the other end and lifted it out, and two more come out a lot easier when I pried on 'em. They was no glass panes, just old heavy double shutters, which I pushed inwards. All was dark inside, and silent. I put my hands on the sill and started to climb in, when Spike snarled, grabbed my trunk's leg and jerked me back. And as he did, something hummed past my head so clost it shaved off a lock of my hair. I grabbed wildly in the dark, and my fingers clamped onto a human hand holding a hatchet, and somebody snarled like a wild animal and jerked savagely.

Electrified by my peril, I yanked my captive half-way through the winder, and in the dim light I seen I had hold of a big half-naked yeller man with a shaven head. Before he couldst wrench loose, my fist smashed like a caulking mallet against his jaw, and he folded down across the winder-sill, out cold.

I found myself shaking all over, with a cold sweat, at the narrerness of my escape. Hadst Spike not smelt danger, I would of crawled right on into the dark where that bloody hatchet man was lurking, and my ivory head would of been lying on the floor inside. I listened, but heered no further sounds, and Spike didn't ack like he smelt any more Orientals. So I rudely yanked my victim out through the winder and let him fall loosely to the ground. I knowed he wouldn't come to any time soon.

I looked at Spike and he smelt the air, but said nothing, so I clumb boldly through the winder and helped him through after me. We groped our way amongst packing-cases and bags of stuff, and if they had been any more hatchet men in that part of the warehouse they couldn't of helped hearing me when I busted my shin on what felt like a keg of nails.

Then I heered Spike whining softly in the dark, and I made my way over to him, and found him standing at the bottom of a stair which led up. He was smelling the steps and now he went up 'em as quiet as a ghost, and I follered him as stealthy as I could. He couldn't know who I was hunting, but he knowed men of some kind was at the top of that stair.

At the head of the stairs I seen a gleam of light, and a few seconds later I was crouching against the door there, under which the light was shining, and wondering why I hadn't noticed that light from the outside.

They was a key hole in the door, and half-way expecting to get a hat pin in my eye, I peered in. What I seen turned my blood cold. I'd found Jack Randal.

The room was an inside one; no winder, but a kind of skylight. Just the one door, as far as I could make out. It was lighted with European made lamps, and they was five men in it. One was Tao Tsang hisself, setting in a corner like a yeller idol, nothing alive about him but his snaky eyes. Two was slant-eyed yeller giants, like the hatchet man downstairs; one was a tall lean man dressed in decorated silk garments that must of cost plenty. The other'n was Jack Randal. He was hanging from a hook in the ceiling by cords which cut into his flesh so his wrists was trickling blood.

"You have eluded us long, my friend," the man in silk was saying, in English as good as mine. "But to every road is the end appointed. You were shadowed from the moment you entered Fusan. Our spies saw you enter the hotel, and they saw you steal forth to the Alley of Rotting Houses, as now you know. Have you had a sufficient time to reflect over the folly of crossing the honorable Yellow Cobras?"

"Kill me and get it over with, you swine!" Randal gasped between his teeth.

The Manchurian shook his head.

"Not so easily," he purred. "The Yellow Cobras do not spare their enemies. Look!"

One of them slant-eyed devils brung up a brazier full of glowing coals. The Manchurian—if that's what he was—took some strips of steel and put their ends in the coals, and started blowing on the coals to make 'em glow red. I'd been getting madder and madder; I shook all over like I had the aggers, and the short hairs on my neck bristled. This was the last straw. With the howl of a blood mad wolf, I launched myself against the door, and the impact tore it clean offa the hinges. I crashed into the room on top of it, and Spike trampled me in his headlong charge.

I was up in a flash, just as Spike sailed from the floor and clamped his iron jaws on the throat of the hatchet man at the brazier. They went down together, and the other'n drawed a knife as I rushed him. It licked past my throat, drawing blood, and I felt his ribs buckle like cardboard as I smashed left and right to his body. Over his crumpling form I leaped at the Manchurian, and I seen a dull gleam in his hand, and heered the crack of a shot so clost to my ear the powder burnt my face. The only reason he missed at that range was because Jack, swinging in mid air just behind him, hadst pushed him off balance with his feet, just as he fired.

Before he could pull the trigger again, I grabbed his wrist and as I bent it with all my strength, the bones in his arm cracked like rotten sticks. A groan bust from his lips, but with his left hand he forked at my eyes, his long nails ripping the hide from my face. Maddened by the pain, I ripped a slungshot right to his jaw and he looped a loop before he lit on the back of his neck, cold as a mackerel.

Turning towards Tao Tsang, I seen him scuttling for the wall, and Jack yelped: "Stop him!"

Tao Tsang was too quick for me, but not for Spike. Just as he reached the wall, Spike soared through the air and crashed smack between his shoulders. Tao Tsang went down with a squall like a wounded cat, and Spike drove quick and deadly for his throat, getting his jaws tangled in the flowered silk robes the Chinee wore.

"Stop him, Dennis!" begged Jack, spinning like a pendulum at the end of his cords. "Don't let him kill the old devil—he's our only chance!"

"Belay there, Spike," I ordered. "Set on him."

Spike done like I said, and Tao Tsang laid there shaking with fear. I cut Jack down, and he was so stiff he couldn't stand up. Whilst he was getting the circulation back in his arms and legs, I took a look at the Yeller Cobras. The two men I'd socked was still out, naturally, and the hatchet man Spike had struck was stone dead, his throat tore clean out.

"Le's get outa here," I said to Jack, and started for the door, but he stopped me.

"Wait!" he said. "Don't you hear something?"

Downstairs a door opened softly, and there sounded a mutter of voices.

"That's the crew," I said. "They've follered me here, somehow." I started to give 'em a hail, when Jack grabbed me.

"Wait!" he said again. "There were ten or twelve men who slipped into my hideout and overpowered me. Only three of them came here with me—those two hatchet men and another. I don't know where the rest went, but that may be them returning."

I glanced at Spike. He'd heered the sounds too. He pricked up his ears, and then commenced to rumble deep in his throat. My hair stood up. It was enemies he smelt, not friends. Where'n thunder *was* that cussed crew?

Jack wheeled to Tao Tsang.

"I'll bargain with you," he said. "I know there's a secret door in that wall somewhere. You were trying to get to it. Lead us out of here and we'll let you go, and say nothing to the police about what's happened."

"White devil!" hissed Tao Tsang. "I give you nothing but death!"

"Set the dog on him, Dennis!" snapped Jack.

"No, no!" The Chinee turned fish-colored as he twisted his head and looked at Spike's other victim, then at Spike's dripping fangs. "I will guide you to safety!"

"Hustle!" rapped Jack. "I hear them at the foot of the stairs."

I made Spike get offa Tao Tsang and I got a good hold on his clothes. The Chinee fumbled at the wall, and a panel slid back, disclosing a dim lit passage. We slid through in a hurry, and he slipped back the panel, just as we heered a lot of men come into the outer room. A clamor of voices come dimly through the wall. They was a bolt inside the panel, and Jack slid it to.

"Lead on," I hissed in Tao Tsang's ear; "one false move and I'll feed you to my man-eatin' bulldog."

"Keep the animal from me," said he sullenly. "None traverses this corridor but myself. It comes out under the wharf."

We went along that narrow passage which was built in the thick walls of the warehouse, down a even narrower flight of steps that went clean down below the foundations, and through a underground tunnel that must of been built by somebody's original ancestor, it looked so ancient. It ended in a iron door, and Tao Tsang opened this, and we come out under a wharf and found ourselves standing knee deep in filthy water. They was a faint hint of dawn in the air, though I couldn't realize nearly a whole night had passed—things had happened so fast.

We clumb up on the wharf, and I demanded: "What'll I do with Tao Tsang?"

"Let him go," said Jack. "We'll be out of the neighborhood before he can get back to his thugs and bring them after us. We'll run for it—what was that splash?"

"That was me lettin' Tao Tsang go," I answered as we made tracks for elsewhere. "I'm afraid they ain't a chance of him drowndin', though. I throwed him as far as I could, but the water's so blamed shaller under that old pier—"

"How on earth did you ever find me?" he marveled.

"On account of that Eurasian bein' a fight fan," I grunted. "I'll write you a letter all about it."

"Address it San Francisco," he said, "because that's where I'll be. There's the pier, and the steamer I sail on."

"Ain't you goin' to get your things at the hotel?" I asked.

"To heck with 'em," he said. "I've got some money sewed inside my undershirt. All I want to do is to get aboard that steamer. And I'm not forgetting what you've done for me tonight, Dennis."

"Aw, forget it," I growled. "But you wait till I see Bill O'Brien and that blasted crew. I can't understand it; it's the first time them lubbers ever let me down."

Well, I seen Jack safe aboard his steamer, and as I turned away from the wharf, I met a rooin which I rekernized as Bill O'Brien. His clothes was in tatters, and he was bruised and battered. Before I could give him a cussing for not follering me and helping me lick the Yeller Cobras, he said bitterly: "So! You runs out and leaves your shipmates to fight your battles alone! Where at's your clothes? You want to get arrested runnin' around like that? No wonder the cops was chasin' you."

"What you talkin' about?" I demanded. "What fight?"

"The fight you got us into," he said. "That 'un with the cops, on account of which most of the *Python*'s crew is now in jail."

"Why in the name of Judas did you fight the cops?" I squawked.

"You said: 'Get the cops,'" he replied icily. "So when we seen 'em runnin' after that carriage you stole, we pitched in and—"

"I didn't mean get 'em that way!" I howled. "I meant—"

"You oughta say what you mean," he snapped. "We been fightin' all the cops in Fusan all night, while you go sky-larkin' and joy-ridin'—where you goin'?"

"Aboard," I snarled. "Whilst I battle a gang of Oriental thugs, the cops and my shipmates amuses theirselves by brawlin' in the alleys instead of comin' to the aid of worthy citerzens. They is no chance for a honest man ashore. Besides, the seat is tore out of my pants."

In High Society

I been unpopular at the Waterfront Arena in Frisco ever since the night the announcer clumb into the ring and bellered: "Ladeez and gents! The management regrets to announce that the semi-windup between Sailor Dorgan and Jim Ash can't come off. Dorgan just knocked Ash so cold in his dressin' room they're workin' on him with a pulmoter."

"Well, let Dorgan fight somebody else," the crowd hollered.

"He can't," said the announcer. "Somebody squirted tabasco sass in his eyes."

Them was the general facks of the case, only it wasn't tabasco sauce. I was laying on a table in my dressing-room, getting a rub down, when in come a learned-looking gent with colored spectacles and a long white beard.

"I'm Dr. Stauf," he said. "The Commission has sent me in to examine you to see if you're in fit condition to fight."

"Well, hustle," said my handler Joe Kerney. "He's due in the ring in about five minutes."

Dr. Stauf tapped my huge chest, looked at my teeth, and give me the general once over.

"Oh," he said. "Ah ha!" he said. "Your peepers is on the blink. But I'll fix that!" He took out a bottle and a glass dropper, and pulling back my lids, dropped a lot of stuff in my eyes, saying, "If that don't fix you, my name ain't Barl—Stauf."

"What is that stuff?" I demanded, setting up and shaking

my head. "Seems like my eye balls is kinda expandin', or somethin'."

"A very beneficial drug," says Stauf. "You got eye strain from shootin' craps under a poor light. That drug will make 'em as good as—*yow!*" Without warning my white bulldog Spike had grabbed him by the leg. He went into a spin wheel, and to my dumfoundment, the colored spectacles and the white whiskers come off, revealing the convulsed features of Foxy Barlow, Jim Ash's manager.

"What kind of a game is this?" I roared, leaping offa the table. Joe Kerney snatched up the bottle and smelt it.

"Belladonna!" he yelled. "In three minutes you'll be stone blind!"

I give a horrible yell of rage and plunged at Barlow, who with a desperate convulsion tore his mangled leg outa Spike's bear-trap jaws and rushed out, howling bloody murder.

"Why didn't we rekernize him?" squalled Joe. "We mighta knowed them rats would try to rooin you before we got into the ring. But even Spike didn't know him till he smelt of him—"

I shoved him aside and charged blunderingly out into the hall, where I seen a bathrobed figger I knowed was Ash emerging from his dressing-room. My eyes were dilating so fast he was just a kind of blur.

"You dirty double-crossin' son of a half-breed pole-cat!" I roared as I rushed and throwed my right mauler at his jaw like a man throwing a hammer. By sheer luck I caught him flat-footed, and when Joe had helped me dress, and led me outa the Arener, they was still trying to bring him to.

Joe took me to his room, and for twenty-four hours I was blind as a bat; then when I got so I could see at all, everything was so blurry and dim I couldn't get around by myself.

"What gets me," I said bitterly, "is how come them dumb-bells ever thought up a trick like that. Ash ain't got no sense, and neither has Barlow."

"I understand Ash's cousin from the East put him up to it," said Joe. "I ain't seen him, but he's a fighter, they say, and smart as they come. Red Stalz was tellin' me Ash told this cousin he was goin' to fight a man he was afeard he couldn't lick, and the cousin told him to slip you the blindin' drops. But that bonehead Barlow put so much dope in your eyes you'd of gone blind before you could get in the ring, even if we hadn't discovered the fake. The cousin intended you should lose your sight after the fight started, of course. But Barlow muffed it."

"Well, what am I goin' to do whilst I wait for my eyes to get normal?" I complained.

"Buy you some glasses," advised Joe, so he guided me down to a eye specialist where I spent most of my scanty roll on a pair of spectacles with big wide horn rims. Joe gawped at me.

"By golly," he said, "I didn't have no idee glasses would change a man's looks like that. Why, you look plumb mild and retirin'. Look in the mirror."

I done so and was disgusted. If it hadn't been for my cauliflowers, I'd of looked like a perfessor or something.

"How long I got to wear these blinders?" I asked the specialist.

"Oh, maybe a week, maybe longer," he said. "You've had a terrific overdose of belladonna. I can't say just when your pupils will regain their normal state."

I went back to Los Angeles, and after I paid my fare I was broke and no chance for a fight with them eyes. To add to my troubles, whilst I wa setting broodingly in my room at the Waterfront Hotel, the landlord come in and told me if I didn't pay my back rent he was going to throw me out. I evaded the question by throwing *him* out, and then wandered morosely down to the pool halls to see if I couldn't borrow a few bucks from somebody.

"Dennis," said Jack Tanner, which I struck up first, "I'll swear I ain't got a dime—but listen, you could box a exhibition, couldn't you? Reason I ask, I seen a gent over to Varella's gym while ago tryin' to get some heavyweight for some kinda society exhibition. Let's go over and see can we catch him."

So we went over to the gym, and Jack said: "There he is, talkin' with Varella." With the aid of my glasses I seen a elderly gent in a high silk hat with a goldheaded cane. Varella seen me, and said: "Hi, Dennis, I'm glad to see you. Maybe you do sa beeznizz with deez gentleman, yes, no? Deez is Dennis Dorgan, Meester. Maybe you use heem, eh, so?"

"I didn't catch the name," I said.

"I am Horace J. J. Vander Swiller III," said the gent, looking at me through one of them there monercals. "My word, what a peculiar-looking individual! With the clothing and general appearance of a wharfside hoodlum, yet with the facial aspect of a man with scholary inclinations."

"Aw, it's these dern glasses," I said. "Without 'em I'm a man among men. Lookit!" I took 'em off and Horace III gasped.

"My word!" he said, "what an incredible difference it makes! Put them back on, please! Thank you. I think you'll do—now. As I have told Mr. Varella, I am looking for a pugilist to appear in an exhibition match at my club—the Athenian. He must be a heavyweight and should be fairly well known."

"I've busted snoots from Galveston to Singapore," I said.

"Indeed? Well, I understand you have some reputation, at least. I have secured Mr. Johnny McGoorty for your opponent—"

"The mugg which has just come to the Coast from Chicago?" I asked. "Well, what's the general purpose of the go, and what's my cut, if it's any of my business?"

"You and Mr. McGoorty will each receive five hundred dollars," said Horace. "The exhibition is in the nature of a fete for Mr. Jack Belding, who is being entertained by our set."

"You mean Gentleman Jack Belding which claims the heavyweight title?" I said.

"I understand the New York Boxing Commission has recognized his claim," said Horace. "Mr. Belding is a most delightful gentleman, not at all like the accepted idea of pugilists."

"So I hear," I growled. "He was a college star and a amateur athlete before he turned perfessional; been playin' the sercierty racket strong back East, I hear."

"Mr. Belding is as much at home in a drawing-room as in the ring," frowned Horace. "A highly cultured young man, with good connections, and a credit to any social set. This fete tonight is the climax of the club's program of entertainment for our honored guest. He has agreed to act as referee—in fact, he himself suggested the exhibition, in order to give the ladies of the club an opportunity to witness a typical ring match, without the painful brutality and bloodshed attendant upon a real fight."

"Then it's to be a very tame affair?" I asked.

"Certainly. Of course, we shall expect you to instill a good deal of harmless action into it, and go through the maneuvers of feinting, guarding and countering as realistically as possible, but without striking any damaging blows or descending to any of the brutal strategies so common in actual combat."

"All right," I said. "For five hundred bucks I'd rassle a Bengal tiger. I reckon I can see good enough to cake walk through a exhibition."

"Wait," he said. "Your garments will never do. You will be forced to mix somewhat with the guests before you don the habiliments of your profession, and possibly after the bout."

"What's wrong with these duds?" I asked impatiently. "I bought 'em at the best slop-shop on the Barbary Coast."

"They may do for the waterfront," said Horace, "but even you must see that they are impossible for the exclusive Athenian Club."

"Well, they're all I got," I growled. "If you don't like 'em, why don't you buy me some other kind?"

"So I will," he said. "Come—let's away to a haberdashery."

"Aw, a gents' furnishin' store'll do," I said. "I ain't particular."

Well, he hauled me into a ritzy joint and they done their worst.

"Something a bit sporty, I should say," said Horace. "An apparel which will suggest the collegiate—the virile yet scholarly playboy of the upper class."

Them clerks went for me, and before I knowed it, I was fitted out in a checkered golf knickers, a silk sport short as they called it, with a fool little boy tie, a jacket with a belt in the back, fancy gold socks, low quarter canvas shoes, and a Panerma hat with a turned-down brim. Then Horace had my tousled hair slicked back with some kind of muck that smelt like a—well, never mind.

"Look at yourself in the mirror," they said proudly. I done so and then set down on a goods box and put my head in my hands.

"I'll never live this down," I groaned. "Get me some false whiskers so I won't have to kill any of my acquaintances which might rekernize me in these riggin's."

"The metamorphosis is remarkable," said Horace. "Those garments, coupled with your spectacles, have transformed a wharfside ruffian into a refined-appearing person who might well pass for an athletic student in some large university—wait! One thing more—a pair of mauve-tinted kid gloves to conceal, as much as possible, those huge hairy hands. Now! I flatter myself I have prepared you rather well for the gaze of my club members and guests. The costume is unique—original—suggesting the casual invasion of the field of physical action by a studious and introspective individual of the better classes. You might have just stepped off the golf links of some fraternity."

"And I mighta just stepped out of a circus," I snapped. "I look like any pansy couldst slap me on the wrist and break my neck."

Spike just set down with his back to me and looked into space and wouldn't pay no attention to me at all.

"Don't ack that way, Spike," I said irritably. "I know you're ashamed of me, and I'm ashamed of myself; but we gotta have some dough."

"You'll have to leave that brutal-looking dog somewhere," said Horace. "Yet, no, on second thought, you may bring him along. He will add atmosphere to the occasion."

"Second thoughts or first," I said bitterly, "Spike comes along or I don't go. You done got me into these monkey-clothes, Double J III, but you ain't goin' to give Spike the air."

So we got into his auto and the shawffeur drove us out to the club. It was a scrumptous place. The members was all rich as mud and the club house looked like a castle or something. We drove into the grounds which was surrounded by a high stone wall, and I seen they had a ring pitched on the lawn out to one side of the club house, with chairs all around and lights strung over the ring and amongst the trees.

"Some of the ladies are in the tea room," said Horace. "I am to bring you in and introduce you to them. They are greatly interested in psychology, and since Mr. Belding has proved such a fascinating gentleman, the club ladies are taking a keen interest in persons connected with the ring. You will be a new and interesting type to them. As soon as Mr. McGoorty arrives I will bring him in, also. Try to act as gentlemanly as possible, and reply courteously to the ladies. Remember, they represent the very heights of culture and sensitive refinement."

"I'm always a gent," I growled. "I never socked a lady in my life."

He shook his head like he had his doubts, and we went into the mansion where a butler met us and took Horace's hat and cane. He tried to take my Panerma too, and Spike clamped onto his leg, and you oughta heard him holler. I pulled Spike off, and Horace frowned. "A most vicious beast."

"Naw, he ain't," I said. "He just thought that egg was tryin' to steal my hat."

"Will he not, then," said Horace, "attack Mr. McGoorty in the ring?"

"Naw," I answered. "He knows his business, and mine too;

but if somebody in street clothes was to sock me, he'd sure go for 'em."

Horace acted kinda nervous, but he led me into a locker room and showed me some silk togs he'd laid out. I hanged my straw hat on a chair and I seen Spike looking at it very mysterious.

Then Horace steered me in another room where half a dozen ladies in evening gowns was sipping tea, and he said: "Ladies, this is Mr. Dorgan, one of the participants in the exhibition match."

They all lifted their large-nets and looked at me like I was a jelly-fish or something.

"Indeed!" one said. "So you are a professional pugilist, Mr. Dorgan?"

"Yes'm," I said.

"Somehow you do not seem the type at all," said another'n. "Don't you find the profession rather strenuous for one of your evident studious nature?"

"Yes'm," I mumbled, having only a vague idee of what she was talking about.

"Do sit down and have some tea," they said. "You're a college man, of course, Mr. Dorgan—to what fraternities do you belong?"

"Well," I said vaguely, "I'm an A.B. mariner."

They all giggled.

"What a delightfully original sense of humor, Mr. Dorgan," one of 'em said. "Tell me—how does a man of your apparent scholarly tastes come to be in such a brutal profession? Do you not find it hard to hold your own against the more primitive types?"

"Well," I said, "I just walk in and start firin' away with both maulers for the head and belly till the other thug drops."

They looked kinda nonplused, and one said: "How many lumps of sugar in your tea, Mr. Dorgan?"

"Nary," I said, "I takes my pizen straight." I picked up the cup, smelt the stuff suspiciously, waved the cup at 'em gallantly, and saying jovially, "Well, here's mud in your eye!" I tossed it up with one gulp. I never forgets my etiket.

A kind of dumb silence reigned and one of the ladies said: "Mr. Dorgan, what is your estimate of Einstein?"

"You mean Abie Einstine of San Diego?" I said. "Aw, he's clever enough, but he couldn't punch a dent in a pound of butter, and he ain't got no guts."

At this moment Spike riz up disgustedly and stalked off towards the dressing-room with a mysterious gleam in his eye. The dames was looking at me kinda bewildered, and to my relief up come Horace with a young fellow, and said: "Here is Mr. Dolan of the TRIBUNE, who is going to write up the exhibition for his paper."

"Hello, Billy," I greeted, getting up and holding out my hand, mighty glad to meet one of my own kind again.

"This is Mr. Dorgan, Mr. Dolan," said Horace, as Billy held out his hand with a blank stare.

"Mr. Dorg- —holy mackerel! It's Dennis!" he gasped.

"Yeah, who else?" I growled embarrassedly, and Billy stared at me like he couldn't believe hisself.

"Ye gods!" he said. "You look like a mildly insane college professor on a drunk! Dennis Dorgan, in golf panties. Well, I'll da-"

"Perhaps you and Mr. Dorgan can talk more freely in the smoking-room," suggested Horace with a nervous glance at the ladies, which was beginning to glare. I was glad to go, and Horace followed us.

"Stay out of sight until the bout starts," he snapped, "and don't try to mix with the guests in the dance afterwards. I should have known you couldn't fit into polite society. Stay here till the bout is ready to begin."

"O.k. with me, pal," I said, pouring me a drink out of a bottle I found on a table. "Billy, did you bring your camera?"

"No," he said. "Why?"

"I just wanted to warn you not to take no pitchers of me in these duds," I said. "Who's that?"

Horace had just entered with a tall, hard-looking young thug.

"Mr. McGoorty, Mr. Dorgan and Mr. Dolan," said Horace. I stuck out my hand but McGoorty just gaped, and then started laughing like a hyener.

"Sailor Dorgan?" he whooped. "The man-eatin' bear-cat of the West Coast? The iron-fisted, granite-jawed terror that was born in a Texas cactus bed and cut his teeth on a Gila monster? Oh boy, this is too much! How come they let you outa the kindergarten for this mill, Drogan?"

"Listen here, you lantern-jawed son of a—" I begun bloodthirstily, but Horace said, "Gentlemen, I beg of you! Come, Mr. McGoorty, I will introduce you to the ladies."

They went out and I ground my teeth to hear McGoorty snickering as he looked back at my golf britches.

"Billy," I asked, "where at have I saw that mutt before?"

"I don't know," said Billy, "he just recently arrived from Chicago. Look out this window, Dennis, the shebang's getting under way."

Big cars was discharging their cargos on the lawn, and the seats was filling up with a colorful array, as they say. The cream of Los Angeles sercierty was there, and by squinting my eyes, I made out a tall figger surrounded by a fluttering group of admirers.

"Gentleman Jack, and isn't he putting on the dog?" said Billy sardonically. "He's certainly made the society racket pay. 'College Star Wins Ring Laurels'; 'Favorite Son of the Four Hundred Reaches Heights'; 'Young Society Leader Cops Title'. I've read and written such headers as those till I'm sick of it. I hope he gets his head knocked off in his next fight. Come on, I'll help you into your togs."

"Oughtn't you to be minglin' with the crowd and gettin' interviews and things?" I ast.

"Apfelstrudel," he sneered. "These society exhibitions are all alike. I could write them up asleep."

At this moment Horace appeared. "Come, come!" he said sharply. "The affair is about to begin. What is delaying you?"

"I thought maybe Gentleman Jack wanted to get acquainted with me and McGoorty before the brawl," I said with mild sarcasm.

"Tush, tush," frowned Horace. "A man of his position can hardly be expected to hobnob with the inferiors of his profession."

We went into the dressing-room and I got into my trunks and bathrobe and called Spike. He come out of a adjoining shower room with a satisfied look on his face like a job well done.

"Are you going to wear your glasses into the ring?" Billy asked.

"Yeah," I said. "I couldn't see to get there without 'em. I'll take 'em off before we start sparrin', of course."

Billy laughed. "I'll swear," he said, "I had no idea glasses could change a man's looks so. Even in fighting-togs you look like a book-worm."

Just then Horace come back in to tell us it was time to go

on. Me and Billy and Spike followed Horace out onto the lawn between the chairs full of men in dress suits and women in low-cut gowns, and I heered a dame say: "Tee hee! Fawncy a poogilist wearing glawses! What an odd-looking person!" And some bird said back to her, "Odd is no name for it, my deah. I fawncy he will find it rawthat difficult to hold his own, even in a friendly exhibition."

I clumb into the ring gnashing my teeth slightly. McGoorty was already there, with some gent in a dress suit acting as his second.

"Club members, ladies and gentlemen," said Horace, "this is the feature event of the series of entertainments we have offered in honor of our distinguished guest, Mr. Jack Belding."

Everybody applauded, and Horace said: "These gentlemen, Mr. Dorgan and Mr. McGoorty, are about to engage in a friendly exhibition, in the course of which they will demonstrate the science of the profession, thus giving this select audience an opportunity to observe the finer points of the game without being shocked by the display of brutality so characteristic of the ordinary pugilistic affair. Mr. Jack Belding will act as referee."

Belding clumb into the ring and bowed, and the crowd applauded wildly, especially the dames. He was the main show; me and McGoorty was just there to give him a background to show off with.

He called us to the center of the ring and give us instructions, like in a regular go, with a great show of being realistic and all, and I heered the skirts murmuring to each other: "Isn't he splendid?"

But I was glaring at McGoorty which was snickering in his sleeve till I jerked off my glasses and threw aside my bathrobe. McGoorty gasped at the sight of my huge body and ferocious features, unmasked, and I heered a sudden murmur sweep around the ringside.

"Heavens!" exclaimed one dame. "It's a gorilla!"

We retired to our corners, and I give my glasses to Billy, impatiently ruffling up my slick hair. Without the spectacles McGoorty looked just like a white blob setting in his corner.

The gong sounded and Gentleman Jack leaped lightly to the center of the ring, snapping his fingers and saying so the dames could hear: "Snap into it, boys! No stalling, now!"

At close range I found I could see fairly well. So we went to work, exhibition style, with lots of showy feinting and blocking and foot-work—well, I gotta admit most of it was McGoorty's. A slugger never shows up well in a exhibition. And then I was handicapped by my short-sightedness. I ain't slow, but I ain't clever, neither.

McGoorty flitted around me, working his left jab fast and purty to my face, and every now and then crossing his right. But when he done that I generally nailed him with a right to the ribs, so he begun to use long-range tactics more and more.

I clinched him and growled wrathfully: "Hey you! These folks didn't come here just to watch you make a fool outa me. They come to see a scientific exhibition. How'm I goin' to do my part if'n you keep so far away all the time I can't even see you?"

"That's for you to figger out," he sneered, which so irritated me that I ripped in a thoughtless left hook that rattled his teeth. I followed it with a smoking right to the belly, and he grabbed my arms with a grunt.

"This here's a exhibition!" he hissed fiercely. "You go easy, dern your hide!"

Gentleman Jack tapped our shoulders, saying: "Come, come, my men, break!"

With heroic self-control I overcome the impulse to bust him in the snoot, and the rest of the round went along polite-like, with us tapping and dancing and jabbing.

We started the second round the same way, and I found that the exertion was making my eyes worse. I blundered around more than ever.

"Dorgan," snapped Belding, "you're lousy! Get in there and show some class, if any, before I pitch you out of the ring."

I heered a dame say, "Isn't Mr. Belding masterful?" and I was so irritated I walked in and hit McGoorty harder'n I intended to. He grunted and shellacked me with a left to the chin, I retaliated with a staggering right to the head, and the next minute we was at it hot and heavy. What with the sweat and heat and all, I couldn't hardly see well enough to tell McGoorty from Belding, but as long as he stood up and traded punches with me, I could locate him. I heered a vague murmur from the ringside and Belding hauled us apart.

"Stop it, you boneheads!" he hissed. "This isn't a fight! Go easy, or I'll toss you both out, and you won't get a cent."

"Go roll your hoop, you toe-dancin' four-flusher," snarled McGoorty, but we eased down and coasted through that round and the next.

As we come up for the fourth, I went into a clinch and said: "I just now remember who you remind me of. Are you any kin to Jim Ash of Frisco?"

"First cousin," said he. "And what about it?"

"So!" I bellered, breaking away. "You was the smart gazabo that put him up to blindin' me, hey? I'll show you!"

And with that I smacked him in the mush with a left hook that cracked like a bull whip. He spat out a mouthful of blood and teeth and come back fighting like a wildcat. The ladies and Horace J. J. give a despairing howl, but I give no heed. I was seeing red and McGoorty was frothing.

We was in the midst of a whirlwind of leather, from which sweat and blood spattered like rain, and the impact of our smashing gloves could of been heard for blocks. Having stopped a slungshut uppercut that nearly tore his head off, McGoorty dived into a clinch, got my ear betwixt his teeth and begun to masticate it like he was eating cabbage, whilst I voiced my annoyance in langwidge which brung more screams from the sercierty folks.

I shook him off, caressing him with a left hook that broke his nose and started the claret in streams, and he begun to give ground. Belding was yelling and cussing us under his breath, but we give him no heed.

By this time McGoorty was just a white blur, but I kept sinking my maulers into the blur and I felt it buckling. Blood was streaming from my nose and smashed lips and crushed ears. Every now and then when I landed solid something splashed into my face which I knowed was McGoorty's gore. The ringside was a bedlam, where the sercierty folks was getting a first-hand glimpse of the polite science of pugilism.

My eye-sight was getting worse all the time, and if McGoorty had kept tin-canning, he could of licked me, but he tried to stand up and trade with me. Feeling his blows getting weaker under my murderous flailing, I put all my beef behind a right hook, and landed solid. I felt McGoorty fall away from me, but the next instant a blob bobbed up in front of me, and I socked it violently. Instantlty a most shocking medley of screams busted loose! Sensing that something was wrong, I shook my head violently to get the sweat and blood outa my eyes, blinked 'em industriously and bent down towards the blur which was now writhing on the canvas. My straining sight cleared a little, and to my dismay I seen *two* figgers on the canvas! That last blob had been Gentleman Jack Belding!

I started to help him up, beginning a explanation, but with fire in his eye he leaped up and swung a terrific right to my jaw. I hit the canvas on the seat of my trunks, and I heered Spike roar. The next instant a white streak shot across the ring and Gentleman Jack yelled bloody murder. With my blurry gaze I seen him whirling like a dancing derfish, trying to dislodge Spike which had a death grip on the seat of his britches. Rrrrrp!—went something and there was the champeen of the East Coast with no more pants on him than a Hottentot!

All over the place the sercierty belles was screaming hysterically or laughing like she-hyenas, and things was just about like a madhouse. Gentleman Jack give a howl like a lost soul and sprinted for the ropes, and I heered Horace yelling: "Call the police! I'll have them arrested! I'll have them sent to prison for life!"

At that McGoorty bounced offa the canvas and went through the ropes like a jackrabbit. I grabbed Spike under one arm and went through the other side. It was like taking a jump in the dark, everything outside the ring was like a deep fog. I stepped on something, and from the way it squeaked, I believe it was Horace. I mighta trompled others in my blundering dash for liberty, I dunno. My one idee was get back to the dressing-room, grab my clothes and beat it before the cops come.

The big club house loomed up dimly before me, and I made out what looked like a open door. I blundered through it, continuing my headlong flight—crash! I felt myself falling through space, and Spike flew outa my grasp. Wham! I hit on my neck hard enough to bust a anvil. I reeled up, wondering if they was a unbroken bone in my body. I'd fell on solid concrete, and somewhere near Spike was whining and scratching on wood. I tore off my gloves, and begun to blink and squint around. I made out where I was. My blame near-sightedness hadst made me step into a trap-door that led into the basement. I was in the basement. Next to me was a big coal bin and Spike had fell into it.

I was fixing to help him out, when I heard somebody else enter the basement in a more regular manner than I had—somebody which panted and cussed in a familiar voice. I peeked around the corner of the coal bin squinting closely. It was Belding which had sought refuge in his pantsless condition. He was cussing like a mule skinner and trying to arrange such clothes as Spike had left on to him. And I descended on him like a wolf on the fold.

"Sock me just because I made a honest mistake, would you?" I roared, and we went to the floor together.

I wouldn't had much chance with him in a regular ring bout, but in a rough-and-tumble brawl I had the advantage, even with my bad sight. He done his best and tried to gouge out my eye, but I butted the wind outa him, and whilst he was trying to get his breath, I socked him on the chin so hard it curled his hair. I then throwed him and fell on him, and was pummelling him heartily when I was aware that we was not alone. In a modern clubhouse they is no such thing as privacy.

A number of hands sought to drag me off my prey, and I shook 'em off and rose, glaring and blinking around like a owl. I dimly made out Horace—considerably mussed up—Billy Dolan, and a bunch of raging club members.

"You ruffian! You gangster! You pirate!" screeched Horace hysterically. "The Athenian will never live down this scandal! See to Mr. Belding—the brute has nearly murdered him. And grab this scoundrel and hold him until the police arrive!"

Then come a clawing noise and what looked like a black goblin come scrambling over the edge of the coal bin. It was Spike, covered with coal dust. Seeing me surrounded he charged with a roar, and the Athenians scattered like a flock of quails. Gentleman Jack run up a stair that musta led into the front part of the house, because a chorus of feminine screams and laughter, and a despairing howl seemed to indicate that he'd run into a flock of dames again. In a second the basement was empty except for me, Spike, and Billy Dolan. Billy took my hand and led me across the basement and up a short flight of stairs into a big closet.

"Wait here in this linen pantry till I bring your clothes," he said.

So I waited there, and shivered and cussed, whilst sounds of pursuit stormed all over the house, which I later learned was the club members chasing McGoorty, and purty soon Billy come back with them fool golf clothes. I put 'em on in a hurry, and he led me outa the house and across the grounds and out through a small back gate. We walked down the road and didn't stop till we was some distance from the Athenian. Then Billy started to laugh.

"What a scoop!" he said. "I said all society exhibitions were alike—I might have known that with you mixed up in this one, it would be different. If I don't scarehead this! Those snooty sissies of the Athenian—and Gentleman Jack! This is a chance

I've sometimes dreamed of. Wasn't he a scream running around before those snobby dames in his B.V.D.'s? Ha ha ha ha!"

"Lend me ten bucks, Billy," I said. "I'll pay you back as soon as I can see good enough to fight. I don't believe it'd be wise to try to collect that five yards from the club."

"I wouldn't advise it," he said, going down into his pocket after the ten. "By the way, the reason I didn't bring your hat was that your dog seems to have chewed it up in the shower room before the fight."

"And as soon as I can get into my regular clothes I'm goin' to give him these monkey-riggin's to play with," I growled. "Gimme them specs, Billy."

"Sure, I'd forgotten about them," said he, handing them to me.

I throwed 'em down on the sidewalk and ground 'em to dust under my heel.

"Gee whiz, Dennis," protested Billy, "you can't get around without them."

"I'll let Spike lead me till my sight gets better," I grunted. "If it hadn't been for them I wouldn't of got into this mess. From now on I sails under my right colors, which nobody can mistake me for a college perfessor or somethin'."

Playing Journalist

As I come into the back room of the Ocean Wave bar, Bill O'Brien, Mushy Hansen, Jim Rogers and Sven Larson looked up from their beer and sneered loudly. And Bill O'Brien said: "There he is, the big business maggot!"

"Lookit that Panerma hat and cane," snorted Jim Rogers. "And a fancy collar on Spike."

Mushy sighed mournfully. "To think that I should ever live to see Dennis Dorgan blossom out into a dern dude!"

"Look here, you barnacle-bellied sea-rats," I said in some wrath; "just because I'm tired bein' a roughneck and tries to dress like a gent ain't no reason I should swaller all them insults. The bar man told me to come back here. What you want?"

"If you can take time off from your big executive deals," said Bill scathingly, "'Hard-cash' Clemants here is gotta proposition for you."

The aforesaid gent was setting there smoking a big cigar, as hard-boiled and pot-bellied as ever.

"No use," I said. "I ain't fightin' for nobody. I been tradin' punches with cabbage-eared gorillas ever since I was big enough to lift my mitts, and—"

"Just because he had the dumb luck to bet on the right horse down at Tia Juana, he thinks he's too good to fight any more," sneered Rogers. "Takin' the bread right outa his mess-mates' mouths, he is—"

"You shut up!" I roared, brandishing a large sunburnt fist under his nose. "How'd I get the dough I bet on that nag? By goin' fifteen rounds with the heavyweight champeen of the Navy, under a sun that melted the rosin on the canvas. *You* set up in the shade and sucked a soda pop and fanned yourself, and then collected the dough you'd won by bettin' on me. I had the luck to put my end of the purse on a fifty-to-one shot which come in first. Bread outa your mouths! You've already won enough dough bettin' on me—well, anyway, I'm through with fightin', and Clemants nee'n to try to—"

"He ain't trying to sign you up for no fight," said Bill impatiently. "If you'd shut up a second, he'll explain."

"Yes," snapped Hard-cash, chewing down vicious on his cigar. "It's a personal matter. I came to you, because I have to have a man I can trust. What you lack in sense, you make up in honesty.

"Do you fellows know my son, Horace?"

"Naw," we said.

"You wouldn't," he snarled. "He's a sissy. Mizzes Clemants has kept him in fashionable schools most of his life, and he's turned out to be an effeminate sap. Wants to be a musician. A musician! Ha!"

"Well, what about it?" I demanded.

His veins swelled and his eyes flamed, and he chawed his cigar with a noise like a horse chawing cactus.

"What about it?" he roared. "A son of Hard-cash Clemants making his living playing on a *harp?* Not even a jazz band, mind'ja. A derned harp! I want him to be a credit to me. I want to make a man out of him. I want—"

"Well, well," I said impatiently, "what can I do about it?"

"Just what I'm fixing to tell you," he said, and the others leaned across the table expectantly. "He won't play football, or pool, or box, or drink whiskey, or do anything a normal youngster ought to do. He won't have nothing to do with the fight-promoting business at all.

"He's been brought up too soft. He ought to had to fight his way like I did. Ought to been raised tough like I was!

"Not long ago he wanted to marry the daughter of a bookkeeper who was as poor as a Piute Injun—well, I busted that up, and got him to going with Gloria Sweet."

"That was a hell of an improvement," I remarked.

"Well, there's no danger of Gloria trying to marry him," said Hard-cash. "But that ain't the point. The point is, I want you and your pals here to take Horace on a cruise down in the Gulf of California and make a man out of him."

"Maybe Horace won't want to go," I remarked.

"He won't," said Hard-cash grimly. "You'll have to persuade him."

"Shanghai him?" I demanded.

"To put it bluntly," said Hard-cash, "yes. I'll pay you a thousand dollars, and the expenses of the cruise, and furnish a yacht. It's tied up now down by Hogan's Flat. I want you to sweat some of his romantic ideas out of him. Make a deck-hand out of him. Put callouses on his hands; and hair on his chest. Make him forget such junk as books and music. Make a man out of him like his father was at his age."

"Aw, tripe," I said. "You make me sick. You've blowed about yourself till you got a reputation for hard livin' and hell raisin' that you're beginnin' to believe yourself. I know you. You never done a day's work with your hands in your life. Your callouses ain't nowheres near your hands. You got your start as a kid, promotin' fights between newsboys in your old man's stable. Fight your way! You gypped your way. Raised rough! You're too derned crooked to been raised rough."

He got purple and his eyes bugged, but I continued: "Now because this kid don't measure up to what you *think* you was at his age, you want him kidnapped and beat into somethin' you think'll look somethin' like you. You're goin' to bust into the kid's life and get him all messed up, tryin' to change his idees and ambitions, just because you think he ain't worthy of the hard-boiled, two-fisted reputation you've lied yourself into. Nothin' doin'."

"Dennis!" begged my mates, "think of the dough!"

"Think of the devil!" I replied with a touch of old world gallantry. "He's got to get somebody else to do his dirty work. I ain't."

"But, Dorgan!" expostulated Clemants, mashing his cigar in his fingers.

"Nothin' doin'," I said firmly. "Anyway, I'm too busy. I'm a man of affairs now. Billy Ash, of the *Tribune,* give me a assignment to visit the trainin' camps of Bull Clanton and Flash Reynolds yesterday, and write up my impressions of 'em. I heard him give instructions that what I wrote was to be printed just like I writ it. And here it is in the paper."

I proudly drawed forth a copy of the *Tribune,* unfolded it, and waved it before their wondering sight. "Right on the sport pages, with my name to it," I said. "Billy said bein' I was so well known on the West Coast people would be interested in my opinion. This article ought to sell a whole block of ringside seats. So long. I'm goin' over to Reynolds' camp and see how he likes what I writ about him."

And tilting my new Panerma to them, I stalked, swishing my cane like I seen Billy Ash do, and follered by Spike in his new gold-plated collar.

I thought to myself as I hailed a taxi, I bet Billy admired my work, and maybe I'd get a steady job as a sports' writer. Clemants was promoting the Clanton-Reynolds brawl, which was a couple of weeks off, and he was pushing the ballyhoo hard, trying to ruin the advance sales for Shifty Steinmann's show, which was to take place a week later, a non-title brawl between Terry Hoolihan, the middle-weight champion, and Panther Gomez. It was war to the knife between Clemants and Steinmann, each one trying to get control of the boxing business in Frisco. I hoped Billy would let me interview Hoolihan, who was training over in Oakland. I'd never seen him, as he'd just recently come to the West Coast from Chicago.

I dropped Spike off at my hotel, on account of him always fighting dogs that hang around training quarters, and then I went on to Flash Reynolds' hangout. As I entered his quarters, no great distance from the waterfront, I was busting with modest pride. I knew he'd have saw my article by then, and I wondered what he'd say. What he did say smit me with dumfoundment.

Loud voices emerged from the gym, and as I opened the door, I seen Flash and his manager and handlers and sparring partners bending over a paper spread on the table, and they was cussing in a way to curl a Hottentot's wool. They wheeled, and Reynolds give a blood-thirsty yell.

"There he is, the dirty double-crossin' so forth!" he hollered, shaking his fist at me with the paper in it.

"What's the matter?" I demanded.

His manager held his head in his hands and moaned, and Reynolds done a war-dance and squalled like a cougar.

"Matter?" he howled. "*Matter?* Did you write this?"

He brandished the paper at me, and I said modestly: "Sure I did. Don't you see my name at the top?"

"Listen at this!" he howled. "'Today I seen Reynolds and Clanton go through their paces at their training camps. Reynolds is a classy boxer, and would be better if he could punch hard enough to dent a hunk of butter.'"

Reynolds was here so overcome by emotion that he paused in his reading long enough for a few more fantastic dance steps.

"'Reynolds is fast and clever,'" he presently read on. "'It's a pity he has got a glass jaw. But I do not think he is quite as yellow as some folks think, though only time will tell. I would pick Clanton to win by a k.o. in the first round, only Bull is slow as a ox and ain't got very much sense. Bull is got a very powerful punch and it's a pity he is as dumb as he is. It will probably be a fairly good fight and I won't try to pick the winner at this time, but it is my honest opinion that I could lick both of them in the same ring."

Here Reynolds was overcome again and could only howl wordlessly so the goose-flesh riz up on his handlers.

"Well, what's the matter?" I demanded. "I said you was a classy boxer, didn't I? How much flattery you got to have? You want me to lie about you?"

At that he give a most awful scream.

"I'm on to you!" he squalled. "Clanton's manager hired you to write this to upset me, and make me nervous. But it won't work. I was never cooler in my life!"

And to prove it he ripped the paper to pieces, throwed 'em on the floor and jumped on 'em, throwed back his head and howled like a panther, and impulsively rushed across the room and throwed his right at my jaw with everything he had behind it.

I crashed into the wall and rebounding from it, caught him smack on the button with a right hook, and he went to sleep. Ignoring the frenzied shrieks of his manager, I turned and stalked out, and run full into Bull Clanton, who evidently thought my remarks had been inspired by the Reynolds crowd, and was coming over to clean out his enemy's camp.

By mutual understanding we clinched and rolled hither and yon, to the great damage of the artificial shrubbery, and presently breaking free, we riz and traded punches with great energy and violence, until finally I hung my famous Iron Mike on his jaw, and he crashed down amongst the ruins of a potted palm, and remained motionless.

Shaking the sweat out of my eyes, I glared about, and perceived that a familiar figger had arriv on the scene of carnage and was staring at me with open mouth. It was Billy Ash. He started towards me, calling me. My previous experiences hadst embittered me, and disillusioned me. I dimly realized that my innercent remarks was causing trouble, and I supposed that Billy meant to hop all over me about 'em, verbally. I wasn't in no mood to be criticized further, and at the same time, I didn't want to slug Billy. So I turned and hurried away, ignoring his shouts.

I made a flying leap and landed on the running-board of a speeding taxi, the driver of which yelled loudly in startlement, and cussed.

"You shut up," I admonished, twisting a bony knuckle in his ear. "You take me somewheres quick!"

"Where?" he quavered, turning pale.

"To the lonesomenest and most uninhabited place you know of," I said. "I craves solitude."

Well, he said nothing but stepped on it, and I was so engrossed in my gloomy meditations I took little notice of which way he was going, till he pulled up near a dim old street lamp, and said: "This is the lonesomest place I know."

I was still so bewildered at all which had took place, I paid him off like a man in a transom and he hurried away like he thought I might cut his throat.

I then looked about, and presently rekernized where I was. I'd been so busy trying to figger out why Reynolds and Clanton had got mad at me, that I hadn't paid much attention to anything. But now loud and blood-curdling shrieks brung me out of my daze.

I was on a strip of lonely waterfront called Hogan's Flat, a desolate stretch which the only inhabitants was fishermen's shanties. They wasn't even any of them near by, and the only sign of life was a yacht moored a short distance away from a busted old wharf, kinda ghostly-looking in the darkness. From this yacht come sounds of vi'lence and a voice hollered "Help! Murder! Perlice!"

Thinking I rekernized the voice, I hurried towards the wharf, just as a man clumb down the yacht's gangway into a boat, and begun pulling frantically for shore. As he drawed near I could hear him panting and puffing, and leaning over the wharf, I rekernized Bill O'Brien.

"What the blank dash blank?" I demanded picturesquely.

His face was a white oval in the semi-dark as he looked up and gasped: "Is that you, Dorgan?"

"Who else, dope?" I asked impatiently. "What's up?"

He clumb shakily up alongside of me, and he was a rooin. His clothes was tore, he had a peach of a black eye, and a lump on his head as big as a egg.

"Lemme get my breath," he puffed. "It's that hyener of old Hard-cash's."

"What?" I started convulsively. "You mean to tell me—"

"Me and the boys ain't got dough like you has," he defended. "After you left, we talked it over, and we told Hardcash *we'd* do the job, without you. He tried to get the boy on the phone, so as to lure him to the yacht, but the servants said Horace had went out, leavin' word that he was goin' to a night club with Gloria Sweet. So Clemants loaned us his car, and we went to that night club, and sent word in that the young man with Gloria Sweet was wanted outside—everybody knows her, even if they don't know Horace. Well, he come out, and we got him out into some shrubbery, and whilst I got his attention by askin' for a match, Mushy hit him over the head with a belayin' pin, and we dumped him into the car and brought him here.

"He come to just after we got him on the yacht, and Dennis, I dunno what the old man wants him to be made into, less'n it's a ring-tailed tiger. That dern boy is hell on wheels. I tried to explain the matter to him, but he was like a buzz-saw crossed with a spotted hyener. Old man Clemants said he was too mild-mannered, but in all my sailin' of the Seven Seas, I never heard such cussin' as Horace done. First we tried to be gentle with him, and then we fit for our lives, and he knocked Mushy and Sven and Jim stiffer'n a job boom. He was killin' me when I got hold of a hand-spike and managed to daze him for a second. I got him locked up in the cabin now. Listen!"

Across the waters I heard a dull reverberation like somebody beating on a steel drum with a maul.

"That's him poundin' on the door with his fists," said Bill with a slight shudder. "He'd rooint it already, only it's made outa bullet proof steel. Everything on that yacht is bullet proof, it bein' the one old man Clemants used to run rum in.

"After I got him locked up, I seen he was too big a job for me and the rest to handle, and I was afeared to let him out. So I started out to find you—"

"Every time I leaves you saps alone you gets into a jam," I said bitterly. "This reminds me of the time on the African coast when I had to jump overboard and swim ashore to help you let go of a wild cat you'd tried to capture. Come on."

We got in the boat and paddled out to the yacht. The pounding had ceased, and Bill got nervouser than ever, and said he bet Horace was trying to figure out some way to sink the yacht with all hands on board. When we clumb the gangway I seen three recumbent figgers stretched out on deck. Sven and Jim was motionless, but Mushy Hansen was muttering something about saving the women and children first.

"What are you goin' to do?" asked Bill, shivering like he had the aggers. Horace sure had him buffaloed.

"I'm goin' in and talk to Horace," I said. "You stay out here."

"It's suicide," said Bill, whereupon I give a scornful snort, and unlocking the cabin door, I went in. I halted in amazement. I hadn't never seen Horace, but I sure had formed a mental pitcher of him different from the snarling, square-jawed, cold-eyed young pirate which now faced me. I dunno when I ever seen a more formidable physique. He was of only medium height and weight, but his thick neck, square shoulders, deep chest and lean waist was such as ain't often seen, even in the ring. His face was remarkable hard, and his eyes glittered in a most amazing fashion. I was froze with astonishment.

Our guest give vent to a noise which sounded like something in a zoo when he seen me, and begun to move towards me with a sort of supple glide, clenching his square fists. "Another, eh?" he snarled, in a blood-thirsty voice.

"Wait, Horace," I told him. "This has been a mistake all around—"

"Ha!" He laughed like a rasp scraping on a hunk of iron. "I'll say it has—for you. The gamblers put you up to this, didn't they?"

"I dunno what you mean," I said, in some irritation. "If you want to know, the name of the bird which plotted all this, is Hard-cash Clemants."

The mention of his old man's name seemed to make Horace madder than ever. He foamed slightly at the mouth, to my horror.

"Oh, he did, did he? I might have known it!" he gritted. "Well, when I get through with him, the old—"

"Now, now, Horace," I reproved. "That ain't no way to talk about your—"

He turned on me like a hungry leopard.

"How much did the old crook pay you?" he asked viciously. "Well, you'll need it for a lawyer. I'll see that you thugs get ten years apiece for this business."

"Now, you wait," I said sternly. "I had nothin' to do with this, and I ain't goin' to have my mates jugged. I'm goin' to let you loose, but you got to promise to keep your mouth shut."

"Sure," he sneered—"till I get to the nearest police station."

"I see they's no arguin' with you," I said, annoyed by his stubbornness. "I repeat I'm goin' to let you go, but I'm goin' to fix it so you can't lead the cops back here. I'm goin' to put a sack over your head so you can't see where at you are, row you ashore and turn you loose some distance from here."

"The hell you are!" he bristled, cocking his fists.

"Be reasonable," I urged. "You think we want to go to jail? Now here's a sack, and if you'll hold still a second—"

With a hair-raising screech he lept at me and caught me on the jaw with a tornado right swing. I was knocked backwards onto a table, and he was right on top of me, ripping rights and lefts to my body and head. I was bigger'n heavier'n him, but he was all steel and whale-bone. One of his smashes closed my eye, another'n tore my ear, and yet another'n started blood from my nose in streams. Rallying myself, I knocked him clean across the cabin with a left hook under the heart, but he come back fighting, and in self defense I crashed my right to his jaw with all my beef behind it. He hit the floor, out cold.

I grabbed the sack and pulled it down over his head, calling for Bill O'Brien, who come in pale and shaky and stared at the recumbent warrior like he couldn't believe it. But he helped me tie him up, and then we lowered him into the row boat and took him ashore.

We had some trouble getting him up on the wharf, because he was coming to, and beginning to twist and writhe in his sack like a eel with the belly ache, but finally we did, and just as we dumped him down, to rest a second, we heard a auto tearing across the Flat. Bill helped: "The Cops!", but before we could run, it swirled up to the wharf and stopped with a screech of brakes, and out boiled a familiar and pot-bellied figger. It was Hard-cash Clemants and he was foaming at the mouth. His face looked kinda green by the dim street lamp which was the only illumination on the Flat.

"You jackasses!" he bellered. "You blunderers! Where's my son?"

"Don't get sourcastic," snarled Bill, wiping some blood off his scalp. "We're givin' him back. A thousand bucks ain't enough for us to risk our lives. This cannibal don't need no yacht-tour. He needs a cage in a zoo."

"What are you babbling about?" squalled old man Clemants. "While I thought you half wits were grabbing Horace, he eloped with that bookkeeper's daughter! They've married and beat it to Los Angeles! Her old man just phoned me."

"Then who's this?" hollered Bill. I jerked the sack offa our captive's head, releasing the choicest flow of profanity I ever heard. Hard-cash screamed and recoiled.

"My God!" he yelled. "That's Terry Hoolihan, the middleweight champion!"

"And when I get through prosecutin' you in the courts," Hoolihan promised blood-thirstily, "you'll all be breakin' rocks the rest of your lives."

"But he was the one that was with Gloria Sweet—" begun Bill dazedly.

"Horace wasn't with her!" hollered Hard-cash, doing a war-dance on the wharf he was that crazy. "He just left word to that effect, to fool me! He's been using Gloria as a blind all the time! He's been out with that girl Joan, nearly every time I thought he was with Gloria. I tell you, he's married her! Joan, I mean. A bookkeeper's daughter! My God!"

"Well, what's the difference between an honest bookkeeper and a crooked fight promoter?" asked a harsh voice, and we all whirled—except Hoolihan which was still tied and couldst only twist his head around, which he done. It was Billy Ash, and he was madder'n I ever seen him. He walked up to Hard-cash.

"You say one word against that girl and I'll knock your fat head into the bay," he said between his teeth. "The kid happens to be my sister. I don't know what she saw in that sap of yours, but they're married now, and you're going to kick in and help them."

"I'll see you in hell first!" roared Hard-cash. Billy laughed harshly.

"You know what happened tonight?" he said. "Dennis here tangled up with your two prize stumblebums and knocked them both stiff in Reynolds' training quarters."

Hard-cash jumped convulsively.

"What? Oh my God! Is it in the papers?" he squalled like a stricken elk.

"Not yet," said Billy. "I was the only newspaper man there. But you open your yap about Horace and Joan, and I'll scare-head it in the morning paper. You've been building up these bums till the public thinks they're championship material. You've spent plenty on the ballyhoo. It would look nice, wouldn't it, a big headline how old Dennis here cooled both your prize pets? How many tickets you think you'd sell?"

Hard-cash began to shake all over and mop his brow with a palsied hand.

"Don't do it, Billy," he begged. "I've got too much money tied up in this fight. If I don't clear some dough on it, I'm sunk."

"Well," said Billy, "your scrap with Shifty Steinmann is none of my business. But if you don't kick in with some dough for those kids, I'll spill the beans all over the place."

"Sure, Billy, sure!" soothed Hard-cash hurriedly. "I'll mail them a big check the first thing in the morning."

"Ain't nobody ever goin' to turn me loose?" wrathfully demanded Hoolihan. "Wait till I get my lawyer! I don't know what you thugs have been talkin' about but I know Clemants hired me shanghaied to try to interfere with my fight with Gomez. I'll see somebody behind the bars for this!"

Billy turned on him. "Yeah?" he sneered. "How'd you like for your wife back in Chicago to know you're playing around with Gloria Sweet?"

"Hold on," begged Hoolihan. "Don't let that get out. You never saw such a jealous woman in your life. She'd shoot me! Let's just all forget about it, pals."

Whilst Bill O'Brien untied Hoolihan, Billy Ash turned to me.

"Dennis," he said, "why did you run away from me for? I've been chasing you all over the city. That article of yours was a knock out. I'd like to have you do a series of them. A laugh in every line! People wouldn't need the comic strips, with them in the paper."

"I dunno what you're talkin' about," I answered, nettled. "That there article represented my best efforts, to say nothin' of a dozen lead pencils and a stack of paper. Anyway, I'm through!"

"Hard-cash, I want you to get me a fight in the prelims of the Reynolds-Clanton match."

"You mean you're goin' back to fightin'?" exclaimed Bill O'Brien with joy. "And me and the boys can win dough on you some more?"

"I mean I've found the only way I can get along with my feller man is to bust him on the jaw," I answered; "and I might as well be gettin' paid for it."

The Destiny Gorilla

When I come into my dressing room just before my fight with One-Round Egan, the first thing I seen was a piece of paper stuck to the rubbing table with a knife. Thinking somebody was playing a joke on me, I picked it up and read it. It wasn't no joke. It said: "Flop in the first round or your name is mudd." They wasn't no signature, but I rekernized the earmarks. They was a gang of tinhorns working the port, picking up small time dough by dirty methods. They thought they was keeping their tracks hid, but I was on to 'em. They was snakes rather'n wolves, but they'd go to any lengths to make a few dirty dollars.

My handlers hadn't arriv yet, so I was alone. I tore up the note and thowed the pieces into the corner with appropriate remarks, and when they arriv, I said nothing about it. But I was fighting mad when I clumb into the ring, and glaring about the ringside, I centered out a group which I had a good idee was responsible. This group was composed of Waspy Shaw, Bully Klisson, Ned Brock, and Tony Spagalli—cheap gamblers, all of 'em. They smirked at me knowingly, and I knowed I was right, and I controlled a passionate urge to climb the ropes and make hash out of 'em.

At the tap of the gong I was watching Shaw, a hatchet faced, cold eyed, flashy dressed mugg, instead of Egan. Waspy half rose from his seat as the gong sounded, and give me a meaning nod. This so infuriated me that I forgot all about my intention of letting Egan stay a few rounds to give the crowd their money's worth. With the whang of the gong still echoing, I rushed across the ring, ignored Egan's straight left which cut my lip, and buckled his knees with a murderous left hook under the liver. I instantly brought the same hand up to his jaw, and his head went back between his shoulders like his neck was broke. I then sank my right under his heart, and the massacre was over.

The crowd roared in amazement and admiration, and I turned and sneered at Shaw and his henchmen which had leaped to their feet and was glaring with their mouths wide open. Shaw was white and shaking like a leaf. I give 'em a loud, rude and jeering guffaw, and bounding over the ropes, departed for my dressing room.

My handlers made some gestures at rubbing me down, and then hasted back to the ringside to see the rassling match which was coming on next. Not caring for no such amusement, I donned my street clothes and left the building by a side door, attended by Spike, my man-eating bull dog.

As I stepped into the shadowy street, a figger loomed up in front of me, gnashing its teeth. I rekernized Waspy Shaw and made ready for to clout him, but he seemed to be alone.

"You needn't cock your fists," he said, choking with passion. "I ain't startin' a fight on the street. I'm goin' to get you my own way, you double-crossin'—"

"Avast!" I roared threateningly. "I never double-crossed you, you low down, dirty—"

"Didn't you see my note?" he demanded. "Then whyn't you follow instructions? Didn't you have sense enough to know we was bettin' heavy on Egan?"

"Heavy!" I snorted. "If you had one grand sunk altogether it was too heavy for your britches, you cheapskate! Instructions? Why, blast your hide! I ain't workin' for you. What do I care if you lose your dough bettin' against me? You got a hell of a nerve! But you get this, Waspy Shaw, you can't scare me worth a cent. I know it was you and your mob what crippled Joe Jacks in a back alley because he wouldn't throw a fight for you, but I just invites you to try that on me. Call your gang; I'll varnish this pavement with their brains. And get to lee 'ard of me; I hates the smell of carrion."

"You'll regret this," he promised. "I'll get you, Dorgan, and it won't be like we got Joe Jacks. Waspy Shaw never forgets." And so saying he turned away, pausing only to look darkly back over his shoulder, and say: "Remember! Waspy Shaw never forgets!" The dramatic effeck would of been a lot more impressive had I not at that instant planted my boot in the seat of his britches with great force. Waspy hit on his all fours in the gutter, and his bloody-thirsty shrieks was music to my ears as I santered with calm dignity up the street.

As the night was still young, I begun to look for acquaintances in the various saloons and billiard parlors, and eventually found myself in the Free and Easy, which was right next to the Yellow Kitten Cabaret. I decided to go into the Yellow Kitten and watch the girls dance, it being a joint noted for the beauty of its femernine performers, but something the bartender said got under my hide—I forget what it was—and I wasted maybe a hour trying to show him the error of his ways. At last, wore to a frazzle by his stubbornness, I was on the point of climbing the bar and demonstrating the truth of my argument by ramming his bungstarter down his neck, when I felt myself rudely bumped into somebody.

I give no heed, thinking it was a drunk, but presently I was bumped again, and this time so violently that I split my licker.

I turned and looked into the scarred and bellicose face of as tough a looking mugg as I ever seen.

"Listen," I said, "ain't they enough room at this bar for both of us?"

"Who wants to know?" he demanded in a tone which put my teeth on edge. I then noted that another mutt just like him was crowding against me on the other side, and still another'n was standing near by. They must of thought I was a lot drunker'n I really was.

"You know who wants to know," I said, "the rat that hired you told you."

And without warning I handed him a terrible clout on the jaw. When you see a man is set on picking a fight with you, they is no sense in wasting time on formalities. Give it to him first and heavy.

As he hit the floor I wheeled, ducked the swing of a bottle, and hit the wielder in the belly. A pair of brass knucks whanged against the back of my head, staggering me, then a howl of agony told me Spike had went into action.

The man with the bottle busted it over my head without effect other than to irritate me, and then, seeing one of his mates out cold on the floor and the other'n fighting for his life against a while devil-dog, began to back up. He give a agonized grunt as I sunk a fist into his midriff, then broke away and run, with me in groggy but ferocious pursuit. I was plumb berserk and wanted his blood. He dashed into a back room, then, finding me close behind him, turned at bay, snarling like a cornered rat, and lifting a blackjack. But I give a roar and plunged in, and before he could bring it down on my head, I caught him on the chin with a clout that had all my beef behind it.

Them walls was just shells. He catapulted back against the partition so hard he crashed right on through it, with me on top of him, carried by the force of my tremendous blow. We crashed headfirst into the room on the other side, and I heered a woman scream, but I was so blind mad I give no heed. I was on top of my enermy amongst the dust and splinters and I had him by the throat and was banging his head against the floor, meanwhile snarling: "Arrrggghhhhrrrrrr!"

Presently, realizing that he was limp as a rag, some sanity penetrated the red mist that I was in, and I let go and looked around me. I was in a room which had a distinctly feminine air. There was a dressing table and mirror like chorus girls uses, and some frilled and spangled costumes hanging on the wall. And there was a girl, too. She was backed into a corner, with one hand over her heart, and her eyes as big as saucers. She was in a dancing costume, and I realized that I'd busted right into a dressing room of the Yellow Kitten. The hole I'd knocked in the wall was rimmed with awed faces, and Spike waddled through with a satisfied grin, and a piece of bloody britches in his mouth.

I riz and tried to take off my cap, only to find I didn't have none on.

"I begs your pardon, Miss," I said with my usual quiet dignity. "It ain't my habit to burst in on frails this way. I'll take my leave, and lug this hunk of shark bait with me."

"Do—do you know who that *is?*" she said in a small, awed voice. "That's Gorilla Baker; and you've just licked him!"

"Indeed!" I said politely, glancing at my victim with a little more interest. "I reckon you don't know who I am, Miss, or you wouldn't ack so surprised about me laying this thug out."

I got him by the collar and hauled him back through the hole in the wall, where he was took in charge by the inmates of the joint, who took him and my first victim out back and poured water on 'em to revive 'em. The thug Spike hadst assaulted had been took to a sawbones for stitches and other repairs.

I stuck my head back through the aperture to apologize some

more to the frail, when into the room stormed the owner of the Yellow Kitten, tearing his scanty hair and wringing his hands.

"What is this?" he howled. "Verdamnt, I am ruined! Those wild men of the Free and Easy will bankrupt me! What has happened now? Ach, Gott, what a hole in mine wall! A train would go through it! Was that the crash I heard? I'll sue them—"

"Oh, be quiet, Max," said the girl. "It can be repaired, and I'll pay for the job myself."

"You won't neither," I said indignantly. "I'll pay for it—"

"Ahah!" howled Max; "so you are the ape that breaks down mine wall!"

"Yeah, I am!" I replied belligerently, starting back through the hole; "and if you don't like it, I'll—"

"Himmel!" he howled. "Keep avay! Help!" He run like a rabbit, despite his build, and I bowed to the girl, and said: "Pardon me some more, Miss; I ain't goin' to intrude on you no further. I'll send a carpenter around tomorrer—"

"Wait!" she said, coming towards me and taking my hand. "Don't go; come on in. I want a good look at man who can knock Gorilla Baker through a solid wall."

"Yeah," said some of the heads which was still peering in from the Free and Easy, "go in and talk to her, Dennis; we'll all come in!"

"Scram, you alley rats!" I roared, turning on 'em in righteous wrath. "Go some place else before I forgets I'm a gent!" I moved on 'em and they fled, shrieking with terror; or maybe they was laughing.

"Sit down," said the girl, pulling me up a chair. I done so. The fight had cleared my head, and as I looked at my companion, my heart pounded vi'lently in my great, strong, manly bosom. She was so purty she made me dizzy. She set down on another chair, and scanned me admiringly, which caused me to involuntarily expand my huge chest and flex my massive biceps.

"You must be Sailor Dorgan," she said. "And is this Spike your famous fighting dog?"

"Well," I explained, "I don't fight him in the pits, but they ain't a dog in the Orient can stand up to him four rounds. Shake hands with the lady, Spike."

He done so, but rather coldly. The softer passions mean very little to Spike; sometimes it seems like he ain't got no sentiment at all.

"I'm glad to meet you both," she said, "I've heard so much about you. My name is Teddy Blaine. I dance here at the Yellow Kitten. I'd just come off my act when you burst through."

"I'm sorry," I said, "if I'd of knowed the wall was so weak, I'd of knocked him the other way."

"Didn't you break your hand?" she asked.

"Naw," I said, holding up my enormous mauler for her to see. "Just skinned the knuckles a little. I soaks my fists regular in salt brine and whiskey."

She touched it timidly and admiringly felt my iron biceps.

"Gee, you're strong!" she sighed. "I could go for you in a big way!"

"Well," I said, "you ain't so bad, yourself. Suppose we go out somewheres and put on the feed bag for a starter?"

She sighed and shook her head, and her beautiful eyes was wistful and shadowed.

"I don't dare," she said.

"What you mean, you don't dare?" I demanded. "I hope I'm as much of a gent as the next son of a—"

"It's not that," she said quickly, laying her hand on my arm; and shivers went over my huge body at the contack. They is no doubt about it; true love at first sight is a fack; I have experienced it maybe fifty times during my life. I trembled with emotion, and wished I could knock somebody's head off for her.

"No, it isn't that," she repeated. "Anybody can see you're a gentleman. No; I'm a victim of persecution." And with that she bowed her dark head in her slim hands and wept.

I stared at her shocked and horrified. Somehow I discovered my manly arm had got around her supple waist.

"You mean," I said in accents of dumbfounded horror, "you mean to say some low swine has been persecutin' a girl as purty as you?"

"Yes," she sobbed, impulsively laying her head on my massive shoulder.

"Tell me who he is," I urged; "I'll stomp him into mush."

"He's made my life miserable," she whimpered. "He tends bar right across the street at the Yorkshire Tavern, and he has a room at my boarding house. He watches me all the time, and beats up every man who tries to call on me or have a date with me. He's nearly killed half a dozen nice young men.

"He hires the waiters to watch me, and they tell him if I talk to anybody, and he comes over from the Yorkshire and sees me home every night. I never have a chance of getting away from him."

"Who?" I asked.

"He says if he can't have me nobody can," she moaned. "All the boys are afraid to date me up. He's a brute."

"Who, dern it?" I demanded with some impatience.

"Big Bill Elkins," she said.

"Bill Elkins, huh?" I ruminated.

"I knew you'd be afraid of him," she sighed. "Everybody is."

I jumped like she'd stabbed me. "Who's afraid of Bill Elkins?" I squalled outragedly. "I never said no such thing. I was just repeatin' his name. They ain't enough people in the world named Elkins to lick me. Come on, get your hat, you're goin out with me."

"I'm afraid," she whimpered. "He never has socked me, but he might! Then, think of the scandal—you two fighting over me in the public street. He watches this place while he works, and we'd no more than get outside before he'd come surging across the street, roaring like a mad bull. I'll just have to endure his persecutions—unless you could take him off somewhere and beat some sense into him."

"Which is just what I'm goin' to do," I said grimly. "You wait here; when I get back, you'll be a free woman. You'll be Dennis Dorgan's girl, instead of Bill Elkins'."

"Oh, if you only could!" she cried, springing up with her eyes sparkling, and throwing her arms around my neck. "Knock his props loose, for my sake!"

And with that she give me a smacking kiss that sent me outa the Yellow Kitten rolling through a rose-colored fog. I seem to remember stumbling into people trying to dance, and stepping on folks's feet, but eventually I found myself in the street, with the breeze blowing through my damp hair.

I looked up at the stars which was visible among the street lamps, and I said: "To think that a mugg like Gorilla Baker was the cause of me meetin' my true love! When I meets him again, I shakes his hand and gives him a ten-spot. It's Fate, no less. It's destiny, which works not only with vi'lets and moonlight, but with gorillers as well. Gorilla Baker was the tool of Destiny!"

I then went across the street towards the Yorkshire Tavern.

Just as I started in through the swinging doors, I heered Spike growl, and turning quickly, I seen the light from the bar falling on the dark face of Tony Spagalli.

"What you doin', you rat?" I rumbled, drawing back my fist. "If I thought you was tailin' me—"

"Don't hit me," protested Tony. "I ain't do nothin'. Can't a man walk along a public street?"

"So long as he ain't tryin' to shadder me," I grunted. "You can tell your boss that I fixed the thugs he set onto me, and if he gets under my feet, I give him the same treatment. Now get outa my way."

I strode on in, leaving him glowering after me.

I paused a moment within the door, glaring suspiciously at the assembled throng which was guzzling at the bar, gorging free lunch, and shooting craps. As I looked, a big man come through the crowd. He had his coat on, and wore the air of a man which has just quit work for the day. I stopped him.

"Are you Bill Elkins?" I asked.

"Yeah; and what about it?" he demanded.

"I wanta word with you," I said.

"I ain't got time," he said. "I gotta date."

"No, you ain't," I grinned fiercely. "That's what I got to talk to you about."

He started; his square brick-colored face got darker and his narrow eyes glinted.

"What you talkin' about?" he demanded, with a sort of low growl rising in his throat, whilst his big fists closed involuntarily.

"I mean," I said, "that your persecution of Teddy Blaine is at an end."

His eyes begun to blaze with a wild light.

"So you been talkin' to my girl!" he begun in rising roar; "I'll—"

"You'll get a chair over your head in about a minute," I snarled. "Shut up that beller. Want every rat in this joint to hear us scrappin' over the girl? If you got the guts, come out where we can be alone, and fight it out, the best man to get Teddy."

"You're right," he growled. "We won't bandy her name about in this lousy saloon. I know just the place for our brawl. You won't be the first smart sailor I've licked there on account of Teddy. I may be crazy, but if I can't have her, nobody is goin' to get her. I figger if I keep the men away from her, she'll come to me at last."

"A busted jaw will come to you at last," I assured him. Let's go!"

"No, you don't," he snapped. "That bench-legged cannibal stays here. I've seen some of the men he's chewed up. First swing I took at you, he'd rip my guts right out of me."

"I'll leave him at the American Bar," I said. "The bartender there's a friend of mine."

So we left Spike tied in the back room of the American Bar, and very reproachful he looked, too, and then we set out for the place Elkins knowed about. No word was passed between us as we passed through the narrow streets and emerged into a open space. It had onst been a residential section, but now all the houses had fell down or been moved away, and trees and underbrush was growing all around. Elkins passed through a grove of trees, and stopped, and I seen it was a ideal place.

It was a wide sandy glade, like, with a ring of trees all around it. The moon was still hanging above the tops of the trees, and the middle of the glade was as light as day, though a ring of black shadows all around us. Elkins ripped off his coat and shirt and I done likewise. It was very quiet; somewhere a night bird sang out, and I heered a twig snap back amongst the trees.

Elkins come for me without a word, his teeth gleaming in the moonlight, and his eyes blazing like a madman's. He was a big man, bigger'n me, and taller.

I stepped to meet him, and we met in the middle of the moonlit space, slugging with everything we had. Elkins had onst been a prizefighter, and he knowed how to handle his fists. But he was the slugger type, just like me, and anyway, we was both too crazy mad for any fancy stuff, even if we'd been capable of it.

Toe to toe in the moonlight we flailed and battered, till the blood and sweat run down our breasts and wet the sand under our feet. The only sounds was the thud and crunch of our blows, our pantings, gasps, and the rasp of the sand under our feet.

My head was singing and the black trees was reeling like a merry-go-round. Like in a nightmare I seen Big Bill Elkins before me, sweat glistening in hair on his mighty chest, his face ghastly in the moonlight. One of his brows was split so the lid hung down over his eye. Blood streamed from his nose and the corners of his mouth, and his left ear was mangled.

His left side was raw beef where I'd pounded under his heart.

I wasn't in much better case, though my wind was better. One of my eyes was closed, my lips was mashed, and most of the skin was missing from the left side of my jaw.

But I felt Elkins staggering, and I bored in and battered him back across the glade, till we was under the shadow of the trees, and I was slugging blind, hardly able to see him. He was just a big white blur in front of me. Then he throwed his arms about me and hung on, his breath whistling in my ear.

"Time out!" he grunted. "Lemme get my wind, and I'll tromp you into the dirt!"

"Alright," I said; my wind wasn't much affected. I had more endurance, and besides, I hadn't been subjected to the terrible body beating I'd give him. But I ain't one to take advantage. I wants to give the other mugg a even break and knock the stuffing outa him on even terms.

So I stepped back, and Elkins staggered over and slumped down in the sand. His belly was heaving like a loose sail in a typhoon, and you could hear him panting all over the place.

I set down on a log, just at the edge of the shadows, and I said: "Elkins, you ought to know this business couldn't keep up. You can't win a girl by these here caveman tactics—*ooook!*"

The last exclamation was involuntary. Unexpected as the stroke of a cobra in the dark, a naked arm encircled my head and jerked it backwards. Simultaneously a keen edge was pressed against my throat. I didn't have time to do nothing. I just set there, with that steel biting into my flesh so a trickle of blood stole down my neck. I knowed if I moved, my jugular and wind pipe would be severed before I couldst get my hands up. All I could see was the moon gleaming through the black branches overhead.

"Don't move—I cut off your head," hissed a voice I rekernized as that of Ahmed, a Malay killer. Somebody laughed. Then he moved into my cramped line of vision—Waspy Shaw. Brock and Spagalli and Klisson was with him. They stood right over me, and give loud jeering snorts of mirth.

"Well, Dorgan," said Waspy, "you ain't so smart. We been tailin' you ever since you come out of the Yellow Kitten. Didn't figger Tony might be listenin' to what you was sayin' to Elkins, eh? Nice of you and him to come away out here where they won't be no interruption."

"What kind of business is this?" rumbled Elkins, lurching up and striding over towards the group.

"None of yours," snapped Shaw. "We're not after you, Elkins. I guess you won't object to what we do to this gorilla, from what we seen while we was sneakin' up on you. This had worked out just right. Glad you was thoughtful enough to leave that murderin' dog of yours behind, Dorgan. Guess you think you're smart, hey?"

I was seeing red, but with a razor-edged knife at my throat, I seen it was a time for diplomacy, so I merely said: "Go ahead, and do your worst, you yellow-bellied pole cat. I ain't afraid of you. I aims to kick the head offa you yet."

"What you aims cuts no ice," sneered Brock. "Shall we give him the works, Waspy?"

"You ain't meanin' to slug him whilst he's helpless?" inquired Elkins.

"You keep outa this," advised Klisson.

"Yes, it ain't your put in, Elkins," said Shaw. "You better beat it. Hold him, now, Ahmed, and if he so much as wiggles, let him have it! I'm goin' to—"

What he was going to do won't never be known because at that instant Elkins, with a roar, grabbed Ahmed's wrist with one hand and smashed him on the jaw with the other'n. Ahmed flopped, and Elkins come down on top of him from a smash of Klisson's blackjack.

Almost simultaneous I riz like a spring released, blood streaming from a shallow gash in my throat, and hit Klisson so hard he looked down his own spine as he done a tail-spin. Brock throwed a arm around my neck from behind and begun battering at my head with his brass knucks, whilst Spagelli run at me with a knife and Waspy Shaw pulled a gun. I ducked quick and throwed Brock over my head; his flying body hit Spagalli and carried him to the ground with Brock. Waspy Shaw chose this instant to open fire on me, and his first bullet combed my hair; his second notched my ear, and then I kicked the gun outa his hand and caved in three of his ribs with a right hand smash. As he crumpled I hooked my left to his jaw for good measure, and when he hit the ground he was as cold as a pickled herring.

I then turned to look for Brock and Tony, and heered a sound like a native tom-tom. In falling they had rolled over Elkins, and without rising, he had grabbed each of them by the neck, and was banging their heads together, chanting: "She loves me!—she loves me not!"

He throwed their limp carcasses from him, and addressed me: "Don't stand there like a gawk. Come on, and let's get started where we left off."

"But I don't want to fight a man which has just saved my life," I growled.

"Nuts to that!" he roared boisterously. "This ain't a matter of likes and dislikes. It's to decide who gets Teddy."

"That's right." I admitted. "Well, get up and let's get goin'."

He started to heave up, then give a howl and crashed down again, cussing horribly.

"I think my blank-blank leg's broke," he said, with passion. "How in the triple-dash blank can I fight you with dashety-dash leg busted?"

"Lemme feel it," I suggested; and he yelled and swore lustily as I done so.

"Ankle seems to be broke or strained mighty bad," I said. "Must of happened when Klisson knocked you down. Come on; I'll help you home. We'll finish this fight after it heals."

"But in the meantime you'll be steppin' out with my girl!" he yelled.

"Aw, I won't neither," I protested angrily. "I won't go about her, till you're able to fight again."

"You're a white man," he said, "help me up."

So with one of his arms around my shoulders, and with much grunting and groaning and cussing, we moved off through the moonlight. Behind us the glade was littered with corpses, all of which was beginning to writhe and moan with signs of returning consciousness.

It wasn't no cinch getting Big Bill Elkins home. I had to might near carry him, because he couldn't set his injured foot to the ground. But finally we made it, and come into the Yorkshire Tavern in the wee small hours just before dawn. I wondered if Teddy wasn't getting tired, waiting for me in her dressing room. I hadn't anticipated being gone so long.

The streets was deserted, nobody in the bar but the swamper. He gawped at us.

"You fellers been fightin'," he accused us. "What's happened to your leg, Bill?"

"I been kicked by a canary bird!" roared Elkins. "Shut up and get me some linimint."

"Alright," said the swamper. "I didn't have no idee a canary bird could kick that hard. But wait a minute!" He fumbled in his britches pocket and dragged out a crumpled note. "This is for you; it was sent over here from the Yellow Kitten."

Big Bill grabbed it, tore it open, glared at it, then give a terrible scream. He waved it wildly at me, strangling so he was black in the face. I grabbed it and read:

> Dear Bill:
>
> I guess this will teach you that you can't make a girl by beating up all her admirers. When Dorgan knocked Gorilla Baker through the wall of my dressing room, I knew Providence had sent me a tool to work with. I played up to the Sailor and ribbed him up into challenging you for a fight, just to get you out of the way long enough for me to marry the boy I've been nuts about all the time—Jimmy Richards, the boy who played the saxophone down at the All Night Inn. The poor boy was so scared of you he didn't dare come about me while you were around. So I fixed it up this way, and by the time you read this, we'll be married and on our way. It was a dirty trick to play on the Sailor, but a weak woman has to use her wits when she's up against gorillas like you. So long, and I hope you break a leg!
>
> Love,
> Teddy

"Married! A saxophone player! Teddy!" moaned Elkins, and laying his head on my shoulder, he bawled like a bull with the belly ache. "She has scornt my love!" he wept. "She has handed me the gaff! I'm a rooint man. I'm scorned and deserted. Oh, Death, where is thy stingaree?"

I was too paralyzed to say anything; a saxophone player! When she could have had me.

"When you get through soakin's my shirt with tears," I said at last, "lemme know. I craves to go forth and drown my unrequited love in blood and cauliflower ears. This is all Gorilla Baker's fault. If it hadn't been for him, I'd never have got into this mess. He can't make a monkey outa me this way. When I get through with him, I bet he'll be careful whose wall he falls through the next time I sock him."

A Knight of the Round Table

You could of knocked me over with a capstan bar that night in the Peaceful Haven Fight Club when the referee lifted Kid Harrigan's hand along with mine at the end of the bout, thereby declaring it a draw. I felt like I had won by considerable more'n a shade. I had battered the groggy Kid all over the ring in the tenth round, and I ain't a man to be robbed with impunity. Still, if I'd had time to think I very probably would not of socked the referee. But I am a man of impulse. The referee done a nose-dive into the laps of the first row customers, and I impulsively throwed Harrigan after him. Then they was a period of confusion in which me, buckets, chair laigs, infuriated customers, cops and my bulldog Spike was so mixed up it was like trying to untangle a Chinese puzzle. And when I at last walked out of the police station my heart was full of bitterness and disgust.

I retired to the rear corner of a beer-joint where me and Spike sot in solitary grandeur, sipping our beer and brooding over our wrongs. And while we so sot, in come Bill Stark. It was easy to see that he too was not tranquil in his mind. He ordered a stein of Schlitz, and when the barkeep didn't understand his request, Bill repeated it in a blood-thirsty yell which caused several customers to dive under their tables. He brung his fist down on the bar so vi'lently that the wood cracked, and glaring around, inquired in a loud rude voice if anybody there objected to his presence. The customers maintained a kind of pale silence, and then he sighted me, and steered for my table. He sot down and guzzled his drink in silence, eying me ominously, and then he lowered his stein and wiped his mouth and said: "The game's goin' to hell!"

He glared at me like he hoped I'd contradict him, but I was heartily in according with his sentiments.

"Yeah," I said bitterly. "You're plumb right. Do you know what that referee over at the Peaceful Haven done to me tonight?"

But he was b'iling over with his own woes. Bill was a battler of the old iron man school. His style was to walk into his man and let fly with both fists till somebody dropped. He was about my size, with close-cropped sandy hair which habitually bristled belligerently, and one of these here raw-boned weather-beaten faces which hadst long ago had what little beauty it ever possessed pounded out of it. He was all raw-hide and scrap-iron, and about as easy to hurt as a anvil. Just then he had, as usual, a black eye and various skinned places on his ferocious countenance which didn't add none to his looks.

"Look at me!" he howled, pounding on the table till the glasses danced on the bar. "A victim of personal bias! Tonight I met that bum One-punch Driscoll over at the Pleasure Hall. One-punch! Ha! I was a stumblin' block for white hopes when he was in knee britches. I took everything he had for six rounds, and in the seventh I blasted him with a left hook to the belt. And what happens? What *happens?*" he screeched, foaming slightly at the mouth.

"How should I know?" I retorted irritably. There I was, winnin' in a walk, when that—"

"I'll tell you what happened!" he roared. "That blame referee called it a foul! He disqualified me, which never fouled nobody intentional in my life! It wasn't no foul! It was square on the belt-line—"

"Referees is all blind and deaf and dumb these days," I said. "One give me a equally dirty deal over at the Peaceful Haven tonight."

"I got a good mind to quit the cussed game," he said bitterly.

"Me, too." I said.

"I'll leave 'em flat," he said, seemingly becoming more and more taken with the idee. "I'll make my livin' some other way."

"How?" I asked, being merely curious and not sarcastic. But Bill was in such a rabid mood that he misunderstood my intentions.

"I can get by!" he roared, glaring at me. "I got brains. I don't have to punch jaws for a livin'. I ain't like you."

"What you mean by that?" I exclaimed, stung. "I can make my livin' outside the ring as good as you can."

"Yeah," he sneered; "in the forecastle of a tramp windjammer. You been sailin' and fightin' all your life. You ain't got sense enough to do nothin' else."

"Oh, is that so?" I roared. "Well, lemme tell you somethin': I'm quittin' the game tonight, and I ain't goin' to sea, neither."

"Ha!" he snorted. "You couldn't live six months ashore without fightin' for your bread and beans."

"No?" I exclaimed, maddened. "Well, I got a hundred dollars which says I can do it as good as you can!"

"Done!" he yelped, dragging out his roll. "We'll give the stakes to Joe, there, to hold. Hey, Joe!"

The bartender come over wiping his hands on his apron, and we explained the bet to him, and give him our hundreds.

"As I get it," he said, folding up the bills and tucking them away, "if either one of you steps into a ring within six months, t'other'n wins the dough."

"Right!" snapped Bill. "And if Dennis goes to sea within that time, either, I likewise wins."

So we had a drink to seal the wager.

"I'm glad," said Bill, "that you decided to shake the rosin dust off your heels. With all your faults, still you're too good a man to waste your years in the modern ring which is become the prey of vipers and serpents in the guise of referees. Let's go into partnership," he said; "with my brains and brawn, and your brawn, we ought to do well."

"Done!" I said. "And let's stick to it, and not be beguiled by the slick tongues of promoters. On top of our bet we make a gents' agreement not to fight no more, eh?" So we shook hands and had another drink.

"What's our capital stock?" he inquired, and I took inventory and found that putting up that hundred had nigh cleaned me. I had a dollar and sixty-five cents. Bill had five dollars.

"We got to look for work," he said, picking up a paper and shaking it out; and he hadn't scanned the want ad columns more'n a minute, when he said: "Hey, Dennis, this might be somethin' for us." I looked over his shoulder to where his finger was p'inting, and read: "Wanted: two strong, able-bodied men who can keep a secret and do heavy work; good wages with chance of sharing in immense fortune." And it give the address.

"That mention of 'heavy work' don't appeal to my idees of dignity," said Bill. "But till we make a stake we can't be choice. I'll stake us to a room tonight, and early in the mornin' we'll hop over and grab that job. I tell you, Dennis," he said, waxing enthusiastic, "I bet we'll turn out to be big financiers yet. We starts at the bottom and climbs up the ladder to fame and fortune, and when we has enough money saved, we goes into some good legitimate business, like racin' horses or openin' a bar. We'll be wearin' diamonds yet. I tell you—"

He was still talking my ear off when I went to sleep, and he hauled me out of bed before daylight next morning to go apply for that job.

The address was a dingy building in a purty hard looking neighborhood. There was a lot of vacant houses around it, and the house which answered the address in the ad didn't seem to be occupied. We banged at the front door and got no answer so we went around to the back. To reach the back part we went through a very narrow alley and come out into a enclosed court, which was surrounded by brick walls on all sides. The house we wanted backed against this court. They was half a dozen men there already—big, hard, tough-looking eggs which looked us over and discovering that we wasn't from their neighborhood, give us a mean glare.

"What you mugs doin' here?" the biggest one demanded.

"We come to apply for a job," answered Bill, with remarkable restraint for him.

"Well, pull your freight while you're able to," said the tough egg, shoving out his jaw. "The job's already took, see?"

"So are you," said Bill, standing him on his neck with a left hook to the button. The others come for us with yells of rage, not knowing who we was. They was a whirl of action in the court for a few minutes, punctuated by the impact of bony fists on human conks, and the rip of britches' laigs in Spike's iron teeth, and then as the poet says, the tumult and the clouting died, and we had the place to ourselves. The lamentations of the tough eggs was fading away down the alley, a living testimonial to the folly of a mere half dozen men attacking Dennis Dorgan, Bill Stark and Spike.

"The nerve of them mutts," snorted Bill, "interferin' with our rise to fame and fortune! Knock on the door, Dennis."

I done so, and presently it opened a crack, and a voice demanded: "Who are you?"

"We come for that job," I answered. "We seen a ad in the paper—"

"Oh, yes, oh, yes!" said the voice. "Come in!"

The door opened and we seen the man which was talking—a lanky, old-like man in a long-tailed coat and a shiny high silk hat.

"I am Professor Gallipoli Antipodes Jeppard," he said. "It was I who put the advertisement in the paper."

"I'm Dennis Dorgan and this is Bill Stark," I said. "And this is Spike."

He pulled out a monocle without no lens in it, and looked at Spike.

"Remarkable!" he said. "Ugliness exalted to such completeness that it becomes a sort of beauty. The perfection of homeliness! Cave canem!" he said.

"E pluribus onion," said Bill.

"Quit tryin' to put on the dog," I muttered. "This here gent is educated. Well, Professor," I said, "what about the job?"

"To be sure," he said. "Of course. Follow me!"

The room we was in was musty looking and nothing in it. He led us through a hall fixed the same way, with the wallpaper hanging in strips, and down a flight of steps into the basement. Light come in through some busted windows, and there was dirt on the floor and cobwebs all over everything. Outside of that they was nothing down there but some old spades and picks.

"I wish you to dig a hole in this basement floor," he said; "a circular hole, ten feet in diameter."

"How deep?" Bill asked.

"That depends," answered the Professor. "I am at present unable to designate the exact depth required with any measure of accuracy. Let us say the hole is to be excavated to a depth sufficient to fulfill its purpose."

"Uh-well, all right," said Bill. "What's our wages?"

"Three dollars a foot," answered the Professor promptly. "To be paid when the task is completed."

"Alright," said Bill, spitting on his hands and picking up a spade. "We'll start right now."

The Professor sot on a step and watched us without saying nothing. It wasn't easy. First we had to get through the floor, which was bricks and concrete, and when we done that, a few feet down we hit the rock foundations of another house that the present building had been built on the site of. We sweated and we heaved, and by noon we hadn't accomplished hardly enough to show. We knocked off and went and et some dinner at a nearby restaurant, and come back and buckled to again.

The Professor said it didn't make no difference to him what hours we put in, just so we put in plenty; he was paying by the job, and not the day, and the sooner we got through, the sooner we'd get paid. All he asked was that we keep our work a secret and tell nobody what we was doing.

"It will rock the world when completed!" he said, rubbing his long bony hands together. "We will all be famous! The world will acclaim us!"

That heartened Bill up mightily, and he said lets sleep right there in the basement and work day and night till we got through, and that was alright with me.

But that digging was hell because of the foundations under the basement which seemed to go down for ever, and they must have been a dumping ground on the site before the first building was put up, because the soil was full of rocks and cans and broken glass and everything else. The Professor insisted on the hole being exactly round, and exactly ten foot across. Every now and then he'd stop us and measure it to find out if it was just right, and that slowed us up. But he said it was necessary, and that we was doing a great thing for science and humanity.

Well, all that digging give us enormous appetites, and by supper time the next day our funds was exhausted. I dunno where the Professor et. Most of the time he was setting on the steps watching us, or fussing over the hole. I dunno where he slept at night, either. Somewhere up in the house, I reckon, though I never seen any furniture up there anywhere. It looked like nobody had lived in that house for years. Me and Bill slept in the basement on some rags the Professor found for us to make a pallet out of, and it was better'n some of the forecastles I've slept in. Spike kept the rats cleaned out, and it being summer time, we was comfortable enough.

We'd dig all day, except for taking time to eat, and then we'd work by the light of a old lantern until we was too tired to hit another lick. They we'd lay down and sleep till maybe daylight, and be up and at it again.

Well, when we riz the third day of our job, and us with no money, I was inclined to grumble some, because I was hungry, but Bill said: "Fame and fortune don't come easy. Maybe today he'll decide the hole is deep enough. We can go awhile without eatin'."

So we sot to work, but by noon I couldn't stand it no more.

"Lissen," I said to the Professor which was setting on his step as usual, "as Napoleon said, no slugger can win bouts on a empty belly. Suppose you advances us some dough to buy grub with. Spike here has stuffed hisself on rats, but bein' neither a bulldog nor a Chinaman, I got to have some regular grub if I'm to go on excavatin'."

The Professor studied awhile, and then said: "Leave the matter to me, my friends. In my scientific zeal, I have forgotten the human aspects of the adventure. I shall sally forth and replenish the larder. It is true that my financial resources are at present practically zero, but the superior mind rises above such trivial handicaps."

He pulled out, and Bill hit a few licks with his pick whilst he digested them remarks, and presently he said: "Did he mean he didn't have no dough?"

"It sounded like it," I said, digging my pick under a fifty pound hunk of broken concrete.

"Hmmmmm!" said Bill; and his hair commenced to bristle.

Presently the Professor returned and placing some articles before us, said, with a magnanermous wave of his arms: "Feast and satisfy the inner man, my friends!" He'd brung us a can of spinach and a box of salted crackers.

Well, old-timers like me and Bill has long learned not to kick at what we gets, but to be thankful we gets anything. We licked up that slush purty quick, but as we started back to work, Bill said: "Did I understand you to say you was broke?"

"Alas, my friend, to frame it in the argot of the common herd," said the Professor, "such is the case."

"Then how," demanded Bill, halting with his pick in the air, "do you expect to pay us?"

"That, my friends," said the Professor, looking mysterious, "is a matter which adjusts itself automatically. Never fear, my good friends; you shall be paid. My honor upon it. When your task is completed, wealth and fame shall pour into your laps as into mine! The work is hard, but the reward shall be proportionate. I assure you!"

Well, that encouraged Bill, and he sailed into that cussed hole with renewed vigor. We worked hard all day, and for supper the Professor dragged out more crackers and spinach. He sung the praises of the latter muck, and told us how much energy it generated, till I had a hysterical desire to cram the can down his gullet. The hole was getting so deep we had to rig a ladder to climb out of it, and me and Bill argued about what it was for. Evidently what we was to find was going to pay for itself. I believed we was sinking a shaft down to a vein of gold the professor knowed about somehow, and Bill thought he had got hold of a map showing where some pirates had planted their loot. Our tempers was frazzled on account of all the spinach we had et, and we nigh come to blows arguing about it.

The next day dawned and with it the Professor with more spinach; dinner and supper it was the same. I would of give my ear by that time for a sirloin steak fried with onions, and I gagged every time I seen a blade of grass, it reminded me so much of spinach.

We was so weak from starvation that we knocked off about sundown that day. Bill looked at the hole, which was beginning to resemble a well, and allowed the Professor owed us a smart passle of dough, but from the way he kicked his pick across the basement, I believed some of his fervor was feigned.

We was so tired we fell into our rag pallets immediately. The Professor had went to wherever he slept at night. I was awful tired, but so hungry I couldn't get to sleep. Anyway, I knowed when I did go to sleep, it would be to dream of mountains of spinach which I was forced to tunnel through with a blunt toothpick. I was laying there with my eyes about half-shut, when suddenly I seen Bill rise up stealthily, glance over towards me kind of furtively, and pull on his shoes. Spike lifted a ear to him, and Bill shhhh'd him very energetic with his fingers to his lips, and then snuck up the stairs and was gone.

Then I riz. I didn't know where Bill had went and I didn't care; but I had to have something in my belly more substantial than spinach and hydrant water. I put on my shoes and me and Spike sallied forth. It was the first time I'd been out of that cussed old house for days, and for the first time I realized how much like a jail it'd been. Riches and fame, I reflected, hauling in my belt another notch, comes neither soft nor easy.

I headed out of that neighborhood and into a more respectable section, looking for a acquaintance I couldst borrow a few bucks offa, when who should I run into but Jack Pendleton, a wealthy young sportsman who hadst won many a kopeck betting on my massive maulers.

"Just the man I'm looking for!" he exclaimed, slapping me

heartily on the shoulder. "Dennis, how'd you like to pick up fifty bucks?"

"My pockets is empty and so likewise is my stummick," I said; "but if it's got anything to do with mayhem inside the squared circle, I gotta be counted out."

"What?" said he. "You mean you don't *want* a fight? Great Jupiter, to think I'd ever live to see the day! Why, that's like hearing a fish say he didn't like water!"

"T'aint a matter of personal likes, Jack," I said. "Between you and me, my knuckles is itchin' for the feel of leather again. But I've retired from the game, and me and Bill Stark is got up both a bet, and a gentleman's agreement for neither of us not to fight no more."

"Shucks," said Jack. "I'm sorry. After all, this job I had in mind wasn't an actual fight, but more like a freak exhibition. You see this is ladies' night in my club, the Corinthian. It isn't a sporting club, by the way. It's what you'd call a high society racket, and it's part of my social burden that I have to belong to it. Well, we're giving a lawn-fete, and the committee of entertainment racked their minds to hit on some unique form of amusement which hadn't been run into the ground by every other club in town, and as a joke I suggested having a couple of heavyweights stage a boxing match in medieval armor. To my amazement they took it seriously. One of the members hired two suits of mail from a museum, and the go is to be staged tonight—in about an hour, in fact.

"One of the other members just phoned me that he had found a man who would take part in it, and I've been trying to dig up another fighter who was at leisure."

"You mean box in them iron togs like them old knights wore?" I said.

"Exactly!" laughed Jack. "Crazy, isn't it? But I think what appealed to the club members was the fact that no gore would be spilled, and no damage done. Those gentlemen of the Corinthian aren't accustomed to violence. I wish you'd come in on it. Your real name won't be used, and with a helmet on, nobody'd ever know you'd taken part in it."

"Fifty bucks," I mused; "and Bill wouldn't never know." Then I sighed. "No, Jack," I said, "I'm afraid I can't do it. It's too much like—" I broke off with a involuntary howl that made Jack jump. We was just passing a cafe, and a luscious aroma of fried steak and onions was wafted to my quivering nostrils. It drove me clean out of my mind.

"What did you say?" Jack gasped.

"I said gimme that fifty!" I gibbered. "Every man has a limit to his endurance, and this here's mine! What shall it profit a man to gain fame and fortune after he's rooint his belly on spinach? Gimme the fifty in advance, and I'll fight the Japanese navy with tin britches on!"

Jack peeled the bills off his roll, but he said: "You're not going to eat this soon before the fight, are you?"

"You watch me!" I advised. "I got a hour before the brawl commences, and I aim to put in every available minute of that time stowin' grub down my starvin' hatchway!"

Well, thereafter I kinda floated away in a dreamy paradise of porterhouse steaks, gravied onions, French fried pertaters and beer, from which blissful state I was finally aroused by Jack's insistent urgings that we wouldst be late for the brawl. So I riz and follered him into his car which was parked nearby, follered by Spike which bulged considerable in the belly. He had appreciated steak and gravy hisself after a steady diet of cellar rats.

I didn't ask Jack who the other thug was, because my opponents is a matter of indifference to me. I laid back and helped Spike enjoy the ride until we pulled up at the back of a big club house. I could see over the stone wall, and seen a big lawn to one side, and they was a lot of women in evening gowns and diamonds and men in dress suits, and everything was lit up by Japanese lanterns in the trees, and servants in white monkey jackets carrying drinks and sandwiches around on trays, and right in the middle there was a ring fixed up, with chairs all around. They was a big tent pitched on the lawn a short distance away, and they had a kind of alleyway built outa striped canvas running from the tent to the ring. Jack said the idee was to let the fighters in their armor get into the ring unseen, so as to spring a surprise on the guests.

We went into the club house and through it, and ducked across the edge of the lawn and into the tent without anybody paying much attention to us. Most of 'em was dancing in a kind of fancy pavilion. The tent was to serve as dressing rooms, it being divided into compartments with partitions of colored canvas. Jack took me into one of these compartments, and him and the menials of the club begun to get me into my armor.

I just took off my shoes and cap and coat and the junk was put on over the rest of my clothes—things Jack called the breastplate and back plate and corselet and helmet and gauntlets. The gauntlets was iron gloves, jointed so I would work my fingers; and they was iron britches and leg pieces and iron shoes, and altogether it was the damndest looking rig you ever seen. But after I got it all on it wasn't near as clumsy to get around in as I'd figgered it'd be, the weight was so evenly distributed all over my body. But that don't mean I could skip a rope in it! When I walked I sounded like a runaway tin shop, and swinging my fists encased in them iron gauntlets I realized a swat with one of them wouldn't be no lady's kiss.

Purty soon a gent stuck his head in and said the other man was ready—he called him a "gladiator"—so Jack said for me to come on, and we salled forth into the alley way. There was another feller dressed just exactly like me, already headed for the ring, and I follered him, casting kinda dubious glances at his iron-covered mitts, whilst Spike smelt of his steel-sheathed laigs, very curiously.

We went clanking down the alley way like a couple of street cars off the tracks, and clumb into the ring where some fellers in silk tights and embroidered jackets and feathered caps was blowing on horns. The dancing hadst ceased and everybody was setting in the chairs around the ring, looking at it through monocles and lorgnettes, and when us walking steel works come banging and clanging out onto the canvas, they was a refined murmur of surprise and delight, and everybody clapped their hands politely, and some said: "Here! Here!" like they was answering a roll call or something.

We retired to our corners, where they was more fellers dressed in them silk monkey-clothes to ack as our handlers, and Jack got in the center of the ring and made a speech. I couldn't hear everything he said, because of my helmet. I kept trying to raise the vizor so I could hear better, but one of the fellers in tights said keep it down, because the ladies wasn't accustomed to the sight of such pans as mine. I felt slightly insulted, but after all, I was being paid for this, so I sot still and managed to hear the last of Jack's speech.

"And so," said he, "the chivalry of San Francisco is tonight arrayed to display its valor before the gaze of fair ladies as in the days of yore when knighthood was in hock—I mean in flower. In that corner, Sir Lancelot of Market Street!" He p'inted at me, so I attempted to rise and failing, shook my iron-cased hands above my head at the crowd, and they applauded gently. "And in that corner," said Jack, "Sir Galahad of Oakland!" The other mug ariz with a clanking like a blacksmith shop in a earthquake, and again they was cultured applause. "Let the joust begin!" said Jack, retiring to my corner.

Then a scholarly gent in full dress clumb into the ring, and I gathered he was to be the referee, though I doubt if he had ever seen a ring fight.

"Don't go at it too violently," muttered Jack, helping my handlers hoist me offa my stool. Setting down in that rig was a mistake. "Most of these lily-fingers would keel over at the sight of a drop of blood."

"I won't do nothin' to shock their senserbilerties," I promised, and then the gong hit a lady-like peal and me and Sir Galahad of Oakland come clashing to the onslaught.

It was the craziest bout I ever fit. I couldn't see my opponent's face because of his helmet, which, like mine, just had a slit with iron bars over it to look through. Our footwork was slow and ponderous; when we tried to step around fast, it was about like a couple of ten-ton trucks trying to do a tango. Every time we landed a punch it sounded like a sledge hammer hitting a anvil, and Sir Galahad's iron-clad knuckles dinning on my helmet dang near deafened me. They was no need for ducking or guarding because we couldn't hurt each other, and so for three rounds it went, the din getting louder and louder as we begun to warm to our work.

We was now slugging away with earnest abandon, and the ladies putting their hands over their ears, and dints was beginning to show on our armor. It seemed like they was beginning a kind of murmur in the crowd, though I couldn't be sure, because my ears was ringing so loud with the banging and clashing of iron against iron. But I gather that our exhibitions was taking on too much energy for them hot-house orchids of culture, for when I went back to my corner after the third, Jack lifted my vizor a little and said: "Ease up, Dennis! This is getting too realistic for the club-members. They're getting nervous. Yes, I know nobody's getting hurt, but the mere impulse towards injury is too brutal for these people."

So I said alright, but Sir Galahad's handlers must not of thought to warn him. As we come up for the fourth he lashed out with such a terrible right-hander that he cracked my breastplate. I retaliated with a left hook to his belly that made him grunt, in spite of his armor, and he whanged away with a right from the floor that broke some of the screws that held on my head-piece.

Not to be outdid I swung my right to his head with such

terrific impact that it snapped all the rivits of his helmet and tore it off his head, and he hit the canvas with a clatter like a flock of wash tubs falling downstairs.

A scream went up from the shocked guests, and I halted short myself. The breaking off of that helmet hadst exposed the battle-scarred and close-cropped head of *Bill Stark!*

Some of the ladies hollered, the sudden display of them battered features wouldst shock any sensitive person. But I'd forgot my environments temporarily. I wrenched off my own head-piece and glared down at him in surprise and wrath.

"So that was where you snuck off to whilst I slept!" I accused heatedly. "A agreement means a lot to you!"

"What about you, you double-crossin' griller?" he howled, scrambling up with a noise like a boiler factory going into action. "I ain't busted our agreement no more'n you have! I didn't sneak out with the intentions of gettin' a fight. I was lookin' for a square meal. I'd et spinach till I was nigh crazy. I thought you was asleep. A fine pal you are!"

"And a sweet business partner you turned out to be!" I said fiercely. "Fame and fortune, ha! I should of knowed better'n to make a gentleman's agreement with a mug like you—"

"I'm as much of a gentleman as you be!" howled Bill, frothing at the mouth, and to prove it he let go with a left hook that caught me on the ear. Ow, murder! It was worsen't being hit with a brick! His iron knuckles crushed my cauliflower like a cabbage hit with a hammer, and the blood spurted all over the referee's shirt front. At the ringside guests screamed and fainted, and they wasn't all women.

I reeled like a steel mill in a typhoon, and come back with a iron-clad right full in Bill's mouth. Blood and teeth flew in every direction and more folks fainted. The rest was jumping up and screaming and falling over chairs, and hollering for the cops. The referee yelped and run forward and laid hold of me yapping; "Here, here, we can't have this, you know!" It was unfortunate that at that instant I was jerking back my left for a punch at Bill. The sharp iron joint of my armored elbow caught the referee in the solar plexus and he squeaked and curled up on the canvas, and me and the good Sir Galahad come together like a couple of infuriated iron foundries.

In the next few minutes I done more and better blocking and ducking than I ever done before or since in any fight; I didn't crave for one of them iron gauntlets knotted up into a big fist to connect with my unprotected head again.

Bill had the same idee. The noise we had made before wasn't a scratch to the din that now ariz. Our four arms was like that many sledge hammers flailing madly away and knocking sparks of fire with every lick. About the time that Bill's armor begun to come to pieces under my terrific battering, a flock of cops come pouring onto the lawn, summoned by the frantic howls of the club members which was hysterical with seeing a classic tilting joust turn into a bloody ring battle right before 'em. I didn't see Jack, he'd ducked when he seen the fat was in the fire.

A big cop jumped up onto the edge of the ring just in time to stop a chunk of steel that whizzed off Bill's breastplate under my smash like a chip knocked off a tree by a axe. The cop stopped the chunk with his mush and begun a series of loop-the-loops which didn't cease till he rammed his nose to the hilt in the turf.

Seeing this, and hearing the infuriated yells of the other bulls, I fell back and hollered warningly to Bill, snatching up my helmet as I done so. He seen the idee and follered my example. Clapping on our headpieces we went through that army of flat-foots like a couple of armored tanks. Their night-sticks beat a tattoo on our helmets as we charged through 'em, and their langwidge was terrible, but they couldn't stop us nor hurt us.

Thanking my stars that most of my clothes was on under that iron, I headed for the wall, with Spike at my heels. I couldn't see Bill, because just then somebody turned out all the lights—it was Jack, I learned later. I went over the wall like a barrel full of scrap iron, and presently belated wayfarers was dumbfounded by the sight of a knight in full armor careening down the street. I bet they heard my iron shoes hitting the sidewalk half a mile away. I sounded like a string of run-away freight cars in full flight.

I have a vague recollection that a cop on his beat shot at me as I hurtled past, but the slug ganced offa my corselet, and presently I spied a alley and ducked down it. Thereafter, a short time later, anyone watching at the other end would of spied a sailorly individual without cap, coat or shoes emerging furtively follered by a while bulldog. The accounterments of the good Sir Lancelot was reposing in a ash can down the alley.

I hailed a taxi and clumb in, discouraging comments with a glare which caused the driver's hair to stand up, and he done my bidding without no fool questions. So presently I limped down the narrow alley and into the court which joined the house where me and Bill was building our fortune.

A figger was setting broodingly on the back steps, and by the light of the street lamp at the mouth of the alley, I seen it was the good Sir Galahad of Oakland, minus his armor. He spit out a mouthful of blood, disclosing a wide gap where his teeth had formerly been, and stared at me somberly.

"How did you get away?" I asked.

"Jack snaked me out and brung me here in his car," he said. "We looked for you, but couldn't find you."

A short silence ensued, and then he said: "I got here just in time to see 'em takin' the Professor away."

"Away?" I said. "Who? Where?"

"Back to the looneytick asylum he escaped from," said Bill. "They been huntin' him for over a week. They finally traced him by the things he's been swipin' from nearby grocery stores—crackers and spinach!"

"A nut!" I said numbly. "Then he didn't own this place?"

"Naw," said Bill gloomily. "He just moved in without askin'."

"But all that work we done!" I said wildly. "Don't we get no pay—"

"Do you know what we was diggin'?" he demanded, and I said: "No!"

"A tunnel to China!" he said. "The Professor told me as they was takin' him off."

I started to say something, but couldn't think of nothing appropriate enough, so I sot silently, and Bill said: "I'm goin' back to the fight racket; it ain't as crazy as anything else I've tried so far."

"Well," I said, "we both busted our agreement, and both lost that bet, so we each got a hundred dollars in addition to what we got for playin' knights for them saps. The *Python* docks here a week from now, and when she sails," I said, "I'm goin' to be on her. And between now and then I'm goin' to fight every night if the promoters sign me up. I have slaved and suffered and bled in the ring," I said, "but I have yet to meet even a referee which tried to drown me in spinach."

Playing Santa Claus

There ain't nothin makes me madder'n to see a big hulk abusing a kid. So when I seen a big Chinaman beating up a skinny, howling young'un in the mouth of a alley, I ignored the rule which says white men should mind their own business in Peiping. I jerked the big slob away from the kid and booted him heartily in the pants to teach him manners, and he had the nerve to draw a knife on me. This irritated me, and I wiped his chin with a left hook which stood him on his neck in the gutter and caused the onlookers—all Chinese too—to scatter with wild shrieks.

Ignoring them as I generally does Chineses except when I have to sock 'em, I picked up the kid and wiped the blood offa him, and give him my last dime, which grasped in his skinny fist as he run off with his ragged shirt tail flapping.

I then glanced at a nearby grog shop, slapped my empty pockets and sighed in a fillysofikal manner, and was about to go on my way, when I heard a voice remark: "You seem to be a lover of children, my friend."

Supposing somebody was giving me the razz for giving my last cent to a Chinese kid, and being sensitive that way, I wheeled, lifting my upper lip and drawing back my right mauler. "And what of it?" I demanded in a blood-thirsty voice.

"It is most commendable, sir," said the fellow which had spoke, and which I now looked at more closely. It was a tally, skinny, bony-looking man with a shiny, worn black suit on, which the coat had long tails, and a broad-brimmed hat. He had a very sober face and didn't look like he'd ever smole in his life, but I liked his looks.

"I begs your pardon," I said with dignerty. "I thought I was bein' addressed by some low-lifed son of a—uh, sea-cook."

He looked me up and down, ruminating on my massive arms, my broad chest and my battle-scarred features.

"Under many a rough exterior throbs a noble soul," he mediated. "Those cauliflower ears may well conceal a heart of gold. No man who defends a child can be wholly bad, however much he may look like a gorilla—ah, I beg your pardon. I did not realize that I was speaking aloud. I am Dr. Ebenezer Twilliger. I run a mission school back up in the hills." And he stuck out his bony hand.

"And I'm Dennis Dorgan, A.B.," I said, taking it, "generally of the trading ship *Python*, when not wanderin' around loose as I am at present. And this here's Spike, my white bulldog, the fightin'est criter in the Asiatic waters. Shake hands with his reverance, Spike."

Spike done so, and the missionary said: "I gather you are at present unemployed. Would you consider a small job with me? I could not pay you much, but—"

"Anything for a little dough," I said.

"Well," he said, twining his bony fingers together, "I am in the habit of giving the mission children a regular Christmas—"

"By golly!" I said. "Tomorrer is Christmas Eve, ain't it? I'd forgot all about it."

"I came into Peiping to buy some toys," he said; "but a little while ago one of my native assistants, Wang, rode in and urged me to return at once. The people at the mission are afraid of bandits. The bandit chief Kwang Tzu has a hide-out somewhere in the vicinity, and has repeatedly threatened to destroy the mission. Providence," said Dr. Twilliger with a longer face than ever, "and the rumor that we are provided with high-powered Winchesters, has kept him at a distance so far. But in my absence the converts have become alarmed.

"I have procured only part of what I came after, and have found no one to play Santa Claus. My white assistant, young Reynolds, who has always enacted the part, is in Tiensin recovering from an attack of cholera. We have but the one costume which I brought with me from America, the last time I was in the States, and as it was made especially for Reynolds, I fear I would appear far from convincing when attired in it."

I was inclined to agree with him.

"Reynolds is about your build, though nothing like as muscular," he said. "You would do nicely."

"Sure," I agreed heartily. "I'd be glad to do it for nothin', just to give the kids a treat."

"I insist on paying you for your time and trouble," he said, and I knowed he was a square-shooter. "I shall return at once with Wang, leaving my car here for you. That is it standing over there." He pointed at a old Model T Ford which looked like it'd been through a war. They was a big box in the back seat. "Such toys as I have had time to purchase are in that box," he said. "You will complete the purchases," he dragged out a list on a long strip of paper, "and tomorrow you will come to the mission. By starting at dawn you will be able to make it to the mission by nightfall. Here are the proper directions," and he gave 'em to me.

"The Christmas exercises should be well under way when you arrive. I will meet you at the back gate of the compound, with the Santa Claus costume. I wish you to be in the nature of a surprise to the children."

"Alright," I said. "I ain't never heard of Santy Claws havin' no bulldog, but Spike'll have to come along with me."

"Of course," said Twilliger, pulling Spike's ear, which he don't allow many people to do, but wagged his stump-tail and grinned like a saw-toothed dragon.

"Here is the money for the toys," said Twilliger, dragging out a wallet, "also your own money in advance. Is that satisfactory?"

"More'n enough for the job," I said. "But gee whiz, how do you know I won't double-cross you, blow all the money in on licker, and never show up at the mission at all?"

"I am a fairly good judge of men," he said. "I look at your eyes, not at your misshapen ears or broken nose. A man like you could never be a thief, or rob children."

And so saying he turned and stalked away in his old warped brim hat, with his coat tails flopping, and he was awkward and bony and funny to look at, but he'd left a warm spot in my tough old bosom, and I wished some fellers would start something with him so's I could show him how much I appreciated what he said by stomping them into the ground.

Well, I took the list and started making rounds of the bazaars and shops. You'd be surprised how many places in the Orient you can buy American-made toys. I just about bought out the joints, as well as a lot of native trinkets and kites and things that Chinese kids likes. When I'd got through I'd spent all the money Twilliger had give me for the purpose, and some of my wages, too, but I had a lay-out I figgered no Santy Claus wouldst be ashamed of.

I was just concluding a dicker over a doll in a shop down in a quarter when lots of white men hang out—them Chineses will skin your eye-teeth if you don't watch out—when I heard a incredulous gasp, and wheeling, I seen Spike Hanrahan, as tough a mugg as ever walked the deck of a whaler, glaring at me with amazement and disgust. I was struck speechless by his expression, and then he turned and made a bee-line for a saloon across the street. Well knowing his intentions I give a roar of rage and charged after him.

As I come through the door of the bar, I seen Spike holding forth to a astounded and hilarious crowd, and as he seen me, he yelled: "There he is! And lookit! He's got it in his hand!"

I glanced down and noticed with some annoyance that I'd absent-mindedly brung along the doll.

"Lookit at him!" sneered Hanrahan. "A doll! At his age! Dennis Dorgan, the bully of the toughest ship afloat! And *he* buys hisself a *doll!* I got a good mind to slap the big sissy on the wrist—"

With a roar of righteous wrath I handed him a left handed clout which sent him reeling into the bar. He give a bloodthirsty howl and rebounded, with a smash to my ear, and then I crashed over my right to his jaw, and he hit the back door so hard his head went right on through the panels where he remained in a attitude of slumber. I then wheeled on the horrified audience.

"Yes, I been buyin' toys, all day!" I roared with blazing eyes, brandishing the doll defiantly. "And what's more, I'm goin' up to the Twilliger Mission tomorrer to play Santy Claws for the kids. I ain't in the habit of askin' a crew of barroom bums permission for what I do. I'll buy dolls when I feel like it, and I'll set on the curb and cut out dresses for 'em if I feel like it! And if any of you blasted skunks got any smart remarks to make, step up here and make 'em! Yeah, do! And get your bone heads kicked through the wall. Well, whyn't you speak up, you lily-livered, goose-starned, yellow-bellied gutter rats? Whyn't *you* say somethin', for instance?" I barked at a big limey which had been laughing the loudest over Hanrahan's tale.

He gulped like he was trying to swaller his tonsils, and said weakly: "Huh-have a dud-drink!"

With a belligerent snort of disgust I turned and stalked out of the joint, and was striding acrost the street when I heard somebody yelp: "Oh, sailor! Wait a minute!"

I turned around and a small dapper-looking feller come running out of the saloon. He had a thin keen face and was dressed better'n most.

"Well, what'a *you* want?" I rumbled, drawing back my right mauler.

"Wait, wait!" he panted, throwing out his palms. "I don't want to fight. Didn't I hear you say you were going up to the Twilliger Mission tomorrow?"

"Well, what about it?" I inquired, still smarting from the undeserved ridercule I hadst endured.

"Did you ever hear of the Abercrombie Missions?" he said.

"Naw," I said.

"Well," he said, "it's between here and Dr. Twilliger's mission, but off the main road. I send a box of toys up there every Christmas for the kids, but this year, though I have the toys, I have no way of getting them up there. Would you consider delivering them? You won't have to drive out of your way. Men from the Abercrombie Mission will meet you along the road and take the toys."

"Sure," I said, mollified. "I'll be glad to. I leave here at dawn tomorrer. Where at's yor toys?"

"Do you know the deserted temple, called the House of the Dragon, which lies outside the city?" he said. "You'll pass right by it on your way. I'll have the toys there at dawn."

"I'll stop for 'em," I promised him, and then I took the toys I'd bought to Twilliger's car and put them and Spike in. I driv into a alley and slept in the car that night to keep somebody from stealing it or the toys and I dang near froze before morning, but I'm used to hard living. Before dawn we was on our way.

I stopped by the ruined temple which stood in a grove of trees off to itself, and the fellow I'd talked to was waiting, with another man, a big galoot which looked like a sea captain. He was a Greek or something. They had a box which looked exactly like mine, but must of been considerable heavier from the way they grunted as they hove it in. I told 'em to put it on the right side; my box was on the left side.

"A few miles from the Twilliger Mission," said the well-dressed man, "there's a place where the road forks, and there's an old stone idol there. Stop the car and wave this rag—" he gimme a strip of red cloth. "That will be a signal for the men from the Abercrombie Mission. They'll be watching for it. Have you a pistol? There are bandits in those hills."

"Naw," I said. "I don't need no pistol. I never seen the man I couldn't lick with my bare fists."

"Well, bon voyage," they said.

"Bum voyage to you, too," I said courteously, to show 'em I knowed foreign langwidges too. Then I driv off and left 'em standing in the dawn there before the ruins, watching me out of sight, which was soon, because the wind was kicking up dust in clouds that nigh blinded you, even that early in the morning.

I hadn't drove a mile when I seen a squad of soldiers with rifles standing in the road, and a officer in a dinky braided cap held up his hand and motioned me to stop. I done so impatiently, and he clumb on the running board—a dapper young fellow from Canton, by his accent, which had probably went to school at Yale or somewheres.

"What are you hauling?" he demanded, poking the box which had my toys in it. Spike growled at him, and I said: "Stop that! You bust them toys and I'll bust your head. I'm takin' em to a mission up in the hills. I'm Santy Claws." He looked at me very funny, and I said: "Gwan, open the box if you don't believe me. And get through wit it. I'm in a hurry."

He done so, and looked surprised when he seen what was in it.

"I wanted to be sure you were not hauling contraband," he said in better English'n what I generally speaks. "There is great smuggling activity now, and European weapons and ammunitions constantly find their way into the hills. I won't bother to open the other box. You may go."

"I'd like to know who'd stop me!" I growled pugnaciously. Folks says I'm too ready for trouble. I ain't; I merely insists on respeck, and it rasps my senserbilerties to be suspicioned for a smuggler or something. So I driv off in a dudgeon, and presently I come into the open country and the hell begun.

I could easy see why Dr. Twilliger's car looked like a wreck on a lee shore. I never seen such infernal roads. They wasn't rightly roads at all, and they was evidently built for jackasses instead of men and machines. Them narrow-wheeled Chinese carts leave roads in a awful shape.

Them car-springs must of been made outa whalebone; we took jumps I didn't think no automobile wouldst stand. We hit bumps that throwed me clean over the steering wheel, and we fell into depressions that nigh driv my spine through the top of my skull. Spike got throwed out seven times, and once I run clean over him before I could stop the cussed machine. I figgered he was kilt, but he was too tough even for that to hurt him.

I'm afraid my langwidge didn't sound much like Santy Claus; I plumb exhausted my vocabulary within the first ten miles. We begun to wind up into the hills at last—I say wind; that's what the road done. The car jumped and bucked and lurched and pitched, and once it lay over on its side entirely and the boxes come tumbling out on top of Spike, and I wondered if all the toys was busted. But I couldn't do nothing if they was. I put some more knots in the ropes which was tied around 'em, and heaved 'em back in the car, and righted it by main strength, and we went on. Driving careful wasn't getting me nowheres and I got disgusted and took it as fast as the bus would go, and the way we bounced over gullies and hurdled ridges was a caution.

It was a very dry, barren, hilly country, with a few ruins to show where villages was once before the bandits burned 'em out. Down in the valleys I couldst see inhabited villages occasionally, but the road didn't run past 'em.

The sun wasn't very high when I come to the idol at the crossroads. I stopped and looked around for somebody, but didn't see nothing, though I heard a sound like somebody cocking a gun. So I honked the honker and waved the red rag and up jumped five of the toughest, wildest looking Chineses I ever seen. They'd been laying in a deep ravine alongside the road. I hadn't never seen no Chineses like them. They was big and mean looking, and wore ragged clothes and cartridge belts stuck full of knives and pistols, and they had rifles in their hands.

"You all ain't takin' no chances with them bandits, are you?" I said sociably, and they looked at me very fishy with their beady black eyes, and Spike growled. The hair on his neck stood up, and so did he, and acted like he wanted to get out of the car and sample their hides, so I told him to keep quiet.

"Where is it?" demanded one in a guttural voice, and I jerked my thumb towards the back of the car.

"The box on the right side," I said. "T'other'n's mine."

They laid to and lifted it out, and I said, "Well, so long and merry Christmas!"

They grunted something and I drove on, thinking that if all mission Chineses was as tough-looking as them babies, they didn't need to be afeared of bandits or anything else.

Well, just before dark I come into a broad valley, and seen a village away over the other side, and a walled cluster of buildings nearer to me, and knowed it must be the mission. It was just after dark had fell that I drawed up in front of a small gate at the back. Inside I seen a lot of lights, and heard voices singing; they was Christian songs but heathen voices, and it sounded queer as all get out.

Twilliger was waiting for me, and he had a bundle under his arm.

"Good man!" he exclaimed, grabbing my hand. "You got here just at the right time. The children are singing carols. They expect the arrival of Santa Claus at any moment. Put on the costume, quickly!"

He opened up the bundle and out fell a Santy Claus uniform with oil-cloth boots, red cap, whiskers and all. It was kind of moth-eaten and faded, and it fit too close acrost the shoulders and too loose around the waist, but I struggled into it, and pretty soon announced myself as ready to make my deebew. Twilliger was so pleased he nigh done a dance; he kept rubbing his hands and saying, "Fine! Fine!" and patting me on the back.

Well, I shouldered the box—and it seemed to have growed a awful lot in weight—and in we went. We crossed a court and come to the long low building where the singing was going on, and went through a hallway, and Twilliger opened a door and throwed back a curtain and ushered me in very dramatic to a big room which was crowded with Chineses of all ages and sexes. They didn't look a derned bit like them other Mission Chineses.

They sot up a sheer when they seen me, which the missionaries had probably taught 'em. (It sounded like, "Wee yant u hootch-down!") and clapped their hands. The smiles the kid wore when they seen that big box was payment enough for all the trouble I'd went to. And old Twilliger smole all over his face, proving he could smile, after all.

"Children," he said, "this is Santa Claus! Each of you step up as your name is called, and receive the presents Santa has brought you."

They all applauded, American-fashion, and I beamed about me over my whiskers and expanded my enormous chest, and boomed: "Ahoy, mates, stand by whilsts old Santy dishes out the plum duff!"

I had set the box on the floor, and now I cut the ropes on it and stuck in my mitt and hauled out the first thing that come to it.

"Which'un does this'n go to, Ebenezer?" I whispered—and then I stopped. I didn't have no toy in my hand. It was a small oblong package done up in waxed cloth.

"What the heck?" I asked of the world at large, and Twilliger took it and tore it open.

"What on earth!" he hollered. In his hand was a cardboard box of rifle cartridges. I stood plumb froze, and then—

It all happened so sudden I've always been kinda hazy about it. One second the room was quiet, the Chineses leaning forward with puzzled expressions, me and Ebenezer staring at the box in his hand, Spike snuffing the air and growling low in his throat—the only noise which could be heard. The next instant all bedlam bust loose. There was a awful racket of shots and yells, and doors crashing in, and women screaming. It come from outside, but with the noise everybody in the big room seemed to go nuts. Somebody run head-on into me and knocked me down, and my whiskers got knocked over my eyes and I couldn't see nothing. When I got 'em down again and jumped up, all I could see was people running every which way, screaming and wringing their hands.

"What the heck?" I gasped. "Don't they like the presents?"

"It's a raid!" yelled Twilliger, bracing his shoulder against the door which was bending and buckling. "Kwang Tzu's bandits from the hills! Oh, why didn't I keep a better watch? Run, children—out the back way!"

I jumped to help him hold the door, while the Chineses tore out the other way, but just then the door crashed inwards from a assault of rifle butts, and Twilliger was throwed backwards as a swarm of wild figgers come busting into the room. He give a moan of despair, and then he set his jaw and waded into them with his coat tails flying and his long arms thrashing like windmills. I heard a howl that told me Spike's iron jaws was on the job, and then I woke up and plunged in with a roar.

Chineses can't take it, even when they are bandits. With every smash of my iron maulers I felt teeth splinter, ribs buckle and jaws snap. I beat 'em down and tromped 'em under, but they kept coming. I seen Twilliger swamped by sheer numbers, and I seen Spike, his jaws streaming red, go down under the swinging rifle stock of a big one-eyed devil in a padded coat. With a roar of fury I rushed on him, ploughing through a swarm of biting, hitting, clinging bodies, and I was so blind-mad I missed my first swing, and nigh dislocated my arm. The one-eyed thug grabbed my whiskers and his knife went up, but the whiskers come loose in his hand, and he screamed with amazement and forgot to strike, and whilst he stood froze with surprise I handed him a swat that fractured his jaw bone in three places. The next instant a bludgeon crashed down on my head and knocked me to my knees, and a whole shower of rifle butts beat down on me. The lights went out.

When I come to myself I was jolting along tied acrost one of them shaggy little hill ponies, and somebody else was tied on with me. It was a most uncomfortable position, but my head hurt so bad I didn't think much about it. It was very dark, but I could tell that they was men on horses all about me. I groaned and cussed earnestly, and somebody said: "This is no time for vain profanity, brother."

"Is that you, Dr. Twilliger?" I said. "This is a fine jack-pot—"

"Our affliction is indeed sore," he said. "Being borne to some unknown fate, slung across the back of a hill-pony is far from dignified. But we must practise philosophical resignation."

"I'll resign somebody to Davy Jones's Locker," I snarled, writhing vainly at my cords, which bit into my wrists and ankles. "What the heck happened, anyway?"

"We were raided by the bandits of Kwang Tzu, just as he has often threatened," said Twilliger. "They stole upon us while we were making merry. I should have maintained a watch—but the men whose duty it was, begged so hard to be allowed to watch the festivities—"

"Spike!" I exclaimed suddenly. "Them dirty devils killed him! Oh, lemme get my hands on em—"

"Shhh!" whispered Twilliger. "He was merely stunned. As they dragged us out, I saw him open his eyes."

"Good!" I said, with a gusty sigh of deep relief. "I wish he'd go back to Peiping where he'd be safe, but I bet he's trailin' us right now, if he's able to crawl. Did they burn the mission?"

"No, thank heaven. You see, they failed to capture any of my converts. All escaped in the darkness while we were battling with the bandits. They will carry word of the raid, and soldiers will be sent. The bandits knew that, and were in haste to be gone. But the soldiers will help you and me very little, for they have never been able to track the bandits to their secret lair. Nevertheless we prevented the capture and slaughter of the helpless people of the mission. You fought a marvelous fight, my friend," he said.

"Well," I ruminated bitterly, "I was a little help, then. I'm ashamed of myself, goin' out from a tap on the head that a way."

"Why, my goodness, friend!" exclaimed Twilliger; "the marvel is that you're alive! You must have an adamantine skull."

At this p'int a guard reined up alongside us and kicked me in the ribs, grunting something which I took as a order for me to shut up. I started describing his ancestors to him, but Twilliger begged me to keep quiet, so I lapsed into what the poet calls sullen silence.

Laying on my belly that way, head down, I couldst tell very little about what kind of country we was going over, but it seemed to be very wild and rocky and full of ravines. We went up and down till I was sick at my stummick, and we weaved and doubled and wandered around till I begun to think the cussed bandits was lost too, and hoped they was, and would stay lost till they all starved to death, even if I had to starve with 'em.

But after awhile we come up a slope with sheer walls on each side, and come out on level ground, and by twisting my neck, I seen the gleam of a light. They cut me and Ebenezer loose from the horse and throwed us on the ground, and I seen we was laying in front of a big cave, with steep cliffs all around, except for the wide level space in front. This space sloped down to the ravine we'd come up, a few hundred feet away. We couldst see all this in the light of torches which several men was holding. The cave mouth was wide, and they'd built a wall of rocks acrost it, with loop-holes and a heavy wooden gate, like a regular fort. I seen at a glance that a few men with plenty ammunition could hold off a army. Only way to get at it was up the ravine, and once out of that, the attacking force would have to cross the open space where there wasn't no protection of no kind.

They prodded us to our feet, and we was so stiff we couldn't hardly move, but they dragged us through the gate and into the cavern. We could see by the torches that there was maybe fifty of them, and there was a machine gun mounted beside the gate. Inside the cave there was a space of maybe fifty feet, then there was a big leather curtain hung from the roof to the floor. They pulled aside a slit in that, like a tent door, and shoved us through.

They had that inner cave all fixed up like a mandarin's palace or something. It was a big place, though the roof was kinda low. The walls was hung with tapestries and they was carpets on the rock floor. Colored lanterns hung from the rocky roof, and they was a big bronze Buddha, with incense burning, and a fire going in a big brazier. The smoke went up through a vent in the roof—most of it.

And on a wooden dais, covered with furs, there set a big Chinaman I knowed must be Kwang Tzu, the scourge of the hills. He was dressed in embroidered silk, with a pearl-handled pistol in his belt.

"So!" he said, hissing like a snake. "The missionary dog!"

"You'll suffer for this, Kwang Tzu," said Twilliger without a quiver.

"*You* shall suffer," said Kwang Tzu cooly. "You have defied me in the past; that is why my men brought you here, instead of knocking you in the head. Your end shall be leisurely and amusing. Tie them up, and let them meditate, while I finish my repast."

In a second we was trussed up to a couple of stakes near the wall, and Kwang Tzu went on eating candied pork and swigging *kaoliang*. Me and Twilliger looked at each other. His coat tails was in tatters, he had a black eye, and his pants was split. I reckon I looked funny too, with my hair full of clotted blood and my red Santy Claus coat busted out at the shoulders.

"Alas, that I should have brought you to such a pass!" he sighed.

"Aw, hell," I said, "that's all right, Ebenezer. I've had my fun. Anyway, this game ain't played out. I'm workin' cautious at my cords. Lemme once get loose and I'll make a Roman holiday outa this louse Kwang Tzu. Say, what about them soldiers you mentioned?"

"They'll never be able to track us here," said Twilliger. "It has always been a mystery where the bandits hid after their raids. But before we die, I am consumed with one curiosity: how came those cartridges in the box that was supposed to contain toys?"

"Aw," I said morosely, "some fellows gimme that box to deliver to the Abercrombie Mission—"

"Abercrombie?" said he. "There's no such mission in these parts."

"I know it—now," I said bitterly. "They was smugglers, and they bamboozled me into haulin' their ammernishun for 'em. Some Chineses met me in the hills, and I must of give 'em the wrong box. The car had turned over and in puttin' the cases back, I accidentally changed places with 'em. What became of the one I brought to the mission?"

"Just before the bandits broke in," he said, "I kicked it into a closet and locked the door. I didn't want it to fall into their hands."

We'd been speaking in whispers, but now Kwang Tzu ordered our guards to shut us up, which they done by socking us in the mouth with their gun butts. We must have hung on them stakes for more'n a hour, while that fat yeller devil gorged hisself and gloated over us. I was tensing and relaxing my muscles, working at my cords, and I begun to feel the ones on my right leg slipping and giving way. Then Kwang Tzu wiped his fingers and smirked and said: "Now, my friends, for the climax of the night's comedy—*what's that?"*

Outside sounded the clatter of hoofs, a burst of shots and yells. A bandit run into the inner cave squalling like a singed cat. Kwang Tzu jumped up, spitting Chinee at him. It was just getting light outside—I could see the sky through the cleft in the roof—and the racket kept getting louder. We could hear bullets splattering the front of the cave.

Kwang Tzu spat at us. "Dogs!" he hissed as he went by, "somehow the soldiers have found my retreat! After I have dealt with them, I will settle with you! Fools, I will have you both skinned alive!"

With which cheering promise he passed through the slit in the leather curtain and the guards follered him, leaving me and Twilliger alone in the inner cave.

"Listen!" Ebenezer was jerking at his cords in his excitement. Outside was the devil's own din of shooting, yelling and cussing in Chinee. "From the shouts," he said, "they have driven the soldiers back, and the soliders are firing from the ravine where they have taken refuge. Kwang Tzu still holds the winning hand. The soldiers cannot rush the cave in the teeth of his rifles and machine gun. And they cannot drive him from his position. He has water and supplies inside the cave, and in these bare hills there are no supplies for the soldiers outside. They are too far from their base; they must win at once or retire."

Presently the shooting lulled a little bit, and we couldst hear the men yelling, both in the outer cave and out in the ravine. Then the flap in the curtain lifted and Kwang Tzu come in, with a knife in his hand. His face was a yeller mask of hate.

"Dogs!" he said. "You have brought me evil luck! The cursed soldiers have smelt us out, and our ammunition is almost exhausted. I have been betrayed; the men I sent to receive a load of cartridges have not come back. When the soldiers realize that we have no more powder, they will rush in and take us."

"The deeds of the wicked return unto them," opined Ebenezer with considerable satisfaction.

Kwang Tzu spit at him. "*You* will not witness my downfall!" he snarled. "I will cut your accursed throat—" And he rushed towards us.

I twisted my foot free and kicked him in the belly. He shot backwards and hit on his back, writhing and groaning—then he froze with his hands on his stummick, gaping upwards at the cleft in the roof. A yeller face was stuck down in this cleft, and a wild jabbering ensued. I rekernized that face; it belonged to one of the men which took the box at the cross-roads!

Kwang Tzu jumped up like he'd forgot all about us, and hollered, he was so tickled with hisself. And down through the cleft, on the end of a rawhide rope, come the box itself, still tied up like I'd delivered it.

It hadn't touched the floor when somebody screamed up above, and let go of the rope, which dropped down through the cleft, and the box crashed to the carpets. A devil of a commotion bust out above us, yelling and howling, and a ripping noise like people was getting their clothes tore offa them. But Kwang Tzu give no heed. He plumb danced in his glee and hollered: "Dogs, do you know what this is? It is the ammunition I was promised by my agents! My faithful servants were delayed in bringing it—they halted to loot some travellers—but they have evaded the soldiers, climbed the cliffs, and now given into my hands the destruction of my enemies. The soldiers do not know of my machine gun; we shall trick them into charging, and mow them down. Not one shall escape—" He cut the cords, wrenched up the lid, and tilted the box—and out of it tumbled a heap of dolls, jumping-jacks and tin trains!

I thought for a second he'd drop dead. Then he let out a shriek which hushed all the racket outside. And in that hush I throwed back my head and bellered so's I could of been heard a mile: "COME ON, BOYS! THEY'RE OUT OF BULLETS!"

A lot of things happened all at once. The soldiers outside heard me, believed me, and come charging out of the ravine, yelling like injuns. Kwang Tzu screeched, pulled his pistol, shot at me and missed—he was that blind mad—then down through the cleft shot something white and solid, which lit square between his shoulders. He squalled once as he went down, then Spike's jaws found his jugular, and that was the last of Kwang Tzu.

There was a devil of a ruckus in the outer cave, yells, curses, and the sound of gun butts busting over skulls, and then what was left of the bandits came busting into the inner cave with the soldiers right on their heels. They stopped short when they seen what Spike was standing astride of. They throwed down their knives and stuck up their hands. The soldiers grabbed on to them, and the officer in command come over and saluted me and Twilliger, and then he had his men cut us loose. He looked at Spike which was licking my face and nearly wagging his stump tail off, and said some Chinese proverb I didn't understand.

"We are indeed indebted to you," said Ebenezer. "I cannot understand how you arrived so quickly, or how you got here at all."

"We had a tip that a consignment of ammunition was to be delivered to the bandits," said the young officer. "We were scouting the hills, hoping to trap both smugglers and bandits together. We were only a few miles from the mission when it was raided. We heard the shots and came to investigate. When we arrived, the bandits had but recently departed, but we were at a loss, not knowing in which direction they had gone, or how to follow them in the darkness. But the dog, there, who seemed to be just recovering from a blow on the head, began snuffing about, and presently trotted away toward the hills. Remembering how bloodhounds are used in the States to track criminals, we followed him. He led us here without hesitation, but when the fighting started he vanished—"

"He was lookin' for a way to get to me," I grunted, pulling

Spike's old stump of a chawed ear whilst he grinned like a bloody-mouthed dragon. "He evidently clumb the cliffs and discovered them bandits lowering what they thought was the ammernishun, and he routed 'em and jumped right down that cleft onto Kwang Tzu's neck. If I had as much sense as Spike's we do fine."

"What are you going to do now?" asked Twilliger as I limped over to the box on the floor.

"I'm goin' to gather up these here toys," I said. "My Santy Claws suit is rooint, but the kids are goin' to have their toys, just the same. It takes more'n a passel of bandits to spile a Christmas which Dennis Dorgan is bein' the Santy Claws of, by golly!"

The Turkish Menace

It was just about dark. I was wandering idly down amongst the waterfront streets wondering when *The Python* would make port. I was purty tired of hanging around Shanghai, and I wanted to see Spike my white bulldog, which I'd left on board when I come on ahead of the ship to fight a Chinaman they called champeen of the Orient.

Well, the champeen had took one look at my ferocious countenance and jumped outa the ring, and the narrow-minded promoter had refused to pay me any dough.

I was brooding on these wrongs as I stalked along, and suddenly I was aware that something was happening ahead of me. A slim, well-built young man was hurrying along, carrying a briefcase, and just as I looked, out of a alley jumped a big bulky figger and I heered the sound of a blow. The smaller man went down and the other'n grabbed the briefcase and run back into the alley.

Instantly I deduced that the first man had been slugged and robbed—I got a natural talent that way—and with a yell I rushed forward.

The victim couldn't of been hurt much for just as I come even with him he struggled up on his arms and started yelling for the cops, so I didn't stop with him, but charged on into the alley. It was black as a stack of cats in there, but I heered the pound of the fugitive's feet away down the alley so I raced in pursuit.

I could hear him running and I don't know how long I follered him in and out amongst them dark winding alleys, but all at once my feet hit pile of cans or something and I went heels over head into the mud and nearly busted myself.

When I rose, cussing bitterly, I didn't hear no sound of my prey. I groped around, wondering where I was. I'd clean lost my sense of direction and hadn't no idea how to get back to the place I started from. But after groping around and stumbling over refuse and being startled outa my liver by rats running over my feet in the dark, I eventually emerged into a dimly lighted alley and come out onto a street which I realized was a long way from the place I'd saw the feller slugged. I wondered who it was done it. I couldn't see clearly, of course—I just got the impression of a heavy figger about medium size that was kind of stooped.

Well, I was purty tired and thirsty, so I went into a saloon and the first thing I heered was a feller run in and say, "Hey, did you muggs hear the news? Just a while ago somebody slugged Goslin, the paymaster of the Anglo-Oriental Company, and grabbed the payroll!"

"You don't say!" they said. "What was Goslin doin' wanderin' around with it?"

"Aw," said the feller, "he was afraid to leave it in the office safe and he figgered if he toted it home in a briefcase nobody'd suspect nothin'. But somebody musta figgered it out."

"How'd it happen?" they asked.

"Well," I said, busting into the conversation, "it was like this—"

They ignored my contribution.

"He was slugged over on the Wu Tung Road, near a alley," said the first man. "Goslin was dropped at the first lick, he said, but he was just stunned for a instant and got a good look at the feller as he ducked into the alley. He says he'd recognize him again. All the cops is lookin' for a big sailor, about six feet tall, with black hair and very wide shoulders and long arms kinda like a gorilla."

One of the men said, "Well, I'll be a monkey's uncle if that don't sound like ole Sailor Dennis Dorgan."

"Yes," replied another man, "I ain't never seen Dorgan but ever'body claims as how he favors a gorilla."

It had begin to dawn on me that they wuz talkin' about me. Furthermore, I realized now that the paymaster, Goslin, thought I was the gent that slugged him in the alley.

Whereby, a man of lesser intelligence might've lingered around and got caught, I figured out purty soon that I'd be smart to make myself scarce.

I sneaked out of that saloon and took off down the street.

About three blocks away I turned a corner too fast and bumped into a couple of big gents and knocked them into the gutter.

It turned out that they was two friends of mine, Mike Leary and Bill McGlory. At first they wanted to fight me because I had knocked 'em down. But they came to their senses before they made such a fatal mistake.

They soon commenced arguing among themselves, which they had been doing when I bumped into them. I was sort of angered for a while, and then Mike turns to me.

"Lissen at him," growled Mike. "Dennis, he's nuts. You know where he's started right now?"

"Naw," I said. "Where?"

"Down to Kalissky's Arener to rassle Abdullah the Terrible Turk."

I shook my head in wonder.

"Has anybody hit him on the head with a handspike lately, Mike?" I asked.

"Well, whatever the cause," said Mike, "they's no doubt but that he's *none compose mental*."

"What?" I said.

"He's nuts," explained Mike. "Come on, Dennis, sock him on the jaw and we'll hawg-tie him and take him to a veterinarian or a mid-specialist for examination."

"You keep offa me!" exclaimed Bill, stung, swinging his huge fists menacingly. "Lemme alone, gol-dern it! Ain't I got a right to live my own life and express myself any way I see fit? By golly, I'm a human bein' with inallynable rights!"

"Abdullah will tie you in a bow-knot," said Mike. "Won't he, Dennis?"

"Well," I said, "I ain't never seen this Turk, but from what they say, he must be a bear-cat."

"So'm I," snorted Bill. "This last cruise I've throwed every-body aboard *The Dutchman,* and—"

"Who couldn't?" snarled Mike. "Just because you can pile a bunch of water-logged, rum-soaked hulks and lumberin' square-heads which don't know a toehold from a flyin' mare, you think you can rassle."

"You wait," predicted Bill. "I know just how to handle this

Abdullah egg. I'm goin' to use my special hold that I used on the cook of *The Dutchman*. You oughta seen him hit the boards when I tossed him. I kinda crouch, away down, like this, see, and come in very crafty, swinging my arms low—"

"Stop them fool contortions," said Mike disgustedly. "You'll get us in the jug. There's a cop watchin' us suspicious-like right now."

"Where?" I demanded in alarm.

"There," said Mike.

"Come on," I urged, grabbing him and Bill by the arms, "le's be gettin' down to the Arener. We'll be late for the go."

"I thought you was agreein' with me that Bill—" begun Mike in surprise.

"Yes, yes," I broke in impatiently. "Hustle up will you? After all, if Bill wants to rassle, that's his lookout. It ain't really any of our business. Come on!"

So we went down the street and I seen to it that we went in some haste.

Well, we got to the Arener and the crowd was gathering fast. The Turk was a big drawing card. Nobody knowed much about him, or where he come from, but he had a big reputation from his bone-crushing grapples already.

Well, we went into the dressing rooms and Mike and Bill was still argying. They argyed about the color of Bill's tights, and how many water buckets should be took into the ring, and the size of the sponge, and what kind of holds Bill should use—providing he ever got one on the Turk—and they get to demonstrating their holds, and tangled up and fell over a bench and rolled into the water buckets, at which time the promoter entered and told 'em the Turk was already in the ring.

Well, Bill put on his bathrobe and throwed out his chest and Mike picked up the water buckets and things and said, "Come on, Dennis, we might as well get it over with."

"I believe I'll sit here in the dressin' room," I said.

They gaped at me. "What the heck!" said Mike. "Why, I'm dependin' on you to help me cart off the remains."

"Well," I said, "is they any cops out there?"

Mike stuck his head out the door and looked and said, "I don't see none."

Just then Kalissky walked up the hall.

"Cops?" said Kalissky, insulted-like. "I'll have you know I don't need no cops to keep order. You think I'd endanger my customers by bringin' cops here? One of the main attractions of Kalissky's Arena is that here a man can sit down and enjoy a little ease and quiet, knowin' no cop is goin' to suddenly clamp onto him. Should a cop try to get in here he'd get throwed out."

"Alright," I said uncertainly, "I'll take a chanct."

Mike and Bill didn't ask me why I was avoiding the cops, being tactful that way; besides they both always avoids the police theirselves on general principles.

Well, we come up the aisle and Bill bobbed his bullet head right and left, smirking complacently as a roar went up from the crowd, many of which was sailors and knowed Bill by sight or reputation.

"Lissen at 'em," growled Mike. "To think that a egg with a reputation for alley-fightin' that he's got goes and risks his popularity by going up against a rassler which will undoubtedly tie him into bowknots."

Well, the Turk was in the ring, and had already throwed off his bathrobe so the crowd could get a glimpse of his physique. He stood glowering and flexing his mighty muscles, and I'll say he was a formidable figger, nearly six feet tall, and broad and thick as a bull, with gigantic legs and arms and a bullet-head set square on his enormous shoulders. His swarthy complexion, along with his flaring moustaches, made him look even more ferocious. I scratched my head in perplexity. They was something vaguely familiar about the egg, but I couldn't place it.

Well, Bill climbed into the ring and I must say he didn't stack up so impressive against the Turk. He was a couple of inches shorter, and he just wasn't as big a man—not by about thirty pounds.

The referee gave them some last minute instructions and turned them loose.

Bill McGlory came charging out of his corner and slugged that Turk squarely in the stomach. A funny thing happened. His fist bounced back like it had hit a solid piece of rubber and he began shakin' it like it wuz busted.

The crowd screamed and yelled, and about this time the referee caught holt of Bill and gave him a rather stern lecture about how this was a rassleling match and not a boxing match.

The referee stepped back from between them and Bill charged that Abdullah again. This time he grabbed the Turk in a terrible bear hug. The Turk kept on smilin', however, and then he rammed his bullet-like forehead square into Bill's face and knocked Bill into the far corner of the ring! Bill staggered up dazed-like and the Turk charged forward and grabbed him. He lifted him clear above his head, slung him around a few times and let him fly.

Old Bill sailed out of the ring. He appeared to be coming in my direction. I couldn't hardly believe it, but—

Bang! Bill's body dropped out of the sky square on top of me!

Our heads banged together and Bill was knocked out cold, and it even made my head ache a little.

The referee declared the fight over and proclaimed Abdullah the Turk the winner.

Mike and I carried Bill down to the dressin' room through the howling and hooting crowd.

A cold shower brought Bill to and we helped him get dressed. By this time all the crowd was gone and we left Kalissky's Arener.

Bill said he was going to find that Terrible Turk and beat up on him if it was the last thing he ever did.

Just that minute, Bill spotted the Turk further down the street.

"There he is," Bill yelled, and started running after him.

We, of course, started running after Bill.

The Turk looked around and saw us—and evidently thought all three of us was chasing him, for he turned off the street and ran into a alley. Bill yelled vengefully and increased his gait, and we come sailing down the street, people scattering right and left in front of us. As Bill wheeled into the alley, I vaguely noticed a group of men coming up the street, and they halted at the alley mouth to keep from being run over.

Bill zipped by 'em into the alley, then Mike passed in hot pursuit of Bill, and I was right behind Mike. And I heered somebody yell, "That's him! The taller one! He's the black-headed sailor that slugged me and grabbed my briefcase!"

Jerusha! A desperate glance showed me a band of policemen, and a slim, well-dressed fellow with a bandage on his head. Goslin! They yelled and started after me.

Away down the alley I seen a bulky bobbing figger, making tracks at full speed. Bill was so intent on his prey that he never seen the cops, and neither did Mike. But lemme tell you, the time I'd been making wasn't nothing to what I made then! I passed Mike Leary like he was standing still, and began stepping on Bill's heels.

"Lemme 'lone," he panted. "I'm goin' to catch that mugg if—"

"Bill McGlory," I gasped, "if that's the fastest you can run, pull over and lemme by!"

He cast a startled glance over his shoulder, but the next minute I was in the lead, and I held it from then on. If they was any Chineses watching us, I reckon they was convinced all white men was crazy. Bill was chasing Abdullah, Mike was chasing Bill, and the cops was chasing me, and only a few of us was entirely aware as to what it was all about.

Ahead of us the bulky figger hadst vanished, and I heered Bill cussing between gasps. I dived down a darker, winding alley-way, and Bill, supposing I seen Abdullah down there, follered me. But heck, I'd already forgot about the Turk. All I wanted was to elude them bloodhounds of the law. And I done it, temporarily. They was a lot of alleys leading off from the main one, and they was all dark or very dim lit, so I guess they musta took the wrong one.

Anyway, I looked back and didn't see nobody—only Mike Leary, a few feet behind Bill. That look-back purty near ruint me. Ahead of me the alley turned sharply, and in the dark I hadn't seen the bend. When I looked again, I seen it, but couldn't check myself. Right ahead of me was a dark, blank wall, with the arched top of a doorway showing just above the level of the street, with a flight of steps leading down. I hadn't seen 'em till I was right on 'em.

I couldn't stop. I went down them steps headlong like the Flying Dutchman, and rammed the door at the bottom with my head like a torpedo. Crash! If the panels hadst been solider I'd of undoubtedly broky my neck, but as it was, the door splintered and the hinges snapped, and I carried the whole thing on into the room with me. Behind me, Bill hadst checked hisself right at the head of the steps, but Mike hadst caromed into him, and they both rolled down the steps, cussing wildly.

I glared about me. I was lying amongst the splinters of the door in a room which was lit by a lamp set in a bracket in the wall. They was cots and chairs and a table, and they was four men, who hadst leaped to their feet and now glared wildly down at me. They was all big, tough-looking muggs—a Englishman, a Dutchman, an American—and Abdullah. Yeah, there he was, with his moustaches a-bristle.

The rest is kinda blurred. I heered Bill McGlory yell. I seen him leap up and light into the Turk with both fists flying. I seen the others pile in to help their pal, and then me and Mike Leary rose up from the floor and joined the ball.

I found myself paired off with the Dutchman and the American. Mike was beating the Englishman to a pulp over in a corner, and Bill was demonstrating the truth of his statement that he couldst lick Abdullah at rough-and-tumble. I wish I coulda had time to watch that fight; it musta been a pippin from the way they both looked afterwards. But I was too busy myself. The Dutchman had a chair, and after I'd cracked the Yankee on the ear and ripped it nigh offa his head, he reeled back, and then come in again with a pair of brass knucks. He laid my scalp open, and then I belted him one on the temple which dropped him to the floor, and about that time the Dutchman lifted the chair with both hands and shattered it over my head. I staggered, but sunk a left hook to the wrist in my abuser's belly, and he gasped and doubled up in time to catch my over-hand right behind his ear, which finished him for the evening.

At this moment the Yankee, which was as tough as boot-leather, come off the floor and raked a strip offa my face with a wild swing of his brass-knuckled fist. I was beginning to get mad by this time, and I caught him square on the jaw with a right hook that spilled him amongst the ruins of the table, and this time he stayed put.

The next instant the room was flooded with men, and I felt myself being grabbed by a number of hands. I jerked angrily away, and started to begin slugging again, when I seen the room was full of cops, and they had their guns out. Some of them had laid hold of Mike, who was getting up offa the senseless carcass of the Englishman, whilst over in another corner, amongst some upset cots, Bill was apparently beating the Turk to death with a leather bag of some kind.

They hauled Bill off, snorting and blowing, and dragged them both to their feet. They was both ruins, with clothes hanging in rags, and black eyes, skinned noses and the like, but the Turk was by far the most bedraggled.

"What kind of a game is this?" demanded a police officer, looking around in astonishment at the battlefield. Nobody said nothing. Then Goslin came over and looked at me close.

"This is the man, alright," he said.

"Lissen," I said despairingly, "you got me all wrong. I know you think it was me which slugged you, but on the level, it wasn't—"

My desperate eye roved about, and rested on the Turk's bulky figure as he stood, slightly stooped, and like a flash it come to me.

"He's the man!" I exclaimed. "It was the Turk which socked you and grabbed the dough! I rekernize him now! I chased him down a alley—"

"Likely story," snorted the officer. "Put the cuffs on him—"

"Wait a minute!" yelped Goslin, springing forward. "What's this you've got?"

He jerked away something which Bill McGlory was apparently unconsciously holding. It was a leather briefcase.

"Where did you get this?" yelled Goslin.

"Why—I—" Bill begun vaguely, but Goslin had run over to a cot which wasn't smashed, and was hurriedly jerking open the case.

"It's the briefcase I was carrying the payroll in!" he exclaimed, dumping the contents out on the cot. "Look, it's all here! Thirty thousand dollars in greenbacks!"

We stared in stupified amazement at the dough and Goslin wheeled on Bill.

"Are you in on this steal? Where did you get that case?"

"What you mean, steal?" snarled Bill. "Are you callin' me a thief? If you are, I'll bust you in the snoot. That bag musta fell outa that cot me and the Turk busted in our scrap. I got a hold of it about that time. I wouldn't of socked him with it, only he was hittin' me with a table leg."

Goslin and the cops stared in bewilderment, and I said, "Even if you think I stole that dough, you can't accuse Bill and Mike. They didn't know nothin' about the robbery. And they can testify that they found the case here, amongst these thugs. I never been in this place before in my life."

It was a tense moment, as they say in books.

Then, suddenly, Goslin turned to me and offered me his hand.

"I see it all now. I mistook you for the thief when you were really chasing Abdullah, the real thief. And now you are the one who is responsible for recovering the lost payroll. The

Anglo-Oriental Company has offered a reward for its recovery and I want you to come by tomorrow and collect it."

As the cops took the Turk away in handcuffs, I turned to Mike and Bill who were standing there with their mouths open.

I remarked, modestly, "Never forget that it is brains what count in this ole world, gents. Some of us have more than our share, and some ain't blessed with so many."

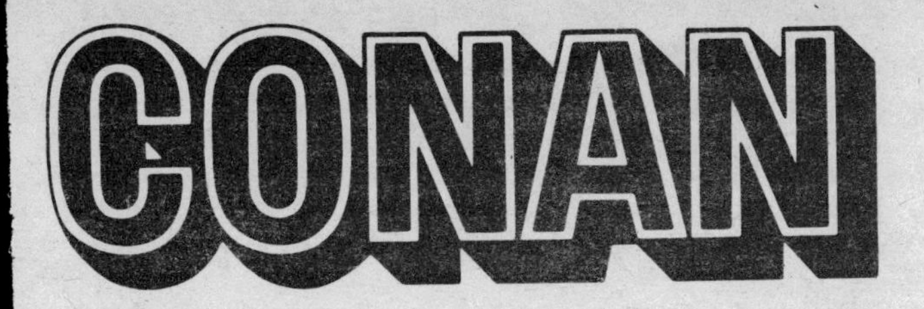
CONAN